Imposter Syndrome

Mark Allan Gunnells

SLASHIC HORROR PRESS

Copyright © 2025 by Mark Allan Gunnells.

All rights reserved.

No portion of this book may be reproduced in any form without written permission from the publisher or author, except as permitted by U.S. copyright law.

ISBN-13: 978-1-7637256-2-1

Edited and Interior Design by David-Jack Fletcher.

Cover Design by Christy Alrdidge of Grim Poppy Designs.

To my work family at the Boiling Springs Public Library.

Selected titles by Mark Allan Gunnells

When it Rains
The Quarry
2B
Twilight at the Gates
Asylum
Before He Wakes
The Summer of Winters
A Laymon Kind of Night
Flowers in a Dumpster
Haunted Places and Other Stories
Social (Media) Life
Lucid

Monday, April 6, 2020

"I'm a fraud," I said to my reflection in the bathroom mirror.

Although I had to admit, I didn't look like a fraud. At least not from the waist up. A nice crisp white button-down and a subdued blue tie, my shaggy hair brushed straight back, face clean shaven for the first time in a month. I had never owned my own blazer so I wore one that had belonged to my father. Slightly too big on my frame, giving me the appearance of a kid playing in his father's closet, pretending at being an adult. The publicist at Doubleday had insisted I "dress up" for the interview, and I thought this should please him.

Of course, from the waist down was another story altogether. I wore a loose-fitting pair of Bermuda shorts and black ankle socks. Turning to catch my entire reflection in the full-length mirror hanging from the back of the bathroom door, I had to laugh. It looked like someone had cut two photos down the center and then taped the top of one to the bottom of the other. Not the most professional of fashion combos, but only the upper part of my body would be visible on camera so no one would be any the wiser.

I bent over the sink and splashed water on my face then gripped the edge of the porcelain basin and stared myself in the eye, muttering, "You can do this, you got this," over and over like some kind of cracked mantra. I felt like that old nerdy *SNL* character, giving himself a pep talk in the mirror. *You're good enough, you're smart enough*, and all that kind of self-help fluff. Then again, I thought that actor went on to be a U.S. Senator or something so maybe I shouldn't scoff.

I ran the brush through my hair one last time, then left the bathroom, making my way down the short hallway into the living room. I had my laptop set up on the round glass-topped coffee table, facing toward the ceiling-high full-wall bookcase with the rolling ladder affixed to it to reach the high shelves. I waffled between thinking that backdrop for the interview would be appropriate for a writer and fearing it was cliché. Probably overthinking it, but overthinking and stressing over inconsequential details was a trademark of mine. Or so several of my exes had told me.

A throw pillow rested on the floor to provide a little cushion, and I settled onto it, my legs folded up yogi style. I knew I would regret it after the interview. Nothing made me feel every minute of my fifty-five years more than having to stand back up after sitting in the floor for an extended period of time. Maybe I should have done this in the small office at the back of the house despite providing a backdrop of nothing but a bare white wall, but it was too late now.

I opened the email and found the one from the producer which provided the invite link so I could remote in. I clicked it, typed the login code from the email, and got a message that read: "Please wait. The host will allow you into the meeting in a few minutes."

Adjusting the knot of my tie, which felt like a tightening noose around my neck, I felt the first droplets of sweat dribbling down my forehead. I wiped them away and considered turning on the air conditioning. Of course, I realized that wouldn't help. It wasn't the temperature that had me sweating, but my nerves. I had never done an interview on a national platform before, especially not one as popular as *The Brooke Simpson Show*. The actress-turned-talk-show-host had the number one show on daytime TV, drawing in millions of viewers every episode. Millions of viewers who would soon be viewing my blotchy face and listening to me babble like an idiot. The producer had provided the questions in advance, and next to the laptop were the printed answers I'd come up with, but I didn't want to sound like a robot spewing forth canned responses. There had to be some kind of middle ground I could tread, where I sounded natural without blathering, but middle ground had never been my forte. I was more a one-extreme-or-the-other kind of guy.

At least it won't be in front of a studio audience, I told myself, and that was a comfort. Sitting here on a pillow in my Bermuda shorts, I wouldn't feel all the eyes on me and I hoped that would help me relax. Of course, the interview may be remote but it was still live. If I made a total fool of myself, another trademark of mine, we couldn't simply cut and do another take.

I tried to employ some meditation techniques, deep breathing and visualization. I was already sitting like a yogi so I was halfway there already. I had dated a Buddhist once who took me to meditate with some local monks, but I admit to being a bit distracted because the only thing I could truly meditate on was the fact that there were Buddhist monks living in South Carolina and I'd never had any idea.

My thoughts were interrupted when the "Please wait" message on my computer screen was replaced with a video box. I found myself looking at a young woman who wasn't quite young enough for the pigtails she sported, wearing one of those Julie-the-Time-Life-Operator headsets.

"There you are, Mr. Justice," she said, her tinny voice coming through the laptop speakers. "Can you see and hear me all right?"

"Um, yes, I can," I said, my voice cracking like an adolescent. "Am I coming through clear?"

"Crystal. I'm Amy, the producer for the show. We've exchanged some emails but nice to finally talk to you face to face. Sort of."

"Same here."

"Okay, just a reminder that Brooke isn't filming in the studio right now. She'll be conducting the interview remotely from her home in Malibu where she's sheltering-in-place. If you've seen the show, you know she likes to keep it loose and light. Less like a traditional interview and more like a conversation. She may go off script depending on how the discussion flows, so don't be surprised if she asks you questions not on the list I sent you."

This terrified me, but I tried not to let it show. I wanted to project an image of cool confidence, but I could feel more sweat snaking down the sides of my face. "Should be fun," I said with another Peter Brady crack to my voice.

"Keep in mind this is network TV, so no profanity or sexually vulgar material. Not that I'm saying you would, but it's a disclaimer I have to give to everyone."

"Fuckin' A!"

The smile she gave me was polite and perfunctory. My jokes rarely landed, another trademark.

"Okay, we'll be going on the air in just a moment. You'll be able to see Brooke on your screen. Do you have any questions before we get started?"

I had a million questions, but the most demanding one that came to mind was, "Do I really have to do this?" So demanding, in fact, that I almost said the words out loud before I could stop myself. Instead, I pressed my lips together and shook my head.

For a moment, Amy stared at me through the screen, and despite the distance that separated us, that stare felt like a laser boring into me. "You'll be fine," she said at last. "Brooke is super easy to talk to, which is why America loves her. She'll put you at ease right away. It will feel like you're having a chat, catching up with an old friend."

I nodded again, saving my voice for the actual interview. If I was able to say anything at all and not merely make high-pitched squeaking noises. My mouth felt so dry I could practically feel tumbleweeds blowing across my tongue, and I wished I'd had the foresight to have a glass of water handy.

"Okay, thirty seconds until you're on air," Amy said then she was gone, leaving me staring at my own image on the screen. I looked surprisingly put together, maybe a little red in the face and shiny from perspiration, but I didn't look like a man on the verge of a mental breakdown which was how I felt on the inside.

I hadn't had time to mentally prepare myself before my laptop screen was filled with the image of Brooke Simpson. Those sparkling green eyes, the mega-watt smile, those ringlet curls that were once deep auburn but now mostly gray.

"I'm so thrilled to introduce my next guest." Her enthusiasm sounded genuine. "Writer Maverick Justice, son of famed author Bentley Justice. Thank you so much for being here."

For three seconds which felt like an eternity, I did not speak. Merely stared at the screen in slack-jawed silence. Then I stammered a moment before finding my voice. "Thank you, Brooke. And please, call me Rick. It's a surreal pleasure to be here."

Surreal was an understatement. Amy had said to think of this as just a conversation between two old friends, but Brooke Simpson wasn't an old friend. She was a world-famous celebrity, and I couldn't remember a time in my life when I wasn't aware of her. In fact, the first movie I recalled watching as a child was *Every Dog Has Its Day*, starring a ten-year-old Brooke. She'd weathered child stardom, managing to avoid all the pitfalls of addiction and tabloid infamy, emerging in the 1990s as the star of a string of blockbuster romantic comedies. When she hit her forties, like too many actresses she found the juicy parts drying up, which was when she turned to the talk show game. This venture too proved a great success, and over the years she had interviewed everyone from movie stars to politicians to business tycoons.

And now she was about to interview me. Surreal didn't even begin to capture the experience.

"I'm so excited to talk to you," she said with a childlike glee that I mused was the secret to her success. Although Brooke was a beautiful woman, she didn't have the sultry charisma that would turn a female star into a sex symbol. Instead, she had an intriguing innocence that made her seem like everyone's kid sister/best friend/favorite babysitter/girl next door. Sex appeal may fade, but relatability was currency one could trade on always.

"Not excited as I am. It's not every day I'm in the presence of Hollywood royalty."

"Please, it's not every day that I'm in the presence of literary royalty. I am such a fan of your father's work. His *Senior & Junior* books were an integral part of my childhood, and when I was thirteen I starred in the adaption of his standalone novel *The Girl from the Future*."

"Yes, I remember. You were great in the film."

I did remember. Mostly I remembered how much I had begged and pleaded with my father to take me to the premier so I could meet Brooke. Eleven at the time, the prospect of meeting a genuine movie star had obsessed me. My father, however, had refused. Said I wasn't going to miss any school for a stupid trip to the West Coast. He was annoyed at having to go as well. Just as he was annoyed at having to do interviews, readings, and book signings. He wanted to simply do the work, send it to the publisher, and be done with it. However, Doubleday insisted he do some promotional events, and attending the premier of one of the most anticipated movies of the year, based on his own work, was not an event they were going to let him miss. So he had gone, refusing to answer any questions on the red carpet, but he was damned if he was going to drag along his star-struck son with him. To appease me, he had promised to get Brooke's autograph for me. When he came home two days later and I asked for it, he confessed he didn't approach Brooke for the autograph because it seemed tacky.

"Growing up in a showbiz family myself," Brooke said, "I felt a lot of pressure to go into the family business, as it were. Did you feel that same pressure, having a best-selling author for a father?"

"Not really. My father never pushed me to write. He let me find my own path."

I was not unaware that so far the entire interview had been about my father, not me. Then again, how could I really be upset when I wouldn't have even been in this situation if it weren't for my father? I could never have gotten here on my own.

"That's great, Rick. I always think it's best when parents let their children discover their own passions. And yet you did end up becoming a writer."

"Yes, between 1991 and 1997 I published four novels with New Blood Press."

"Not a lot of people know that because you wrote under a pseudonym."

"Sort of. I dropped my last name and used part of my first and my middle name. I published those books under Rick Henry."

"What made you decide to go that route? I mean, many would have considered the Justice name to be a great asset in the publishing world?"

"It is true. I was aware almost any publisher would happily publish something by me because of my famous father, but I didn't want that. I wanted to do it on my own, get there on my own merit and not by riding my father's coattails."

"Very commendable. And yet you stopped writing after those four books."

"I turned my attention to teaching instead," I said, amazed at how comfortable and natural this all seemed. Amy had been right, Brooke put me right at ease and now it felt like an intimate chat. "I teach English Lit at Furman University, and I love it."

"And yet..." Brooke said, then stared into the camera. She was known for this signature prompt that encouraged her interview subject to continue with their story. In fact, her autobiography from a few years ago had been called *And Yet...*

Taking the bait, I chuckled and said, "And yet I'm about to start writing again. I honestly never expected to go back to it, but here we are."

"And I'm sure my audience will be excited to find out you will be continuing your father's legacy."

"Yes. I'm sure you know that he published what was supposed to be the final installment of the *Senior & Junior Adventures* in 2000. However, last year he began a new book in the series. Unfortunately, he had gotten only about three-fourths of the way through when he died. Doubleday convinced me to finish the novel based on the notes he left behind."

"We were all devastated when we heard about Bentley's death," Brooke said, her voice becoming somber. "A true loss to the literary world. It must feel like a great responsibility to finish this book for him."

I nodded, feeling the metaphorical weight on my shoulders like a real load of bricks. "I'm going to do my best."

"I've no doubt. And I hear you are writing the book in your father's house."

"Well, my house now. He left it to me."

"How wonderful. You must sense his presence all around you, and wherever he is, I'm sure he is happy to know his work is in your hands."

I hesitated a moment before nodding again. "I only hope I can do him justice, if you'll pardon the really bad pun."

"He must have been so proud that you followed in his footsteps. Do you remember the first time you told him you wanted to be a writer? Or the first time you showed him a piece of your writing?"

This was definitely not one of the questions I'd been fed in advance, and it threw me for a loop. I felt the sweat beginning to bead at my hairline again, and my stammer returned as I answered. "Um, you know, I think I was about ten. I'm not really sure."

"I bet he was super supportive and encouraging," Brooke said, though her voice seemed to fade away in my ears, as if we were losing connection. But the only connection being lost was in my mind, as it drifted from the present moment and into the past...

The boy waits on the floor in front of the fire, feeling the heat baking into his back. He catches himself chewing on his nails and quickly stops. If his father notices, he will yell at him again, tell him only classless hicks chew their nails.

His father sits across the room in the red leather recliner, glasses resting on the very tip of his nose in a way that seems to defy gravity. The boy sometimes wonders if his father puts a daub of glue on his nose to keep them in place, but that is absurd. Yet another absurd thought to come out of what the boy's teachers call his "overheated imagination".

But the pages his father now clutches in his hand might be proof that the boy's overheated imagination could be worth something. The way his father's imagination has paid for this house and put food on table. Mrs. Davidson, the boy's teacher, certainly seems to think it has value.

The boy checks the clock on the wall. His father has been reading the story for almost fifteen minutes. The thing is only two pages, but maybe this is a good sign. Perhaps it means his father is giving the piece serious consideration, the way he would one of the thick novels the publisher sometimes sends him to see if he will provide a blurb.

Finally, his father folds the two sheets of notebook paper in half and places them on the end table next to the chair. He makes his fingers into a steeple beneath his chin and stares at the boy, but he does not speak. His expression remains impassive, unreadable and inscrutable.

As the silence stretches on, the boy begins to shift uncomfortably, his skin itching as if his body is covered with fleas. He feels as if this is another of his father's little tests of will, and the boy doesn't want to be the first to speak because he senses that would prove him the weaker of the two.

One minute becomes two, and the silence seems to gain actual weight, crushing down on his chest like a cartoon anvil. When the boy can stand it no longer, he caves and says, "So what did you think?"

His father maintains his silence for another few seconds then clears his throat. "Where'd you get the idea for that?"

The boy shrugs. "I don't know. I mean, I was in the kitchen one day and for some reason was staring at the toaster. I kind of fixated on the fact that the middle setting between light and dark was 'golden'. So I started to think, what if when you put the toaster on the 'golden' setting, the bread literally turned into gold instead of toast. But I don't know why I thought that. I mean, I've looked at the toaster before and nothing like that ever occurred to me, but this time the idea just hit me and I thought it would be fun to write for Mrs. Davidson's assignment to reinvent fairytales."

His father picks up the pages again, unfolds them and stares at the top of the first page, the red letter circled at the top. "Well, you understand the unexplainable magic of where ideas come from,

I'll grant you that. I can't believe she gave you a B minus for this."

This perks the boy up. While he's proud of the story and his grade, he honestly feels his work deserved at least a B plus, if not an A. If his father agrees then it doesn't matter what scarlet letter Mrs. Davidson put on the story. His father's approval is the only passing grade the boy needs.

"The idea is interesting if a bit juvenile," his father continues. "The execution, however, is clumsy and lacks any internal logic. The prose itself is like elevated Dick and Jane. This-happens-then-that-happens-then-this-other-thing-happens. And the ending is abrupt and without resolution. This is a D minus story at best."

It takes a moment for the boy to process his father's words. The smile that has begun to form on his lips wilts like a deflating balloon. His face flushes with heat, hotter than the fire behind him, and he finds it hard to breathe as if the room has become a vacuum devoid of air.

His father stands and tosses the two pages at the boy. "Don't take easy praise from teachers who don't know what they're talking about. Try harder next time."

Left alone in the den, the boy feels tears prickling at the corners of his eyes, pleading to be set free so they can make tracks down his cheeks. He holds them back, knowing how much it *infuriates his father to see him cry. He gathers up his story, looking down at the words scrawled across the pages in his shaky script. The pride he'd felt earlier sours, curdles like expired milk, the stench plugging up his nostrils and making him want to gag.*

Losing the battle as a few stray tears streak down the sides of his face, the boy crumples the two pages into balls and tosses them into the fire.

I shook my head to dislodge the unwanted memory and saw Brooke's expectant stare on the screen, eyes wide with puzzled concern. I tried to collect my thoughts but I couldn't remember the last thing she had said. I could attempt to fake it with some vague non-response like, "You know how it is" or "What're you going to do?" However, I decided the only way to truly save this interview was to bite the bullet and tell the truth.

"I'm sorry, my mind drifted. Danger of talking with a writer, our brains are always in about a half dozen places at once. What did you say?"

To my relief, she laughed. "No problem. Happens to me all the time, and I don't even have the excuse of being a writer. I was just saying that your father must have been very supportive of your writing."

"Oh, well...he always pushed me to be my best, that's for sure."

"That's awesome, Rick. I know you're just about to get started, so it's probably too early to ask, but when can we readers expect to be able to get our hands on the book?"

"Doubleday has this one on the fast-track, and they want to get it released by the end of the year."

Brooke clapped her hands together and bounced in her chair like an excited child. "The perfect Christmas gift. Is there anything you can tell us about the book's plot to tide us over until then?"

I shook my head and offered her a teasing smile. "Sorry, the publisher would send a sniper to take me out if I breathed a word about what our favorite father/son ghost hunting duo will be getting up to in their latest adventure. You'll simply have to wait and find out."

Brooke squealed and clapped again, her enthusiasm both charming and infectious. It made me excited to find out about the new book, and I was finishing the damn thing.

"I guess that as scary and surreal as everything is right now with the pandemic changing our world, in some ways it should be good for your writing."

"I certainly won't have any excuse not to put my ass in the seat and do the work. Self-isolation is often exactly what the writer needs to see a project through to the end."

Of course, what this COVID thing also brought was crippling anxiety, especially for someone already immuno-compromised, and a fear that the world may never be the same again. In my nearly half a century on the planet, I had never seen anything that shut down schools and businesses and had people hiding out in their homes like this. Probably not a good idea to bring that up on *The Brooke Simpson Show*, where people tuned in to make themselves feel good about life, not like everything had become a sucking black hole of despair.

Yet when I really took a minute to examine Brooke's face closely, I could see the signs of worry there as well. In the way the corners of her smile twitched, the slight furrow in her brow. The state of current events was taking a toll on all of us, no matter how hard we tried to pretend that the New Normal was in fact normal when it was anything but.

"I will be the first in line to buy the book when it comes out," Brooke said. "I've no doubt it will be a huge best-seller. Rick, I want to thank you for joining us today, and I encourage all my viewers to look up your older works."

I could have pointed out to her that my four New Blood Press books were all long out of print, but instead I said, "Thank you for having me on. It was a pleasure."

"Okay folks, stick around. After the break, I'll be showing you how to throw together a gourmet meal with just the staples you have in your pantry."

She held her smile for another moment then let out a soft sigh. "Okay, we're clear. Rick, again I want to thank you for joining me. I wish we could have done this in person in the studio, but you know how it goes right now."

"I'm just honored to be able to chat with you. I thought it was a joke when they told me you were going to interview me. I've been a fan for a long time."

"That's sweet of you to say. You know, I didn't want to bring it up on air, but while it's decades overdue, I feel I owe you an apology."

I frowned. "An apology?"

She chewed on her lips like a nervous teenager, perhaps her version of my childhood habit of chewing my nails. "I met your father only once, at the premier of *The Girl from the Future*. I wasn't lying when I said I was a huge fan of his, but in my early teens I had become an annoyingly precocious thing, letting fame get to me. I didn't want to let him know how much I loved his books because I thought it would make me look uncool, and being cool was the most important thing to me back then."

I nodded along, not really sure what any of this had to do with her owing me an apology, but I kept my silence and waited for her to get to the point.

"Anyway, I remember he approached me before the film started, introduced himself and told me he had a son who was a fan and wanted an autograph. At that point, I had stopped giving autographs because I thought it would make me seem more mysterious and raise my prestige or something silly like that. So I refused, and I'm sorry."

I heard her words, I understood them, but still they didn't make sense to me. They contradicted the reality I knew. "But my father said he never asked you for the autograph, that he thought it would be tacky to ask."

Brooke shrugged. "I guess he didn't want you thinking badly of me. Sweet man. Anyway, I really do have to run so I can get prepared for this cooking segment. Thanks again, and we'll schedule a follow-up appearance when the book comes out."

Before I could say goodbye, she had disconnected the chat. I closed the laptop and sat there for several minutes, my mind turning over this new revelation. And that was exactly how it felt, like a revelation. My father had lied about asking Brooke for her autograph, but why? To spare my feelings, to prevent me from losing faith in someone I idolized? That seemed so out of character for the man.

And yet, as Brooke would say, in some ways it only confirmed the one thing I knew for certain about my father. Which was that I never really knew him at all.

After the interview, I spent a while wandering through the house, getting acclimated. I had moved in three weeks earlier, but the place didn't yet feel like home. In fact, I felt like an intruder and kept half-expecting the police to show up, sirens blazing, and haul me away in handcuffs. I had never been in this house while my father alive; it felt wrong somehow that I should make myself at home in it now.

My father hadn't left me any of his money. That all got split between his alma mater, College of Charleston, for a new library, and the Greenville County Literacy Association to expand their services. This hadn't upset me because I never expected anything from him. Over the last two years of his life, we spoke a total of twice, and neither conversation was particularly pleasant. We hadn't seen one another at all, despite living in neighboring cities. I learned he died when I saw the story online.

So no, I hadn't expected anything. Finding out he'd left me the house he bought five years prior was enough of a shock. As big a shock as learning he'd lied about the autograph all those years ago, making himself look bad instead of Brooke. I couldn't fathom what was going on in his mind when he made the decision.

The house itself wasn't particularly large. One story, two bedrooms, one and a half baths. Much smaller than the house we had when I was growing up; he had downsized in his older age. I knew it wasn't for lack of money. His books continued to sell while other authors he came up with faded into obscurity, and several had been adapted into successful movies and TV shows. Only last year his one adult novel *Fallen Angels* had been turned into a hit limited series for Netflix. So the money he'd donated in his will had been substantial.

But my father had never been interested in the trappings of fame and wealth. He liked being financially secure without the need of a boring day job, enabling him to spend ten to fifteen hour sessions at the keyboard. However, he didn't desire fancy clothes or expensive cars or trips around the world. All he wanted was to be left alone so he could create his stories in peace, which meant all he needed was a comfortable home, a computer, and some quiet.

Of course, raising a son alone had thrown a wrench into the whole peace and quiet thing. He had never missed an opportunity to remind me of that.

This house, I had to admit, must have been perfect for him. Just enough space for a single man without any of the trappings of ostentation he abhorred. As I meandered around the living room, I again noted all the bric-a-brac but lack of any personal touches. No photographs, no mementos from past trips, not even any of the awards he had collected for his writing. Those I had found in a box stuffed under his bed. The only personal items contained in the room were the books. I had gone through a few, titles I knew had been my father's favorites, wondering if I'd find notes scribbled in the margins, but nothing of the sort. Brooke had said I must have felt his presence all around me in this house, but I got no sense of the man here. As if he wanted to leave no stamp on the place, a house but not a home.

I took my laptop and made my way into the back bedroom he had converted into his office. This room was severely Spartan. The walls plain white plaster, no furniture except an old wooden desk in the corner, the one window covered by a blackout curtain. My father had never wanted any distractions while he worked. When he sat down to create a fictional world, he left the real one behind completely. Begrudgingly, I found myself admiring that kind of focus, a trait I had not inherited.

I wanted to upgrade the office as I required more stimuli to get my creative juices flowing. I needed to be able to look out the window, feel some sunlight on my skin. I wanted to have the room painted or wallpapered. I would have done that already, but with the world being what it was, I hadn't been able to get anyone to come out to do that kind of work. And even if I could, it was a risk I wasn't willing to take at the moment. Hopefully by the end of summer things would have settled down enough, but in the meantime I'd have to make do.

The one thing I had changed was replacing the outdated desktop my father had worked on since I was a teenager, with its massive CPU tower and boxy monitor. I hadn't thrown the machine away, but I had put it in the storage building behind the house with the lawn mower and gas grill. I had bought a brand new Dell Latitude 5420 with some of the advance I'd received from Doubleday, replacing my five-year-old Samsung laptop.

As I stepped further into the office to place the Dell back on the desk, I noticed a book sitting on the chair. I stared down at the glossy cover, depicting a burly man with graying beard and a skinny teenaged boy standing back to back in a cemetery, a thick mist surrounding them, threads snaking forward as if reaching for them. *Final Nail*, the last of my father's *Senior & Junior* series.

Though not for much longer.

I picked up the hardcover, confused by its presence. I didn't remember leaving it here last night after finishing up my notes. In fact, I had a fuzzy memory of taking it back to the bookshelf in the living room. Then again, my memory from last night couldn't exactly be trusted. I had stayed up fairly late and had more than a few beers to calm my nerves about the impending interview. This resulted in a semi-drunken state that didn't leave me in a blackout situation but made my recall questionable. I kind of dreaded looking back over my handwritten notes, almost certain they would contain little more than indecipherable gibberish.

I set down the laptop and returned to the living room, tucking the book on the bottom shelf where my father had kept a single copy of each of his titles. They seemed hidden away, almost as if he had been ashamed of them. More likely he simply hadn't wanted to appear prideful in front of guests. My father had a lot of pride in his work, to the point of coming across almost egotistical when talking about it, but he never wanted to *appear* prideful. One of the odd contradictions that kept the man an utter mystery to me my whole life.

I felt my phone vibrating in my pocket, and when I pulled it out I wasn't surprised to see *ET* on the Caller ID. Edwin Tate was the editor Doubleday had assigned to me, the one who had worked with my father on his last three books. I had no doubt he'd watched the interview and now wanted to dissect and critique it. I almost didn't answer, but in the short time I had known the man, I recognized that persistence was one of his strongest and most annoying attributes. If I let the call go to voicemail, he would keep calling and texting and emailing until I simply had to respond. Best to get it over with now instead of merely delaying the inevitable.

"Hey ET, what's up?"

A pause on the line. I got the sense he didn't like my nickname for him, but he hadn't quite worked up the nerve yet to tell me to stop using it. Of course, I could have stopped out of common courtesy, but something about Edwin rubbed me the wrong way and I enjoyed needling him a little bit. A character flaw of mine, sure, but I never claimed to be perfect.

"Hi there, Rick. Caught the interview this morning."

"Figured you would."

"Not bad," Edwin said, perhaps the highest praise I'd ever gotten from him. "You came across as personable and engaging. You even recovered nicely from that little brain fart where you obviously drifted away for a second."

He paused again but I didn't say anything to fill that void. I could feel the *but* dangling in the air and decided to wait it out.

"But there was one thing you said that got me a little worried."

"Which was?" I asked though I was pretty sure I knew.

"You told Brooke you were *about* to start writing again. *About.* That word suggests an event still in the future, meaning you haven't actually started writing yet."

"That would be an astute interpretation, ET."

"I know I don't have to remind you because you said it to Brooke yourself, but this book has been fast-tracked for an end of the year release. When you signed the contract, you assured us you would be able to meet the June 30th deadline."

"And I will. It's only the beginning of April, and it's not like I have to write a whole novel. I just have to finish the damn thing."

"Think how much closer you would be to finishing if you had started already. I have to ask, what exactly have you been doing for the past month?"

I sighed and rubbed at my left temple, where a headache pulsed like a tiny snare drum in my head. "Let's see, other than dealing with the death of my father, moving, and adjusting to a global pandemic, I've been preparing."

"Preparing for what? You father left extensive notes so all you have to do is follow them."

"When I agreed to do this project, I was assured by all parties involved that Doubleday didn't want something simply churned out to make a quick buck but wanted something better than that."

"True, but anything will always be better than nothing."

"I'm going to be starting today," I assured the pesky editor, not to placate him but because that was honestly the plan. "I needed to reread the other books in the series to get all the facts straight. You know how rabid the fans are. If I got even the smallest detail wrong about some past adventure or the name of Junior's second grade teacher, they'd blast us on Twitter like we were the anti-Christ come to drag the world into hell."

This pulled a rare laugh from Edwin. "I can't argue with you there. We still get hate mail from the time the artist accidently gave Junior blue eyes instead of green on the cover of the first printing of the third book."

I laughed along with Edwin, glad for the moment of levity. Our relationship had been entirely too tense this past month. So as not to disrupt this tenuous peace, I didn't tell him that I had only *re*read the first of the series, as I had never actually read any of the others before now. Yes, the son of the great Bentley Justice had not read his father's most famous series. In fact, the only reason I'd read the first one was because when I was fourteen, Doubleday released a special audio edition for the tenth anniversary of the book's original release and thought it would be a great gimmick if father and son narrated jointly. I reluctantly agreed then had to read the book in advance to familiarize myself with the material.

This had proven a disaster, because despite there being a director in the recording studio with us, my father had taken over all directing duties. This mostly consisted of him criticizing every other word out of my mouth. He didn't like my inflection, my emphasis of certain phrasings over others, where I chose to take pauses, how loud I breathed, and above all he kept telling me my voice was too high-pitched and girly for the football-playing Junior character. After an hour of this haranguing, I'd started to cry. My father called me a pussy and stormed out of the studio.

The next day, Doubleday replaced me with a twenty-year-old actress who my father stated—rather loudly, so I could hear—had a more masculine voice than me.

"I'm not going to keep you from your work any longer," Edwin said, putting extra weight on the word *work*. "I was wondering if maybe you could send me chapters as you finish them. I know that isn't part of your contract, you're only obligated to send in the finished manuscript, but I was thinking since time is of the essence, I could potentially edit as we go."

"Sure, ET. Sounds good."

Another pause, this one drawing out so long I thought he might finally tell me he didn't like that nickname, but in the end he simply muttered a goodbye and hung up.

I stuffed the phone in my pocket, feeling rather exhausted after the three-minute conversation. I had the distinct impression that the editor did not care for me. From the very beginning, he had treated me with a vague disdain that at times wasn't so vague. Of course, he had worked with my father for several years so there was no telling what the old man had told Edwin about me. Sometimes I wondered if the folks at Doubleday knew how their star author truly felt about his son's work, if they knew he would be horrified that I had been hired to continue his legacy. If they did, surely they wouldn't have contacted me to finish the book.

But they did, I told myself. *So whatever Edwin's attitude, someone there must have confidence in your abilities.*

If only I could gain a little of that confidence myself.

I knew I should get to the office and start work as I'd told Edwin I was going to, but instead I took a seat in the armchair in front of the bookshelves. The pounding continued in my head, though the drummer seemed to be losing steam. My hand itched to reach for the remote, find something mindless on TV to drown out my senses, but that was an old habit. My father had not kept a television in the living room, and I had yet to put one in here. I wasn't sure I wanted to. I had never before thought about how much people designed their living rooms with the TV as the focal point, but I could see now how much it opened up the room when you didn't have to worry about facing everything toward the screen.

Yet right now I could have used the distraction of a sitcom laugh track to divert my thoughts from themselves. I wouldn't admit this to Edwin, but I had no choice but to admit it to myself—I was stalling. A lot was riding on this book. They had contracted me to finish *Reborn*, the new installment of *Senior & Junior*, but the contract had a clause stating if this book was a success, I would write two more for them. This could jumpstart my stalled writing career, and that excited me.

And terrified me.

I told Brooke I had turned my focus to teaching, which made it sound like a conscious decision. The reality was that I'd fallen back on teaching when my writing career imploded. Over the years, I had buried most of the bitterness and disappointment and found a certain contentment in my quiet life as a college professor. Most of my colleagues and students hadn't even known I ever published any books.

Then my father's death, followed by Doubleday's unexpected offer. It brought up all the complicated feelings of my past, the anger and self-doubt but also the hope and creative drive. I could fall flat on my face and become a failed writer for the second time in my life, or I might actually pull this off and find a way to fulfill my dreams long after I had given those dreams up for dead.

The pressure left me crippled. I found myself in a Schrödinger's cat situation. As long as I didn't start working, I wasn't a failure or a success. I was neither and both at the same time.

I turned and perused the shelves again. The full-wall bookcase was my favorite feature of the house, and I had yet to look through all the titles. I could do that now, but it would be just another diversion from the work that needed to be done. With a sigh, I heaved myself up from the chair.

On the way to the office, I stopped by the kitchen and popped a couple of Advil. The headache had receded but not totally departed. I made myself a cup of herbal tea and then returned to the desk and the laptop.

After pulling up the file for the manuscript, I scrolled to the very bottom. I had not added a single word to my father's work yet. He had made it to page 238, a total of 59,459 words. What fascinated me was the fact that my father had ended his final day of work not only in the middle of a chapter and the middle of a paragraph, but in the middle of a sentence. Bentley Justice's last literary words were, "Junior felt an icy breath on the back of"…

If I didn't know any better I might think my father had died right in the middle of a writing session, which would have been apropos of how he lived his life and exactly how he would have wanted to go out. I did know better, however. He had been found in the shower, the coronary that stopped his heart hitting while he took a rinse.

Which made that incomplete sentence even more of a tantalizing mystery. Who stopped writing mid-thought? And it wasn't even a complicated sentence. Obviously it should finish off, "Junior felt an icy breath on the back of his neck."

Then again, how obvious was that? In every ghost story, someone feels an icy breath on the back of their neck. Perhaps that was why my father walked away from the sentence, because he was disgusted with its banality. I could almost envision him in the shower, trying to think of something a little more interesting and unexpected.

I went back to the beginning of that chapter and did a quick reread. It started with Junior waking up in the middle of the night, hot and sweaty because it was mid-summer in South Carolina and his air conditioning had conked out. He got out of bed, wearing only his underwear, and stumbled through the dark house to the kitchen for a glass of water. Standing at the sink, he heard a sibilant whisper behind him and felt an icy breath on the back of…

Placing my hands on the keyboard, I typed two words.

I sat back, feeling oddly accomplished for only having written two words, but it was a start. I had officially begun this project, finishing a thought that had been frozen since my father's death. "Junior felt an icy breath on the back of his thigh." I couldn't quite decide if that sentence was interesting or goofy, but it was certainly unexpected.

After that exhausting writing session, I took a break and looked back through my handwritten notes. As I had plunged through the series, I'd scribbled down important dates, significant events, even minor details that I thought might be fun to callback for devoted fans who had memorized even the minutia of the books.

In interviews, my father had always said he had never intended for the first book to launch a series; he had written it as a standalone. Reading all six books back-to-back, I found that almost hard to believe. Everything fit together so perfectly, like puzzle pieces, things from chapter one of Book One playing a significant role in the final chapter of Book Six. As if the whole thing had been mapped out in advance.

Of course, my father had also said after the release of *Final Nail* that the series was done and he would never return to it. Yet twenty years later, he did. Not having spoken to the man much in his later life, I had no way of knowing what his motivations were for reviving the series. Creative reasons, a new inspiration that had to be explored, or was it monetary?

Fact was, while his books outside the series were bestsellers, none of them came close to achieving the same level of success as the *Senior & Junior Adventures*. The series about a father and son (never given actual names beyond Senior and Junior) working together as paranormal investigators had become a global phenomenon. Like most of my father's work, the series was marketed as Young Adult Fiction, but adults devoured them as well as young people. It had sparked a media frenzy the previous November when Doubleday announced that my father was at work on a new installment.

Whatever his reasons, my father had turned back to the series, but fate had intervened and now he would never finish it. He had left this world right in the middle of a sentence. A sentence I had finished, just as I was expected to finish the rest of the book.

Putting aside my notes, I turned to the laptop and minimized the manuscript, pulling up my father's notes for the novel. He hadn't outlined in the traditional sense. There were no bullet points, no chapter-by-chapter blueprint. Instead, he wrote a summary of the entire story, a condensed Reader's Digest version of what would become the novel. The summary for *Reborn* was thirty-two pages long. Therefore, I had a clear roadmap of where the rest of the story was meant to go.

So why was I so hesitant to go there?

There was of course my own fear of inadequacy, yes. That could always be counted on as a factor. However, even more than that, I was hesitant to bring the story to the conclusion my father had planned because I simply didn't find it very interesting. In fact, I found my father's proposed ending rather weak and unsatisfying.

Some might accuse me of being overcritical because of my rocky relationship with my father, my rather complicated feelings when it came to the man, but I never denied his talent. I had not read his complete works, but what I had read impressed me with its lyrical prose, deep characterization, intricate plotting. The man may have been a bastard, but he was a gifted bastard.

Yet something about this one seemed like he hadn't even been trying. The prose still had his distinctive lyrical bent, but the story itself felt so lackluster. It did start off with a bang, I had to give him that. Killing off the Senior character in the first chapter would take everyone by surprise. It was a bold move and considering the author had died during the writing of the book would give it an extra boost in the marketing department. People had a morbid streak they liked to deny until they were passing an accident on the interstate.

What came after was a huge letdown after such a promising start. The main plot involved Junior and the ghost of his father working together to try to find a way to resurrect Senior. Things got complicated when spirits from Hell were sent to try to drag Senior's soul back with them. The ending my father described in his summary had to do with Junior discovering these spirits had been summoned by the old woman who lived next door, well established as a sweet spinster in all the previous books but now revealed to be the sister of a woman Senior had dumped in his youth when he met Junior's mother. She had apparently turned to witchcraft after her sister's suicide and used her powers to assure Senior went to Hell. However, once her plot was uncovered, she realized the error of her ways and called off her spirit hoard and even gave Junior the spell that would resurrect Senior.

The whole thing had a strong *Scooby Doo* vibe that left a sour taste in my mouth as if I'd chugged a carton of expired milk. While the series was technically categorized as YA Fantasy, the stories had always been grounded and felt plausible, which was one reason it had gained such a large adult audience as well. This story felt rather cartoonish and lacking in the depth my father always brought to his work. It seemed to me that he had been phoning this one in, not truly invested and perhaps writing for the paycheck. Maybe he had died from embarrassment that he had resorted to such passionless drivel?

Not a very charitable view, and I couldn't deny those notions might have been colored by my less-than-glowing opinion of my father, but I felt embarrassment both for him and for myself that I would be associated with this story. No doubt it would be a huge bestseller, but I had a feeling it would disappoint fans and critics would roast it over a raging fire. And I knew if that happened, my father would not be blamed for it.

I would.

They would say I had corrupted his vision, ruined his series, tainted his legacy. All the flaws in his story would be laid at my feet, even though I was only following my father's guidelines.

Thus my lack of motivation to get started.

I decided the two words I had written were enough for now. I returned to the kitchen and grabbed a beer from the fridge. I would have one, maybe two drinks to relax myself then get back to it, finally tunnel into the book.

I wasn't stalling. I was...mentally preparing. That was what I had told Edwin, but I wasn't any more convinced than he was.

Tuesday, April 7, 2020

I awoke to an atomic detonation inside my skull. I groaned and pulled the covers over my head to try to block out the assaulting light streaming through the window. My head felt three times too large, like a balloon swelling on the stump of my neck. Except my head felt not only big but heavy, too heavy to be filled with only air. More like a balloon full of concrete chips. When I shifted slightly, those chips slammed against each other. My stomach also churned and roiled like the bubbling concoction in a witch's cauldron. For a moment, I feared I might throw up but I couldn't motivate myself to get out of bed and make a dash for the bathroom. Luckily, the worst of the nausea passed.

When I finally felt the pressure in my head had abated enough that I could move without causing blinding pain, I tentatively emerged from my blanket cocoon, squinting against the sunshine that beat through the window like an intruder. On my nightstand I saw five beer cans, two still standing and three toppled, leaking their sudsy residue across the nightstand to dribble onto the carpet.

Easing myself into a sitting position, I winced as the pain reasserted itself in my head, ricocheting inside my skull like a stray bullet. I supposed one stray bullet was better than a headful of concrete, but either way I felt like I was one step away from the grave—not an unfamiliar feeling for me. I reached out and snagged my phone from among the beer cans, grateful it hadn't been doused in beer, and checked the time. Half past ten in the morning.

I swung my feet onto the floor, one landing in a soppy puddle of beer and one on another can. There were three more scatted on the carpet. Apparently I'd made my way through more than one six pack last night. I couldn't recall.

Not that it was a total blackout. I could remember when my two drinks turned into four, my decision to leave the writing for the next day. I recalled at some point scrolling through my Instagram, looking up past boyfriends and lovers, torturing myself by taking a pictorial tour of the wonderful lives they attained once I was out of the picture, literally and figuratively. I may have sent a private message to one of them, the modern equivalent of drunk dialing, but I couldn't say which ex and what the content of the message might have been. I knew I could check, but I wasn't up for seeing how big a fool I'd made of myself quite yet.

Stumbling from the bedroom, shuffling like a Romero zombie, I made my way to the bathroom to relieve my aching bladder. The cabinet under the sink was open, toilet paper and cotton swabs scattered on the floor. I didn't remember coming into the bathroom last night and had no idea what I might have been searching for under the sink. If I ran out of beer, maybe I was looking for rubbing alcohol. A joke, but one I didn't find funny because it seemed less far-fetched than I'd intended.

At the sink, I splashed cold water on my face then glanced at my reflection in the mirror. The haggard stranger staring back at me looked like some kind of deranged homeless psychopath. Vacant, bloodshot eyes gazed from puffy dark circles, a shadow of bristle darkened my jawline, and my bottom lip was swollen. I still wore the button-down from yesterday's interview, though it was now unbuttoned and stained with either tomato sauce or blood. I stripped out of my clothes and stepped into the shower, hesitating briefly as I remembered this was where my father had died. Not that I felt his presence here anymore than anywhere else in the house, but he had spent his final minutes in this spot. Surely that had to leave some kind of impression.

Could a shower be haunted? Sounded like the plot of the kind of book I'd have written back in my New Blood Press days. Which meant the notion was both implausible and cliché-ridden, if past reviews were to be believed.

I let the water pound down on me, hot as I could stand, as I braced my hands against the tiled wall of the shower. As I did far too many mornings as of late, I contemplated my life, its trajectory if I stayed on the current course. I had always been a drinker, but I hadn't drank this heavily since my heady college years. I tried to excuse it because of all the big life changes I'd gone through, the pressure I was under with this book, but the word *alcoholic* kept creeping into my mind like a pesky rat that nibbles the cheese but never gets caught in the trap.

I had looked up online chapters of AA last week, but I wasn't quite ready to take such a drastic step. I had curtailed my drinking before—I knew I could do it again. I simply needed to start turning to the computer instead of the bottle.

After the shower, I dressed in flannel pajama pants and a loose-fitting tee. I found the kitchen a disaster area. Looked like I had attempted to make a lasagna last night and ended up just making a mess. More beer cans sat on the counter. Checking the fridge, I discovered I had gone through the two six-packs I had left. There wasn't much in the fridge at all, but my churning stomach couldn't have handled anything at the moment anyway.

"Okay," I told myself, speaking out loud as if that might reinforce the thought. "Time to buckle down, get your shit together, and finish this goddamn book."

I shut myself in the office, vowing that I wouldn't leave again until I had completed the chapter. No matter what.

But first I needed to order groceries. Even if I currently had no appetite, I would need to eat at some point and the cupboards were bare. It wasn't procrastination when you were taking care of a necessity. Since I wasn't risking the grocery stores these days, I ordered from a local market that provided home delivery. For an exorbitant fee, but with everything going on in the world, any fee would have felt like a bargain as long as I didn't have to go inside with all those people who wanted to stand too close and not wear a mask. I added more toilet paper to my list but figured I wouldn't get it. One of the weirdest side effects of this pandemic had been the hoarding of toilet paper. I resisted the temptation to put beer in my virtual cart, proving to myself that I wasn't addicted.

Once that was done, I checked my email. Still not procrastination, but business. Had to see if Edwin or anyone else from Doubleday had contacted me.

I had only one new email, from Greta Jenson.

A gentle smile curled my lips as I opened her message. Short but sweet, just like Greta herself. At barely five feet, she was a tiny dynamo of tenacity and confidence and intelligence, all wrapped up in a warming kindness. Sometimes she seemed almost too kind, but she confided in me once that an ambitious career woman could too easily be labeled a bitch, and thus labeled would be dismissed. To play the game effectively, she couldn't just be competent and savvy; she had to create a persona of charm and demure gentility. She turned the stereotypical expectations of being a woman into a weapon, getting what she wanted from people yet making them think they were doing her a favor and never realizing how deftly she had manipulated them into capitulation.

Greta was my hero.

She had been the HBIC (a term I learned from her, Head Bitch in Charge) at New Blood, handling everything from author acquisition to editing to cover design, during my time there. A one-woman powerhouse that turned a paperback horror line into a real force in the publishing industry. She had brought me on board, fought for me when no one else believed in me, and though we had rarely seen each other in person since those days, we still kept in touch through email and text and the occasional phone call. She now worked for *The New Yorker* but was never too busy to keep tabs on me.

Her email said she'd seen my interview yesterday and thought I'd done a wonderful job. Also, that she was so happy I was dipping my toes back into the literary waters and couldn't wait to read more by me again.

This bolstered my mood considerably, to the point that even the lingering hangover headache dissipated. I pulled the manuscript up and did not pause to think about what I was going to write, put my fingers on the home keys, and began to type. I let my mind go blank, trying to evoke that special magic that allowed the story to reveal itself to me.

This felt oddly familiar, a sensation I was once intimate with, but had forgotten. In my twenties when I wrote my four New Blood books, I had known this pure delight in the writing process, but other things had corrupted it. I had allowed other things to corrupt it. Critics, mostly, and one critic in particular had pretty much ended my career. The same one that now might be responsible for resurrecting it.

Yet in the beginning, when I first met Greta, I had harbored nothing but hope. Because of all that followed, I often didn't like to think about that initial meeting in her office, but now it felt safe to fall into the memory, like falling back into a nest of soft blankets.

The young man is surprised by how small and dingy the editor's office is. Long and narrow, the desk wedged at the end giving the short woman barely enough room to maneuver between the desk and the wall to flop down in her chair. The floor is scattered with stacks of books and unbound manuscripts held together with rubber bands. The young man has to move a few books off a chair to have a seat himself. It is cramped and hot in here, and the air smells like old Chinese food.

Still, he is in an actual professional editor's office in New York fucking City! Not only had she requested the meeting, she had sprung for the plane ticket. She didn't chip in for room and board so he is staying at some hole-in-the-wall youth hostel, but he is still here goddamn it. He could have asked his father for a loan, he supposed, but he likes to ask his father for money about as much as his father likes to give it. Besides, he doesn't want his father to know about this meeting, not until the paperwork is signed and it is all a done deal. If things don't pan out, the young man's father doesn't ever need to know.

"So," the editor says, leaning back in her chair as far as she can considering she has little room behind her desk to breathe let alone lean, "I don't have to be a psychic to know what you're thinking right now."

The young man smiles. "I'll play along. Read my mind."

"You're thinking, what can this woman do for me when her office is this big a dump?"

He averts his gaze and feels a blush warm his cheeks because she hit the metaphorical nail on the proverbial head.

"Don't worry," the editor assures. "Sometimes I wonder what I can do for myself when my office is this big a dump. However, since we are in the book business, remember the old adage: don't judge a book by its cover. New Blood is a small outfit, I grant

you, but we are an imprint of Simon & Schuster. Which means while our pockets aren't that deep, we are connected to deep pockets. That's why I could get you a free plane ride but no hotel.

"Bottom line is that while we are a publisher on a budget, that budget is slightly larger than other horror paperback publishers like Zebra or Sphere and comes with more prestige. We can't pay King-type advances, but the money isn't anything to shake a stick at. Whatever the hell that saying means. What would you shake a stick at? A wild dog maybe, so am I saying the money isn't a wild dog? Sorry, if we're going to work together, you better get used to my digressions and ramblings. Especially when it comes to matters of linguistics and etymology."

The young man smiles, amused and bemused. The editor talks as if they've already struck a deal, but as far as he knows this is simply a meeting to discuss the possibility.

"Why would you want to publish me?" the young man asks, wondering if the editor realizes who his father is.

"I convinced the bigwigs at Simon & Schuster to start this imprint, but I know they consider horror something of a ghetto genre. I argued I could prove them wrong, and I suspect they simply wanted to get me out of their hair. They gave me this phone booth of an office and a bit of capital to get started, but the most vital thing they've given me is freedom. They aren't going to be breathing down my neck and constantly peeking over my shoulder. I can do what I want with New Blood, and what I want to do is build a quality line of horror that will showcase the potential power inherit in the genre. So the first step in building that is to gather a stable of authors who can provide the goods."

"Okay, but that doesn't answer the question of why me. I mean, I have only published a handful of short stories. I'm not exactly a name in the business."

"Not yet," the editor said, leaning forward with her elbows on the desk. "But I read your stories in The Horror Show and Twilight Zone Magazine, and they both impressed me. Impressed me enough that I reached out to the editors of those magazines to get your contact information, and now you're sitting across the desk from me because I think you've got the goods. You said on the phone you were halfway through a novel, correct?"

The young man hesitates. It had seemed okay to embellish on the phone because at the time New York had felt a long way from South Carolina, and he hadn't truly believed anything would come of this. But now he is here and has no choice but to come clean. "Maybe halfway through is a bit of an exaggeration. I have started a novel, let's say that."

"How far into it are you?"

He hesitates again before answering. "Three chapters."

The editor's expression suggests that isn't the answer she wants to hear but she nods and shrugs at the same time. "We can work with that. I've only signed two other authors so far, and our first title won't launch for another six to nine months at least. Give me the elevator pitch."

"I'm sorry, the what?"

"Describe your story to me in a nutshell. Doesn't have to be blow-by-blow, but just the gist, the essence, the major plot points."

The young man finds himself at a loss. He always has trouble explaining his story ideas, even to himself. That's why he never outlines. He prefers to start with a basic concept then tunnel in and let the story reveal itself. He doesn't always know what a story is about himself until about the halfway point.

"Um, well, you see, there's these two girls. You know…teenagers. They live next door to each other and were best friends until puberty hit. Then, uh, one develops into this real beauty and becomes a super popular cheerleader while the other is, um, this ugly duckling type." *He shrugs, unable to gauge her stoic face. Clearing his throat, he continues,* "The popular one starts joining in with her new crowd in making fun of her former best friend. That's all back story of course that gets revealed gradually, not like, you know, an info dump right at the beginning. Nothing like that."

She staring at him and his collar feels hot, soaked in sweat.

He focuses on breathing. "The action starts the night after a big football game, and the popular one goes to this party on the beach that's supposed to be all the football players and cheerleaders. But, uh, it turns out that um, that it's only her and five members of the football team. They assault her, and she ends up turning to her old friend next door. In the meantime this girl has spent her time in social isolation studying up on the occult and decides to get payback on the cheerleader's behalf. I'm calling it, um, With Friends Like These."

"Supernatural revenge," the editor says, but her tone doesn't make it clear if she approves or not. Her extended pause doesn't help clarify matters. She stares up at the water-spotted ceiling, as if her opinion hovers somewhere up there near the buzzing light. After a moment, she slaps a hand on her desk, causing the young man to jump. "I like it. I can offer you a contract for the book with a clause where I get first refusal rights for a follow-up."

At first the writer isn't sure he has heard correctly. "I'm sorry, did you say you were offering me a contract? You haven't even read a word of what I've written on the book so far."

"Don't need to. I like your writing and I like the concept. That's enough for me. If the book turns

*out to be a dud, we simply won't go forward with
another."*

The young man laughs. "Okay, so no pressure then."

*"Just giving it to you straight. That's one thing
you can count on from me, I never pull the Band-Aid
off slow. However, I don't think you're going to
disappoint. We can talk money and iron out all the
details, but do you want to hitch your wagon to my
star?"*

*The young man thinks it over, or at least pretends
to because it seems he shouldn't come across too
eager. "Okay," he says after a moment, holding his
hand over the desk. "It's a deal."*

When I broke out of my trance two and a half hours later, I had not only finished the chapter but written another to boot, exceeding my goal. I wasn't sure if what I'd written was any good, and I still harbored a lot of doubts about the story itself, but I tried not to focus on any of that. Too much self-analysis could cripple a writer. Instead, I focused on the fact that I had made progress, and that reminded me of one of Greta's pearls of wisdom (she used to joke she was literally going to release a book one day called *Greta's Pearls of Wisdom*): Any progress is good progress.

After saving and backing up my work, I stood and stretched my back. The effects of the hangover were gone, and I felt good. Energized in a way that only creativity or good sex could do for me. It had been so long since I'd had either that I had nearly forgotten this feeling.

My stomach growled at me, like a little dog that had found its food dish empty. I dimly recalled that I had heard the doorbell at some point, maybe fifteen minutes earlier, and when I opened the front door I found my grocery order waiting, stacked neatly in cardboard boxes. I put on latex gloves and brought it all in, wiping down the containers with sanitizing wipes before putting them away. A month prior, this had seemed insane, the act of a paranoid person with a severe case of OCD, but I found myself amazed by how fast I could get used to these things. The New Normal.

I fried up a couple of eggs and ate them on wheat bread, then started cleaning up the mess from last night. Some of the discarded beer cans were not empty, a few almost halfway full, but with an amazing bit of willpower I poured the sudsy contents down the kitchen sink drain. The smell alone made me thirsty, a craving that started as a tickle in the back of my throat then spread throughout my body like an electrical charge.

To get my mind off that tickle, I decided to give the house a good spring cleaning. Top to bottom. I started at the large bookcase with a feather duster I found under the kitchen sink with the other cleaning supplies. I began dusting the ledges of the shelves and the tops and spines of the books, starting at the bottom shelf and working my way up until I had to use the ladder.

The process was a bit awkward. I would have to climb up the ladder to get at the top shelves of a section, climb back down and slide the ladder over, climb back up and do the next section, then repeat again. I didn't mind. The work had the desired effect and got my mind off the thirst. Besides, the wall wasn't so long that it took me hours. In fact, within forty-five minutes I was climbing the ladder to dust the final section.

As I began dusting the tops and spines of the books on the very top shelf at the right corner, I paused and jerked as if struck, almost toppling off the ladder. I blinked several times, as if what I saw were a mirage I could dislodge like a speck of dust in my eye.

The duster fell from my fingers, clattering to the carpet below, but I hardly noticed. With a trembling hand, I reached out and stroked the spines of the last four books on the shelf as if to assure myself they were real and not just a figment of my alcohol-starved brain. They felt solid enough, so I pulled out one of them.

That familiar cover, two young girls' faces side by side, one with a wicked grin and the other a pronounced frown, no doubt meant to mimic the comedy/tragedy mask, both their eyes glowing red. Above the faces, the title: *With Friends Like These*. Underneath, the author's name: Rick Henry. The other three books—*The Freaks Come Out at Night*, *Wind in the Canyon*, and *Skeleton Bones*—were also by Rick Henry.

My father had copies of all four of my books. The spines were pristine and uncracked, the pages a little yellowed from age but otherwise in fine condition. This suggested to me the books had never been read, but the fact that they were here at all left me feeling flabbergasted. They were tucked away on the highest shelf, but I wouldn't have guessed he would have owned them at all.

My father had not been a fan of my writing. He had made that abundantly clear when I was publishing, never missing an opportunity to tell me my prose was too simplistic, my characters one-note, my subject matter embarrassing. Above all else, he seemed appalled I had gravitated toward horror, which he saw as a childish genre appealing to the basest instincts of readers. He also told me on numerous occasions that my decision to incorporate queer characters in my work was going to cost me any chance at mainstream success.

Bentley Justice had not been exactly what I would have called homophobic. In fact, for years he had an assistant who was flamboyantly gay and the two got along famously. However, he seemed less comfortable—*un*comfortable, even—having a gay son. Of course, the fact that he discovered this by walking in on me at seventeen, making out and jerking off a boy from the football team at school, probably didn't help matters.

He seemed horrified and surprised. I remembered I had told him I didn't know how he could be so shocked; hadn't he ever noticed I never had any girlfriends or even talked about girls? What did he think I—

The idea hit me with such sudden force that for the second time I almost fell from the ladder. In my haste to climb back down, I did miss the last rung, stumbled and twisted my ankle. I ignored the pain and ran for the office and my notes.

I had to get the idea down on paper while the inspiration still flared like a fire in my mind.

I REREAD THE EMAIL for perhaps the twentieth time, tweaking and revising sentences here and there. I had written the first draft at eight a.m. and it was now nearly noon and I couldn't stop tinkering with it. I moved the cursor to hover over the SEND button but hesitated, still unable to pull the trigger. I read over the email for the twenty-first time.

Dear Edwin,

I have been giving the novel a lot of thought and I wanted to run something by you. I mean, I want to get your opinion and advice because your years of expertise could really help me out here. I know we have my father's notes for how he wanted this book to go, but honestly I'm having problems with that direction. No disrespect to my father, he was a first-class talent, but something about this story feels off. Like he wasn't really trying.

I got an inspiration yesterday about a possible new twist on this story. Senior would die at the beginning, all of that would remain the same, and he would haunt Junior, at first this being a comfort to them both. However, I began thinking about how we know almost nothing about these characters' personal lives, especially Junior's, which also led me to ponder how much Senior had known about Junior's personal life. So I was thinking that if

Senior was a ghost, he would suddenly have access to parts of his son's life he'd never had before. Here's where the story would start to deviate dramatically, so bear with me.

To start, Junior is gay. I know, I know, it's a YA series, but more and more YA books are starting to open up in regards to diversity, both in race and sexual orientation. When my father first started publishing this series, the inclusion of a gay character would have been unthinkable, but despite the current administration, we are in a new era and the books should progress with the times. Also, some might argue that nothing in the previous books established that Junior was gay. That's true, but here's the thing. Nothing in the previous books established that he was straight either. Nothing! I just reread the entire series from beginning to end, and not only is there never any mention of Junior having a girlfriend, there isn't even any mention of him having a crush on a girl in school or at the movie theater. Nothing, not even in the books that take place when he is a teenager when you would think the issue would come up. My father kept the focus of these books so narrowly trained on the father/son dynamic and their paranormal adventures that their personal lives were a closed door the reader never got to go through. Well, now that leaves the door wide open for me to explore this twist.

Junior is a gay man, but he never told his father because he feared being rejected by him. Senior was always portrayed as a real old school kind of figure, a paranormal-investigating Sam Spade, I believe a NYT review once said. In death, he sees a side of his son's life he never realized existed. Junior even has a boyfriend, a single father with a ten-year-old son, and the two get engaged shortly after Senior's death. This leads to Senior's spirit becoming enraged and the haunting of his son turning from comforting to violent assaults. Some may say this could corrupt the Senior character, but I see this as a redemptive arc where he eventually realizes his anger is misplaced, really anger at himself that he raised his son in such a way *that Junior felt he had to hide such an important part of his life. In the end, we will have a touching reconciliation before Senior passes into the light. And yes, I am proposing we nix the idea of Senior being resurrected at the end. Feels too cheesy to me, and also an emotional cheat.*

This may seem like it's tackling some adult themes for a YA book, but frankly the Junior character is in his 30s at this point and the series has always had a huge adult readership. I think the audience can handle it. I know this is a lot to throw at you all at once, and you may hate the idea. All I ask is that you give it serious consideration and then let me know your thoughts. I'm excited by the idea, but I know you guys at Doubleday have a lot invested in this series so I'm eager for your input.

Thank you for your time and I look forward to hearing from you.

I contemplated changing the "Dear Edwin" to "Hey Edwin" but decided that would sound too casual and we didn't have that kind of relationship. I wondered if I was too heavy-handed in my ass-kissing at the beginning of the message—"I want to get your opinion and advice because your years of expertise could really help me out"—but figured he would respond well to such obvious fawning flattery. I hoped I didn't appear too critical of my father even while criticizing him. I worried that my description of the idea rambled too long, but the original draft of the email was twice as long and I had worked hard to whittle it down. The very last phrase—"I look forward to hearing from you"—was a total lie, because I felt nothing but dread at the prospect of what Edwin may have to say about this.

Doubleday had hired me for a very specific task. Take my father's notes and finish his novel. What I suggested in this email was a major overhaul that wouldn't only change the ending he had in mind, but rewrite a large chunk of what he had produced before his death. Hell, here I was mincing words even with myself. What I suggested was not a rewrite but actually *throwing out* a large chunk of what he had produced and starting from scratch. This wasn't merely a reinterpretation of my father's vision but a brand new vision that had nothing to do with what he had intended for the story. Not to mention that this new vision could be considered quite taboo even in 2020.

"Fuck," I muttered to myself, removing my hand from the mouse. Was I being stupid? Should I just finish the damn book regardless of what I thought of the plot, take the money and run? That would be the sensible thing to do, and maybe I could then write something entirely of my own creation, try to kick-start the writing career I had given up for dead decades ago. I was courting disaster, running the risk of getting fired from this gig. Yes, I still had teaching to fall back on, but whereas I had once convinced myself that teaching satisfied me completely, the deal with Doubleday had reawakened a desire in me, finding buried embers and breathing them back into a fire. If I gave up the dream again, it would be so much more painful the second time around. Possibly unbearably painful.

And I hadn't been this excited about an idea since my first novel, *With Friends Like These*. I felt like I had to at least give it a try. What was the worst Edwin could do? Say no?

Of course, all writers knew that little two letter word could cause some of the deepest pain.

Not allowing myself any more time to waffle, I gripped the mouse and clicked SEND. Instantly I regretted it, wishing I'd given it a little more thought, did one more edit of the message, but I knew that was nothing but my doubt and fear talking. They had very loud voices, but I had to learn to tune them out. The email was sent, now all I could do was sit and wait to find out what the consequences might be.

Feeling shaky, I got to my feet and made my way to the kitchen. I needed food in my stomach, but my nerves left me nauseated. Less butterflies in my stomach and more like pterodactyls. As I stood there, wondering if I might throw up from nerves, the alarm on my smartwatch began to beep, reminding me it was medication time.

I might skip a meal or two, but skipping my Biktarvy was out of the question. Especially now, keeping my immune system as healthy as possible was of utmost importance. I opened the medicine cabinet and grabbed the prescription bottle, shaking one of the pale pink pills into my palm. I stood there for a moment, merely staring down at it.

Amazing how this little pill could keep me alive. It wasn't a cure, there still was no cure, but it enabled me to live a productive and active life, a life that could have been destroyed because of a questionable hookup from a club in my youth. I had only been a kid during the height of the AIDS panic, still struggling with my sexuality and years away from losing my virginity, but I vividly remembered news stories that talked about the "gay plague" and the devastation it brought to the gay community. A certain death sentence, that was what it was called in articles, no cure and no effective treatment. In my teens, I watched documentaries about those years and read the book *And the Band Played On*, learning about all the fear and desperation and pain. And how every story, no matter how unique, ended the same way.

But this pill, a combination of several treatments compressed into one tiny oblong, changed the ending. Too late for millions, but I was lucky enough to have come along at a time in history when HIV was no longer a death sentence. In fact, there were times I could almost forget I had it, when my Biktarvy seemed like nothing more than a daily multivitamin.

Or, to be more accurate, there *had been* times. Then this damn pandemic came along and reminded me just how fragile my immune system was. Immunocompromised, that was the term being put out there in the media. The virus was a threat to everyone, but critical for the immunocompromised. Like me.

I filled a glass halfway with water from the fridge and used it to wash down my "magic pill". That was what Dr. Lundy sometimes called it, joking even the name sounded like a bastardization of abracadabra or a spell from the *Harry Potter* series. I reminded him J.K. Rowling was a blatant transphobe and killed the humor of the moment. Bringing the room down, another Rick Justice trademark.

I picked up the pill bottle to put it back in the cabinet when my cell phone rang. I glanced at the face of my smartwatch and saw *ET*. Jesus, he was getting in touch so much faster than I had anticipated. I wasn't sure I was ready for this conversation, but putting it off wouldn't make me any more ready.

I answered through my watch, which always made me feel a bit like Inspector Gadget. "Hey there, what's shaking?" I said then instantly winced. No one had ever accused me of being graceful under pressure.

Quick as always, Edwin answered, "Well, your email is certainly going to shake things up, that's for sure."

I couldn't tell if he was angry or amused from his neutral tone, but I took a seat on the stool at the kitchen island, bracing for the worst and hoping for the best. Probably more of the former than the latter.

"Yeah, I know," I stammered. "It was just an idea."

"A good idea."

It took a moment for those three words to penetrate my brain as they were the last three words I had expected to hear. "I'm sorry, run that by me again."

Edwin's laugh came through the watch, a sound I rarely heard. "I said it's a good idea. An intriguing and unexpected direction, and one that I think could result in something special."

"I think so too. I mean, after all the books in the series, I think the audience is probably hungry for something fresh."

"Some of them, definitely. Others will want just the same old thing repackaged with a new cover, but that's always the balancing act for any series author. Giving the audience what they expect while also giving them something new."

"I definitely want to be true to the spirit of the characters, but I think I can deepen them," I said, my excitement causing my words to run together and my voice to rise an octave.

"Slow your roll for a minute. I love the idea, but I can't make you any guarantees because I have to run this by the higher ups at Doubleday. The ultimate decision will be made well above my pay grade. I will definitely go to bat for you though, because I like where your head is on this."

"Thank you, ET. I mean Edwin, sorry. I appreciate the support, and I understand it's kind of a radical notion so if they say no then they say no."

"And they very well might, but..."

He trailed off and didn't say anything for a moment. "You still there?" I prompted.

"Yes. Look, I don't want to get your hopes up and do not repeat this to anyone, but the truth of the matter is that no one here at Doubleday was particularly excited by your father's pitch for the new book. I mean, we were all excited by the prospect of a new *Senior & Junior* installment and frankly we had been pressuring him for a while to bring the series back. His sales had been steadily declining since *The Final Nail* and we knew resurrecting his most famous series would turn that around. It is speculation around the office that the pitch he sent us was meant as a joke. Sort of, *Oh you guys want a new book so bad, what about this piece of shit idea?* Maybe he didn't think Doubleday would take him up on it, but honestly we were so focused on the sales numbers we could get, we offered him an obscene amount of money for the book. An offer even the most dedicated artist couldn't refuse. But with your idea, we could get those sales *and* have a book that wouldn't be an embarrassment to the company."

This outpouring of information left me stunned. Some of it I had already guessed at, but a lot of it I hadn't. To think my father, the great literary icon Bentley Justice, suffered the same kind of pressures and financial concerns that even the lowliest small press writers lived under. It humanized him in a way that living in the same house with him until I was eighteen never had, and it certainly explained *Reborn*. So not a passion project, not a story created from a burst of inspiration, but merely a money-grab by the publisher and an attempt to revive a flagging career by my father. Money itself had never been one of his greatest concerns, but he thrived on the recognition and respect being a successful author brought him. If he had sensed that respect waning, he very well might have compromised his artistic principles in order to regain it.

"I hope you don't think I'm speaking ill of the dead," Edwin said as if regretting the brutal candidness. "Your father was a great man, and I admired him greatly. In fact, having been raised by a single mother, he had become something of a father figure to me. And he once said I was the son he—uh, was like a second son to him."

I realized the real end to that sentence was either "the son he never had" or "the son he always wanted", but the knowledge held surprisingly little sting. I had long since accepted that my father viewed me as nothing more than a disappointment and failure. Edwin wasn't confirming anything I didn't already know.

"It's nice you two had gotten so close," I said diplomatically.

"To be perfectly honest, that is partly why your idea resonates so much with me. As close as your father and I were, there were blind spots in our friendship. I mean, we talked about literature and politics and philosophy and our shared love of French cuisine and classic French films, but we never really talked about our personal lives. He never asked me what I did over the weekend or what my vacation plans were, that sort of thing. So he never knew that I'm gay."

Another moment of stunned silence on my end. I hadn't realized Edwin was gay, either. I didn't really know the man all that well, and we had only met in person once, but I had never gotten that vibe from him. Perhaps my gaydar was on the fritz.

"Do you think that would have mattered to him?" I asked.

"I don't know. Your father never seemed overtly homophobic or anything, and he had that one assistant for a while, but sometimes he used the word 'queer' to describe gay people and it didn't quite seem to have the positive empowering spin on it that we've tried to imbue it with over the years."

"Let me guess, he used to refer to me as his 'queer son.'"

"I'm sorry, man."

"I'm used to it," I said, and I was. Back before we had stopped speaking, when I would occasionally call to check in, he'd usually say something like, "So I don't hear from my queer son for months, and suddenly he takes the time to stop sucking dicks long enough to ring up his old man and say hello." He'd claim he meant it as a joke, but I always detected a hard edge there, the words meant less to inspire laughter and more to cut and draw blood.

"I always found myself too afraid to reveal that side of my life to your father. I was afraid he'd treat me differently, be uncomfortable around me. Even when I went through a painful breakup last year, I know your father had to know something was wrong but he never asked and I never broached the subject with him. So I say we were close, but truthfully there was always this wall between us, a line we didn't cross. Our relationship was all on the surface. So that's why your proposal struck such a chord with me. I could relate to it a little too much."

"I think a lot of gay people of our generation can relate to that," I said. "And honestly, as much progress that has been made in the last decade, a lot of younger gay people still go through this sort of thing. Especially down here in the South."

"You're right, which means this book could actually branch out to a whole new audience. I remember when no one cared about what gay people may want to watch or read, so the fact that we are a viable and sought-after demographic these days is kind of a trip."

"Well, gay folk have a lot of disposable income. It's amazing how quickly companies and businesses can become equal opportunity when they realize they can get a chunk of that cash."

"As long as we don't want a wedding cake in Colorado," Edwin said and we both laughed.

I marveled at how easy and comfortable this conversation was. I never would have guessed how much Edwin and I had in common. I mused that the old adage "Don't judge a book by its cover" was Truth with a capital T.

"I'm really glad you like the idea," I said. "You have no idea how scared I was to send that email. I didn't know how you might react."

"I know my persona is a bit gruff and intimidating, but my bark is a whole lot worse than my bite. I think I learned on the playground in grammar school that macho posturing was sometimes the only way to survive. I probably take that a little too far sometimes."

"You're all right."

"So are you, Rick. Okay, so this isn't a done deal yet. Like I said, I have some people to convince who will have to sign off on it. However, I'm going to give it a hell of a pitch. I think the one major roadblock we face is the fact that such a radical change will mean we will lose the window to get this book out by Christmas. However, considering the current state of the world, maybe that's a good thing. If we push it to Christmas of 2021, this whole pandemic thing will likely be behind us and we can send you on a real tour. If all the bookstores aren't out of business by then."

"And if it helps convince the suits, there is still potential here to continue the series. When the book ends, Junior will have a step-son who can also see the dead. He could become the new Junior and Junior the new Senior."

"I like that idea. I could try to sell it not as just a continuation of the series but a complete relaunch. I have a lot of calls to make and emails to send. Stay by your phone, I'll be in touch as soon as I have a concrete answer for you."

Edwin hung up and I stood staring at the little screen of my watch for a moment, running the whole conversation back through my mind. That had gone better than I could have possibly imagined. So much so that I actually wondered if I had imagined it, if the entire call had been a fever dream of wish fulfillment.

Around the edges of this euphoria, I also detected the first hints of panic starting to nibble. My mind went from "I may have actually pulled this off" to "What in the hell have you done?" It was one thing to agree to finish a book that was mostly completed with a clear roadmap to the ending. If Doubleday agreed to my proposal then I would actually have to *write*. To create something wholly new and my own, which hadn't exactly worked out for me in the past.

"Stop manifesting failure," I said to myself, mirroring the words of an old boyfriend who considered himself an amateur psychologist. He had pointed out that I tried to turn every opportunity into a potential disaster, and I couldn't argue there. I needed to change my thinking, which was easier said than done.

I tried to look at this situation from a different perspective. I had the chance here to do something very special and actually resurrect my writing career. However, even if I did fail, if the book was a flop, then I would return to teaching and be no worse off than I was now. From that angle, it really was a nothing-to-lose situation.

My stomach grumbled at me, and I realized my appetite had returned. Making sure the volume on my smart watch was all the way up in case Edwin called back, I gathered the ingredients to make an egg-white frittata.

Later that afternoon, I sat in bed with my back against the headboard, munching on Doritos while streaming *The Color Purple* on the flat screen mounted on the wall. I didn't feel guilty or if I were procrastinating because there was no use in working on the book until I got word from Edwin on whether we were staying the course or taking the detour I had suggested.

Part of me worried that I hadn't heard back from him yet, but I told myself it had only been a couple of hours and this was a big decision for the publisher to make. At least Edwin was my ally in this. While the Suits at Doubleday might not listen to me, surely they would put some stock in Edwin's opinion. That at least gave me a shot.

To distract myself, I focused on the movie. Oprah was currently marching up to the house, about to raise all kinds of holy hell. I loved this movie, had seen it dozens of times over the years, but this viewing made me a little sad. Last year I had bought tickets for an equity production of the musical based off the movie to be performed at the Peace Center in Greenville. The cost was a bit exorbitant but I had chosen great seats, third row center, and considered it well worth every cent.

Then like everything else in the world, live theater was cancelled. Not postponed, but *cancelled*. I was of course issued a refund but I couldn't be compensated for missing out on something I had been looking forward to for almost nine months. Today was the day I would have been in my seat watching the production unfold up on the stage, so to temper my disappointment I tried to get lost in the movie again.

Right around the time Whoopi was discovering the joys of sex, my phone rang. Edwin. I quickly licked the orange dust off my fingers, paused the movie, and grabbed the cell. "Hey," I said, trying to sound casual but instead sure I sounded like a desperate teenage girl who had been waiting by the phone for the boy she liked to call.

"How's it going, buddy?"

"I'm hoping you're about to tell me. Living in suspense isn't all it's cracked up to be."

"The verdict is in," he said but no more.

I could tell by his tone he was teasing me for his own amusement, and this filled me with hope. If the answer had been no, I felt sure he would have come straight out and told me. The fact that he was stringing me along suggested the news was good.

"Who are you, Judge Judy?"

He laughed and said, "It's a go. Doubleday loves the idea, though I did have to do some persuading mostly because of the delay of release. I knew that would be a point of contention, but I pointed out this would give us time to do a real marketing blitz, create a buzz that will have the country salivating for the book."

I didn't admit to him that the idea of that level of expectation filled me with dread. A lot of room to fuck things up and disappoint millions of people. People who wouldn't be afraid to flood social media and decry me as the antichrist of literature and metaphorically burn me at the stake. Of course I had signed up for this.

"So I'm okay to start the revisions then?" I asked.

"Yes. I'll be emailing you over a revised contract in just a bit. The new deadline is December 31st, and we will aim to release in late fall of next year."

"That's doable. Should give me plenty of time to get this done."

"I think so. Now, um, there is something I want to prepare you for. A clause that wasn't in the original contract."

"What's that?"

"Doubleday wants you to send me each chapter as you complete it so that I can offer you editorial notes as you go along. I know I suggested that before, but now it's going to be a requirement."

I thought about this for a moment, wondering if this was something Edwin had fought against...or something he may have proposed himself. It intimated that I wasn't trusted not to screw up the book, but I also reminded myself that they had no reason to trust me yet. I told myself not to take it personally, with the usual amount of success when someone tries not to take something personally.

"I don't want you to think of it as me checking up on you," Edwin said when I didn't respond right away, as if he could read my thoughts. "Everyone is on board with the idea, one hundred percent."

"It's just my ability to write it that has everyone concerned."

Once the words were out of my mouth, I realized they sounded more acerbic than I'd intended so I tried to cut the bitterness with a laugh.

"I assure you, I'm not going to try to rewrite the book. I'm an editor, not a writer. My job is to provide some guidance to keep things flowing smoothly.

I'm not a collaborator but I do hope we can be partners on this. I want you to succeed, and I will do everything I can to make sure that happens."

It all sounded lovely, but I knew I couldn't take this personally either. Edwin wasn't thinking about my success as a person. He wanted the *book* to succeed because that meant greater revenue streams. Then again, he wasn't paid to be my best friend but my editor, so what else could I expect? Perhaps I'd been out of the publishing business a bit too long.

"Partners it is," I said.

"I think we'll make a good team. You know, in all my time with Doubleday, this will be the first book I've ever worked on with a gay protagonist. I'm excited. Representation matters, as the hashtag on Twitter likes to remind us."

This only made the pressure I felt weighing on me increase tenfold. Now I had the task of providing positive representation to the rather demanding LGBTQIA+ community on top of everything else.

"I'll be on the lookout for the new contract," I said, trying to make my voice sound bright.

"Awesome. You'll hear from me soon."

I hung up and sat in silence. The movie no longer held any interest for me so I turned off the TV. "What have I done?" I said to the room. The situation had already been stressful enough, but I had just made it so much more so.

I took my phone and pulled up the grocery store app for delivery, putting two six packs of beer in my cart. I had promised myself I would cut back on the drinking, but I needed something to calm my nerves. This wasn't recreational; it was medicinal. Besides, I had just pulled off a pretty impressive feat. Wasn't I entitled to celebrate a little?

As I went through the online checkout, I recognized all this as rationalization and in my head heard a repeat of my earlier question.

What have I done?

Thursday, April 9, 2020

Another morning, another hangover.

Morning? Barely. It was half past eleven by the time I rolled out of bed, feeling as if my brains had been scooped out and replaced with broken glass and sharp needles. Every movement sent the jagged mess shifting around inside my head, scraping against my skull.

I had overdone it with the celebrating last night. Then again, moderation was not a trait for which I was known. I had been okay until I actually got the contract from Edwin. After that I started a series of toasts. I toasted my future, I toasted Edwin and the folks at Doubleday, I toasted new beginnings, bittersweet endings, the LGBTQIA+ community, those who still read in a world where readers were a dying breed. Hell, I even toasted my father and his literary legacy. Of course, each new toast called for another beer.

Somewhere around the time I started toasting the trees that gave their lives to become the paper on which books were printed, my memory started to become a bit fuzzy around the edges. I woke up naked with porn still playing on my phone. I checked my messages and outgoing call log. People who didn't hit the bottle heavily had no idea of that fear, the fear of having reached out to people in a drunken state and making a goddamn fool of yourself. Luckily I found no evidence of that this time. Thank god for small favors.

After throwing on a pair of sweat pants, I did my version of the walk of shame, which was the trip from bedroom to kitchen to grab some Advil for the headache. Just as I passed the fridge, my bare foot landed on something hard which pressed into my heel. Absently, I lifted my foot and bent down to retrieve a pill from the linoleum tile. The simple act of rising back to an upright position left me dizzy and I leaned against the fridge door so I didn't tumble onto my ass. I frowned down at the pale pink pill in my palm.

One of my Biktarvy. What the hell was it doing on the floor? I must have dropped it yesterday and failed to notice. I blew the dust off the pill and took it to the cabinet to pop it back in the bottle as I got my Advil. Some might think that gross since it had been on the floor all night and I had stepped on it, but those people didn't know how incredibly expensive HIV medications could be.

I opened the cabinet and reached for the tiny squat bottle of Advil then froze with my hand hanging in the air. Straight away, I noticed that among the Advil and Zyrtec and Gaviscon, one bottle was missing. The most important bottle. The one orange bottle with the child-proof cap.

My Biktarvy was not in the medicine cabinet.

I reached in and began shifting the bottles around in case somehow the Biktarvy got shoved to the back. Nothing. I spun around, glancing at all the counter tops, but no sign of my prescription bottle. I had taken my pill the day before, just before Edwin called, but had I put the bottle back in the cabinet? I had meant to, but the call interrupted me. So what had I done with the bottle?

I tried to retrace my steps. This had all transpired before the drinking so those memories were more or less clear. I had taken the call here in the kitchen, sitting at the island. Nothing was on the island except a large wooden cutting board and a bowl of fruit. Just to make sure, I took out all the apples, oranges, and bananas, as if in my distracted state talking to Edwin I may have buried my pills under the fruit. The only thing I found buried was a dead spider.

Panic swelled in my chest like a frightened pufferfish. What in the hell could I have done with my Biktarvy? Considering I might have mistakenly put it in the wrong cabinet, I began opening every cupboard and drawer and rummaging through. When that yielded no results, I repeated the search through the fridge and freezer and even the drawer under the stove for good measure.

When all of this still left me emptyhanded, I stood in the center of the kitchen, turning this way and that, my mind a chaotic jumble of confusion. I closed my eyes and rubbed at my aching temples, trying to pull up any detail I may have forgotten? Had I perhaps grasped the pill bottle like a talisman throughout the phone call? If so, afterwards I started cooking so the bottle should still be in the kitchen. Unless...

Unless I absentmindedly shoved it into my pocket.

This thought had me dashing to the laundry room by the back door. My clothes from the day before were on top of the pile in the hamper. I snatched up my pants and checked every pocket, front and back. Then I picked up the hamper and dumped the entirety of its contents onto the floor, kicking them around like a child throwing a tantrum.

"Fuuuuuuuck!" I screamed, placing my hands on top of the dryer and leaning there. My breath came in hitching gasps and I could feel my heart pounding in my chest. The pills had to be somewhere in this house; they couldn't have simply disappeared.

I began tearing through the house like the Tasmanian Devil from those old cartoons, going through the cabinets under the sink in the bathroom, the dresser drawers in my bedroom, even rummaging through the covers on the bed in case I took the pills to bed with me like some kind of security blanket.

Part of my brain knew I wasn't being rational, that if I took a pause to calm down I could think more clearly and search more systemically, but rationality had flown out the window. All I could think about was how much I needed those pills. Dr. Lundy had warned me over and over how dangerous it could be to skip doses. Once or twice might be forgivable but not advisable, but if I missed more than a couple then the virus could develop a resistance to the drug which would mean dire circumstances for my health.

And if I couldn't find them? What was I supposed to do, contact my doctor and explain I had somehow lost a month's supply and needed a refill early? The damn pills were almost four thousand dollars for thirty. If not for my insurance through Furman University, I wouldn't be able to afford to live as it was.

After going through every room in the house, I found myself back in the kitchen. I glanced over at the silver cylindrical trash can by sink. I walked over and put my foot on the pedal which lifted the lid. No way would I have thrown my pills away, but I had looked everywhere else. I saw nothing but garbage and started to lift my foot but paused suddenly. Something about the contents of the trash can seemed off.

It took me a second to puzzle through my headache and realize what it was that caught my attention. Crumpled paper towels. What looked like an entire roll, piled in to almost the top of the can. Why would I have used almost an entire roll of paper towels last night?

I reached into the can and pulled out a handful. When I did, a pink pill shook loose from one and landed at my foot. I dug deeper into the trash and found more pills, the prescription bottle buried at the bottom.

Baffled but relieved at the same time, I dumped the trash onto the floor and got down on my knees, finding every pill and depositing it back in the bottle. I found a total of twenty-four which seemed about right. I sat on my butt, back against the fridge, the pill bottle clutched tight in my fist as if someone might try to wrestle it away from me, wondering how fucked up I must have been last night to actually pour my pills into the trash. Then on top of that I covered them with mounds of paper towels in some weird attempt to hide them.

I had gone through self-destructive periods before, especially in my twenties and early thirties, but never anything like this. It scared me that even in a drunken state I could have done something so stupid and almost lethal to myself. I wished I could remember what had been going on in my brain that led me to such an act. Perhaps the alcohol had me flying so high that I felt invincible and convinced myself I didn't need the medication.

Whatever the case, I had to stop drinking. Of course this was a refrain I had repeated many times in the past, but this time I had to stick to it. I still wasn't ready to apply the label "alcoholic" to myself, but I had a problem. That much could not be denied.

I had only three beers left from the two six packs I had ordered the day prior, and I poured them down the sink. I recognized this was the same gesture I had done only a couple of days earlier, but that was before I had put my own life in danger during a blackout session of drinking. That was a rock bottom that had a way of waking a poor sap up.

When I was done, I went ahead and took one of my Biktarvy then started cleaning up the mess I had made. I skipped the Advil despite my headache being worse than ever. In some ways, I felt I deserved the pain as punishment for my colossal foolishness.

Later I reclined in the tub, surrounded by mounds of sudsy bubbles, the water as hot as I could stand it but cooling fast. I had always considered bubble baths to be one of life's greatest simple pleasures, and a good soak never failed to help me unwind and relieve stress. Usually I had a book and a beer handy as well. I had a tattered paperback within reach on the edge of the tub, but no beer today. I tried not to focus on that absence, but the book looked so lonesome all by itself. Like it missed its brother and resented me from banishing Beer from the house.

"Beer never did anything to you," I could imagine Book saying. "In fact, *you* were the one who abused *him*. Yet he is the one who gets punished? That makes no sense. You aren't thinking rationally and now Beer and I are paying the price.

You haven't even touched me since you kicked him out, because you know we're a pair that shouldn't have been separated."

"Shut up!" I growled and knocked the book off the edge and onto the tiled floor.

Since early childhood I had anthropomorphized inanimate objects, sometimes constructing elaborate conversations between myself and them. When I was around six, I found an odd-shaped rock in the backyard which, to me, resembled a humanoid figure with a fat bulbous body and a deformed head. For almost a year I carried it around with me, named it Patrick, slept with it under my pillow, and had full-blown conversations with it. That relationship ended when my father got tired of his son talking to a rock "like some kind of goddamn retard" and threw it out. I cried for weeks. Years later when I went to see the movie *Castaway* with a date, I found myself relating so much to Tom Hanks' attachment to Wilson and his devastation when the two were separated. My date had the audacity to laugh and mutter, "He's crazy, that's just a ball." That was our last date.

Sometimes I found it comforting to imbue everything around me with consciousness and agency. Other times, like now, I found it irritating to have objects without mouths—or consciousness—arguing with me. Of course, I wasn't crazy, not in the clinical sense anyway, so I knew the objects weren't arguing with me. Merely a manifestation of me arguing with myself.

I wanted a beer but didn't want to admit how badly I wanted a beer, and therefore I let the book be that voice. Even now I could hear it mumbling down on the floor. As long as I projected that desire onto the book, I could pretend the craving wasn't inside me, in my blood, just like the HIV.

Sinking a little deeper in tub, I reveled in the warmth. I closed my eyes, tried to empty my mind, but found that a difficult task. Too many thoughts ricocheted around in my skull, a chaotic jumble of worries and fears that wouldn't be silenced.

There was the Thirst, of course, but also the fact that I had not written a single word today. I had convinced a major publishing house to give me the opportunity of a lifetime, and instead of using that as motivation to attack the keyboard, I had avoided the office all day as if a man-eating bear waited on the other side of that door. Self-sabotage at its best.

And when it came to self-sabotage, the main thought I couldn't shake was of how I had poured all my Biktarvy into the trash then tried to hide them. Even if I didn't remember it, I had to have done it. I had considered that my alcohol-soaked brain had decided I didn't need them, but the fear that haunted me and wouldn't let go was that I had known I needed them and that might have been *why* I threw them away.

I didn't think of myself as suicidal, but a lot of my adolescent anxieties and insecurities had reared their ugly heads since I accepted Doubleday's offer to finish this book. I hadn't handled those too well in my younger years. Only then it wasn't withholding pills that had put my life in danger, but a glut of them.

The young man lies in the hospital bed, listening to the constant beeping of the machinery monitoring his vitals. To some, that sound may have been the sweetest music, but to the young man it is nails on a chalkboard, a cat running across piano keys, cymbals crashing right next to his ears. It is the sound of failure, a sound he is all too familiar with.

When his father enters the room, the young man groans before he can stop himself. As if things aren't bad enough already, this conversation is bound to make them even worse. He hates that the hospital called his father at all, but he is the young man's next of kin.

At *first* his father stands by the bed, saying nothing, the two engaged in some kind of morbid staring contest that no one will ever win. Finally his father breaks the stalemate and says, "There are better ways to get attention, you know."

The young man barks a laugh devoid of humor. "You think this was a cry for attention?"

"Let's see, you swallow a bottle of sleeping pills then immediately call one of your exes to deliver some melodramatic 'goodbye cruel world' monologue. You would have to know he'd call the police and send them over to your apartment. You wouldn't classify that as a cry for attention? I mean, if you were truly serious about it, you wouldn't have called anyone."

"Is that what you want? Do you wish I had succeeded?"

His father sighs and shakes his head. "Of course not, son. I'm just trying to make sense of this. I don't understand why you felt the need for this extreme gesture. So you lost a book deal. Happens to a lot of writers."

"I lost my book deal because of you. Don't leave that part out."

"Here we go again. How long are you going to blame me for everything that goes wrong in your life?"

"I don't blame you for everything," the young man says. "Only the stuff that's your fault. And this is your fault. Once that article came out, prompted by what you said at that damn convention, that was all she wrote. The fat lady sang."

"You'll land on your feet. Work harder and land another deal, one with a real publisher. Do you think I started out this successful? Hell no, I met with plenty of adversity and rejection early on. I used it to make me stronger and better."

"Leave it to you to use your son's attempted suicide as an excuse to extol your own virtues yet again."

"You twist everything I say around, you always have," his father says, but his voice is soft and without its usual growl. "I was trying to be supportive, to make you see that losing the book deal isn't a reason for you to try something like this."

"For your information, I have more going on in my life than your betrayal leading to the implosion of my writing career."

This catches his father's attention, and he sits in the chair next to the young man's bed. "Like what?"

"Nothing. Just forget it."

"No, you always complain I don't know anything about your life, but that's because you don't tell me anything about your life. Now I'm asking."

The young man hesitates a moment then finally says it, the truth he had sworn only days ago he would never reveal to his father. "I'm positive."

"Positive about what?"

At first the young man thinks his father is messing with him, but then he realizes the man is simply that oblivious to what's going on in the world. "I'm HIV positive."

His father stands abruptly and backs away from the bed. "You've got AIDS?"

"I don't have full-blown AIDS, no, but I do have HIV, the virus that causes AIDS."

At first his father is silent, as if struck mute, and when he does speak, the young man wishes his father had remained mute. "I knew it. I always knew that lifestyle of yours was going to lead to something like this."

"Thanks, Pop. An 'I told you so' is exactly what I need right now. It's the icing on the cake."

"Who gave it to you?"

"Doesn't matter. I've got it, that's the point."

"You probably don't even know, do you?"

Ignoring his father's question, the young man looks at him and asks his own question. "Do you still think I have everything to live for?"

His father doesn't answer, merely turns and leaves the room. Which is answer enough.

I started awake, my entire body jerking enough to send water sloshing over the side of the tub in a mini tidal wave. I often ended up napping during a bath, but this time I didn't feel any more rested or relaxed. If anything, I felt more tense and achy. My neck had bent at an odd angle against the rim of the tub and now I had a massive cramp right where my neck met my shoulder. The bubbles had deflated to a thin scrim, and the water was cold.

I pulled the plug, listening to the gurgle as the water cycloned down the drain, then pushed myself up and grabbed the towel off the rack on the wall. After drying off, I stepped over the tub and stood on the fuzzy bathmat, watching as the last of the water was siphoned away. If only my anxiety could be siphoned away so easily.

I wasn't suicidal. That was what I kept telling myself. Hell, even back when I downed a bottle of sleeping pills like they were mints, I wasn't suicidal. My father had been right. The whole thing had been an attention-grab, and when it didn't work out the way I had wanted (my father's shame of his son only deepened, and the ex I had called did not beg to be my lover again), I had picked up the pieces of my life and reassembled them. That life didn't look like it did before, some of the pieces no longer fit into the puzzle, but I forged ahead and built a new life that I loved even if it wasn't the one I had dreamed I would have.

So no, despite the pressure I was under and the fact that the pandemic had made me remember precisely how precarious my health was, I didn't want to die, not even in my most inebriated state. So whatever I had been thinking last night when I threw away my pills, it couldn't have been a deliberate act of self-destruction.

I had to believe that.

After slipping on some underwear, I sat on the closed lid of the toilet and massaged the cramp in my shoulder. I stared into the tub, musing that I shouldn't have expected I could get any rest in there. After all, my father had died in that tub. It was an enameled coffin.

As I hastily pulled the shower curtain across the rod, the hooks jangling and clacking, the doorbell chimed through the house. I frowned, uncertain who could be visiting. I couldn't very well go check in only my tighty-whities, or to be more accurate my tighty-blackies, so I threw on my clothes as fast as I could.

At the front door I pressed my eye to the peephole but saw no one. My frown deepening, I eased open the door and discovered a small grocery delivery waiting on the porch. I hadn't made any more orders...or had I?

I grabbed my phone and opened the grocery delivery app. This morning I had checked for any embarrassing outgoing messages I may have sent while drunk, but I hadn't thought to see if I made any orders. And it turned out, I had. At 2:25 a.m. I placed the order and requested it be delivered sometime after 3 p.m.

I returned to the door, reluctantly admitting that I needed to reevaluate my conviction that I wasn't self-destructive as I stared down at the two cases of beer.

FRIDAY, APRIL 10, 2020

"FUCK IT ALL TO goddamn hell!"

I highlighted the last two paragraphs I had written then jabbed hard at the DELETE button. Not as satisfying as the old days when you would rip a piece of paper from the typewriter carriage, ball it up and toss it across the room, but it got the job done. "The job" being taking a pile of drivel I had written and removing it from my sight.

I checked the time and saw I had been at it for an hour and a half and so far had written only half a page that I hadn't ended up deleting. Not what one would call productive. My hair stuck up in tufts and corkscrews from where I had been yanking at it in frustration. The ghostly reflection in the computer monitor looked like the quintessential madman. The image was accurate because I felt like the quintessential madman.

I reminded myself that I had always found the beginning the most difficult part of creating a story. Feeling my way into the world, establishing the mood, developing the characters. This took time and patience. Once I had built that foundation, however, and got into the meat of the story, things always tended to start flowing much more quickly and smoothly. I supposed I had assumed it would be easier stepping into an already-established world, that I would be able to skip over all the hard stuff, but that proved not to be the case. If anything, it was harder because I had to make sure I wasn't contradicting anything that came before while creating something wholly new.

And this was a new story, a story more mine than my father's. I had kept his first chapter more or less intact, the scene at the hospital where Junior is by his father's side, holding his hand, as Senior dies. I made a few minor tweaks and adjustments here and there, setting up for some things I would have come later in the story, but for the most part this was still fully my father's chapter, and he had imbued it with a potent emotion that was a great jumping off point.

Chapter two was where I started significant deviations. In my father's original draft, Senior's funeral was attended by a plethora of familiar characters readers would recognize from past books, people Senior and Junior had helped free of paranormal problems, but Junior had stood alone by the graveside, with only the ghost of his father next to him which no one else could see.

In my version, Junior was not alone. His fiancé stood next to him, with his fiancé's son between them, each man with a hand on the boy's shoulder. Senior was not at the graveside but several feet away, standing by a monument of an angel with its stone arms upraised. He stared at his son and these two strangers with a frown, but Junior avoided the gaze.

The last thing I wrote before I started deleting everything had the young boy point toward the angel monument and ask, "Who's that man?"

My problem was I couldn't decide how to have the men react to the revelation that the boy shared Junior's gift of seeing ghosts. I hadn't even figured out if it should be a revelation or something of which the men were already aware. Should there be confusion and denial? If not, would I need to give a detailed explanation of Junior's history with the boy and his father to get the reader up to speed? That could prove awkward right in the middle of a funeral scene.

My smart watch buzzed on my wrist and I turned it off without looking to see who was calling. I felt certain it was Edwin, expecting an update. He had emailed the afternoon prior and I hadn't responded. I imagined he was as nervous and full of regrets as I was.

I tried to put all that out of my mind and focus on the story. I had approached this part from so many different angles and so far nothing felt right. I wondered if I should cut the part where the kid spots Senior, but I wanted to establish his gift early on. Or at least hint at it.

Inspiration comes in many different ways, some of them gradual and cumulative, but often it happened all at once. Of course, I recognized that such eureka moments weren't as spontaneous as they seemed, resulting from a lot of work happening in the subconscious, but they *felt* like a sudden gift from the muses. The proverbial lightbulb.

One such lightbulb illuminated over my head now. I could simply *hint* here. This was a novel, not a short story. I didn't have to load all the information at the beginning. Besides, sometimes a hint was more effective at this stage, peaking the reader's curiosity and leaving them a bit in suspense. I had been overcomplicating a scene that needed simplicity, a common sin among the writer clan.

After the boy points and asks, "Who's that man?", I had his father pat him on the head and say, "That's a statue of an angel." Junior, however, squeezes the boy's shoulder and whispers, "We'll talk later."

And that was it. The perfect tease that gave just enough information while still promising more juicy revelations to come. Once I was past that hurdle, I picked up speed, my fingers dancing over the keys like light-footed spiders. The rest of the funeral scene played out with a sense of numbed grief, leading up to a dramatic moment. When the funeral is over and after Junior helps the boy into the backseat, Junior turns to find his father's spirit standing beside the car.

"Who are these people?" Senior asks in a voice only Junior can hear.

Junior hesitates for a moment before answering, "My family." Then he gets into the car and drives away. End of chapter two.

It wasn't perfect, but first drafts weren't meant to be perfect. It was, however, done and I felt semi-quasi good about it. I thought I'd made the right choice only teasing the boy's gift without delving too deeply into it, and the end of the chapter set up the conflict of the rest of the book quite nicely. Not a bad start, even though I'd had a bad start to the start. The last half hour I had written more than the first hour and a half, but I had gotten it done and that called for celebration.

Of course, the way I normally celebrated was with a beer or five, but not this time. I couldn't allow myself to indulge that particular craving.

But you could, the devilish little voice in my ear spoke up. *It would be so easy.*

And it would be. The two cases of beer that had been delivered to my door yesterday were currently sitting on the floor in the pantry closet just off the kitchen. I should have poured it all down the drain, but I couldn't bring myself to. Seemed like too big a waste. I could always gift it to someone, but to whom? I didn't leave the house and didn't even interact face-to-face with the folks who delivered my groceries. I supposed I could leave the cases at the edge of the property with a sign that read FREE BEER! Laughable, but I knew without a doubt someone would stop and snatch them up within the hour if not sooner.

And yet they are still sitting in the pantry, waiting for you. Waiting for you to admit that resistance is futile, as that robot chick in the skin-tight leotard used to say on Star Trek.

I lifted my left shoulder and rubbed it against my ear, as if trying to dislodge the little devil sitting there, whispering these things directly into my brain.

So no beer to celebrate, but I did feel strong enough now to listen to Edwin's voicemail. In fact, before I grabbed my phone I took the time to email him what I wrote today to get his thoughts. Mostly I wanted to prove to him that I was working.

I was surprised to find the earlier call hadn't been from Edwin at all, but Michael Franklin. A former student of mine at Furman, I had taught him Freshman Composition when he first arrived on campus. Now he was a senior, but over the years we had lunch often or caught up over coffee in the bookstore café. He seemed to have a crush on me, and I didn't encourage it. I also didn't *dis*courage it because no one being honest would deny they liked a little ego boost from time to time. A harmless school boy crush, no danger there. Or so I told myself.

I stood up and left the office as I played Michael's voicemail.

"Hey Prof, how's it hanging? I'm dealing, although it's all so strange schooling from home. I mean, when we all left for spring break last month, we had no idea that we wouldn't be coming back. Hell, I left so much stuff in my dorm, including most of my textbooks. Meanwhile, my parents are trying to figure out if the university is going to reimburse us for room and board since we're spending half the semester at home and not on campus."

Since I was on sabbatical this semester and next so I could focus on the book, I had heard about how the pandemic had sent things into an unprecedented quagmire. No one allowed on campus except security, professors trying to figure out how to adapt their courses for online learning. I imagined the bookstore was scrambling to figure out how to get the rented textbooks returned when students weren't on campus and as Michael pointed out, most had left their textbooks in their dorms when they went on spring break.

"Anyway, I miss being able to chat with you in person. I mean, this is my last semester and now I won't even be in town for us to meet up. I did catch you on *The Brooke Simpson Show*, and you looked great. I know you're probably hard at work on the book as we speak, but give me a call when you get the chance. I want to hear all about the exciting life of a professional writer."

I was about to call him back when I walked into the kitchen and stubbed my toe on something on the floor. I cursed, did a little one-foot hop, and stared down at the object I'd struck. The sight of it caused a chill to radiate from my spine throughout the rest of my body, and I nearly dropped my phone. I blinked several times, as if that would dispel the image like a mirage. Yet the pain in my big toe confirmed the reality of the thing.

A case of beer. Sitting right out in the middle of the kitchen floor. I had left both cases in the pantry closet yesterday, I knew I did. Hell, I had been in the kitchen this morning to fix coffee and toast and that case wasn't there.

So what did that mean? That someone had broken in and moved a case of beer out of the pantry?

I scanned the room for anything else amiss, but everything seemed normal. Nothing out of place but the case of beer. The house suddenly felt too quiet, a suspicious kind of quiet like the hush before a big storm. I stumbled over to the countertop by the stove and pulled the biggest butcher knife out of the wooden block. I felt a little silly, Drew Barrymore circa 1996, but I knew I hadn't moved the case.

Holding the knife out in front of me, I did a quick circuit of the house, checking in the closets and even under my bed. Not only did I find no one, I found nothing else moved or missing. All the doors and windows were locked and showed no obvious signs of forced entry. Part of me wanted to call 911, but what could I say? That I suspected someone had broken into my locked house somehow, without actually breaking anything, and only moved one case of beer? The operator would either laugh me off the phone or accuse me of making a prank call to 911 which could get me into serious trouble. Besides, I had read that another side effect of the pandemic was that the police were only responding to calls that were true emergencies. I doubted my situation, even if the operator believed me, would be deemed an emergency.

I went back to the kitchen, still not quite willing to relinquish the knife, and stared down at the case of beer. It couldn't have simply grown legs and walked itself out here. Which meant someone had to have moved it. If not an intruder that only left one person.

Me.

But I would remember if I had moved the case. Right? I had gone into the pantry this morning to get a new bag of coffee, but I hadn't touched the beer. I had gone in, grabbed the coffee, and come right back out.

I had let the knife drop almost to my side, but I raised it high again as a chilling thought occurred to me. I had searched the house, looking in all the closets, but I hadn't checked the pantry.

Creeping forward, I tried not to let my feet squeak on the linoleum and willed the hand holding the knife not to shake. I was successful in the former but not the latter. The pantry door was open a crack, and I hesitated a moment before knocking the door the rest of the way open with my shoulder. The pantry was small, kind of like the old-time phone booths that Superman would change in, so I could see right away that no one was there.

I noticed another thing right away as well. The second case of beer was missing.

I sat on the sofa, my entire body leaned forward with my elbows resting on my knees, staring at the case of beer which rested on the coffee table where I had moved it. I studied it like a puzzle that could be solved, a complicated Rubik's cube. I had never been able to figure those out as a kid, and I seemed no more capable of figuring this out now.

I felt relatively safe in the house despite this mystery, but the sun was shining through the windows and that made all the difference. Once the sun went down, my sense of safety was sure to become more tenuous.

"It had to be me," I said, my own voice startling in the quiet.

I didn't know how I could have done something like this and not be aware of it, only I often did things without remembering them when I was drunk. Only I hadn't been drunk this time.

Had I?

Could I have gotten so drunk last night that I didn't even remember starting to drink? The scariest part was that the idea felt at least somewhat plausible. But if I had gotten drunk last night, where were the beer cans? The house should be scattered with them, shrapnel left behind after a bloody battle.

I stood abruptly and grabbed the case, hurrying through the house to the backdoor which led onto a small concrete patio. The wheeled trashcan sat at the corner of the patio, and I made a beeline for it to get rid of the beer, which I should have done yesterday afternoon as soon as it arrived at my doorstep. I had tried so hard to convince myself I kept it only to avoid waste. Of course I had kept it to drink it. Any idiot could have called that one. Any idiot but me.

With one hand I flipped open the lid to the trashcan and raised the case with the other to toss it in, but I had another frozen moment. I couldn't move, could barely breathe, as I looked down into the trashcan. The first thing I noticed was the torn cardboard of the second case of beer, ripped apart as if a wild animal had gotten to it. All around the remnants were crushed beer cans. I didn't count, but it looked like all twenty-four that would have been in the case. Emptied and drained, crushed and discarded. Shrapnel.

When my paralysis passed, I threw in the full case and slammed the lid, as if hiding the evidence could wipe it from existence. That never worked. What had been seen could not be unseen, what was known could not be unknown.

Moving as if in a trance, my brain feeling dazed and foggy, I went back inside and headed straight for the office, taking a seat at my desk. On the laptop, I minimized the manuscript and pulled up Google. In the search bar I typed, "Online AA meetings."

By later that evening, my mood had lightened considerably. I had approached attending my first online AA meeting with real trepidation. Held via Zoom, like so much of life these days, everyone appeared in little boxes along the borders of the screen with only a first name and last initial. The majority of the screen displayed whoever was talking at any given time. First a young woman—Stacy

Q.—who welcomed everyone, went through the whole spiel about recovery and higher powers and working the steps and the Serenity Prayer. All stuff I was familiar with from decades of TV shows and movies. I felt like a weird combination of Sandra Bullock from *28 Days* and Sandra Bullock from *The Net*.

After the introduction, Stacy Q. opened the floor for people to tell their stories. I chose not to tell mine, not yet. For my first meeting, I wanted only to be an observer, to get the lay of the land so to speak. I listened to an hour of stories, half a dozen people sharing the darkest moments of their lives that led them to recovery. In some ways, it was the most depressing sixty minutes of my life, and yet in others I found it incredibly uplifting. Here were people who had been far worse off than me, and they had managed to climb their way out of the quicksand of alcoholism.

And that was my biggest takeaway from the meeting. I admitted to myself what had been obvious to others for years. I was an alcoholic. I had thought such an admission would be devastating, but instead I found it liberating. No more denying or pretending which could be exhausting. Once you admitted you had a problem, you could start looking for solutions.

I knew it wouldn't be easy. The stories I heard assured me of that, but they also assured me it was possible. I walked away from the meeting feeling better about myself. I wasn't alone, and that knowledge was everything. One guy, Jason P., talked about waking up in the back of a pickup two states over from his with no memory of the past week. His last vivid recollection had been going to the ATM to get some cash then—BAM!—he was in a stranger's pickup in a Walmart parking lot. Somehow that made me not remembering drinking one case of beer and moving the other seem less frightening.

After the meeting, I got an email from Edwin. The message was restrained, nothing effusive, but he said he had read what I sent him and liked the direction in which I was going. The best bit was when he said, "I loved how you threw in that the kid can see the dead but didn't linger, instead letting it spark the curiosity of the reader." That confirmed my instincts had been right on that part.

All this left me in such good spirits that I decided to have a rare evening writing session. Back when I had been publishing with New Blood, I always wrote in the mornings. It had been a routine that worked for me, so when I got this deal with Doubleday I fell right back into that routine. However, inspiration struck and I thought of a scene where Junior wakes up in the night, his fiancé sleeping next to him, and sees Senior's ghost standing at the foot of the bed.

I sat down at my desk, excited to get the scene on paper. Metaphorically speaking, of course. Unlike my previous time as a professional author, almost nothing was printed anymore. Not contracts, not manuscripts. Everything was electronic. No more self-addressed stamped envelopes, no more spending money on paper and ink. A brave new world.

As I mused on the technological revolution, I opened the file folder on my desktop I had humorously named "Ruining Dad's Legacy" to open the manuscript...

And it wasn't there.

My father's original manuscript was there, but the new file I had made for my revised version was not. I checked the flash drive stuck in the laptop but found nothing. Ditto Google Drive and iCloud. Panic began to flutter in my chest. How could I have forgotten to save my work from this morning? The writing had not come easy, but ultimately I had been proud of it and hated the idea of trying to recreate it. Even Edwin had liked the direction.

Edwin!

I must have saved my work, because I had emailed it to Edwin. I opened my Gmail account, my breath caught in my lungs, and went into my SENT folder. The email to Edwin was right on top, including the attachment.

With a long, shuddering sigh of relief, I opened the attachment, finding my work intact. I saved the file to my computer, the flash drive, Google Drive, and iCloud. My gratitude at being able to recover the document momentarily blinded me to the real question.

How had the file gotten deleted in the first place?

Saturday, April 11, 2020

It felt like a rainy day, even though the sun was shining. I couldn't sit still for more than five minutes, couldn't even seem to stay in the same room for that long. I paced the house, room to room, closing all the curtains and blinds because the light streaming through the windows seemed like an affront to me.

A strange mood to be in, a sort of stir-crazy feeling. In the past several years, I hadn't been what anyone would call a social butterfly. The occasional trip to see a play, maybe peruse one of the Greenville bookstores, a day trip up to Asheville to take in the hippie mountain culture. Mostly though I stayed in, reading or working on my lessons for class, re-watching my favorite TV shows. However, only now was I beginning to see how being on the Furman campus every day had given me a sense of a social life, albeit an indirect one.

The campus bristled with life, students and other professors crisscrossing the grounds and quads, the bookstore café always packed, the dining hall a circus of loud voices and clanking silverware. I couldn't walk from my office in Riley Hall to the library without having a dozen or more people say hello or ask how I was doing, a student with a question about an assignment, a fellow professor inquiring if I wanted to grab lunch later in the week. These things I had taken for granted until my hiatus.

Of course, I had expected even during the hiatus I would continue to be a presence on campus. If this virus hadn't come along and fucked everything up, I could drive down there now. I still had my office, and the head of the English department had encouraged me to write on campus. I think she loved the idea of a member of the faculty having such a high-profile book deal. No doubt imagining the prestige it would add to the Furman English department. She had even talked to me about the possibility of teaching a Creative Writing course when I returned.

If I returned, those had been her exact words. As if she thought my star would rise so high that I'd never have to work again. In truth, the money from this one book assured I wouldn't have to work for at least another year or two if I didn't want. Of course, if they signed me on to do more—

I shook my head, cutting off this train of thought before it picked up too much speed and got ahead of myself. I had barely started this first book, and it would never get finished at all if I kept deleting what I wrote.

As I paced through the living room, I stopped and dropped onto the sofa. The real reason I felt so cooped up today was because I wanted to get out and find a distraction from these thoughts that plagued me. Instead, I was trapped in this house with nothing but my thoughts and the conclusions I had no choice but to draw.

I had gone over the situation a million times and all the evidence pointed to the same place. I had to have deleted my work. There was zero indication whatsoever that anyone else had been in this house, and I couldn't think of any way someone could have gotten in and out without me knowing. Plus I had a history of blacking out.

Of course, I told myself, I hadn't been drunk yesterday when the work got deleted, so could that technically be called a black out? Maybe a fugue state? I had heard stories of heavy drug users who experienced effects of their addiction years after they stopped using. What was alcohol except a legal drug? Legal but no less dangerous and damaging. And I had only stopped drinking within the last few days. I wasn't sure how long alcohol stayed in someone's system, but might it still be coursing through my veins, saturating my brain like a sponge, causing me to do things then forget them?

I felt myself shivering even though it was a warm day and I didn't have the air conditioning on. Withdrawals? Was that a thing for alcohol the way it was for other drugs? I certainly felt like a wreck, worse than any hangover. A case of the cure being worse than the disease?

I stood and rushed across the room, the hurried steps of someone trying to make it to the bathroom before they blew chunks all over the carpet. Only I rushed for the front door. The house felt as if it were shrinking, miniaturizing down to the size of a dollhouse, yet I stayed the same size, being squeezed flat. This sensation went beyond simple claustrophobia. It felt more like I was a roach as a shoe started to press down on the hard shell. I needed to get out of the house, breathe in the fresh air, experience a wide world with no walls.

I made it to the edge of the front lawn and stopped, gulping air and staring up at the sky. Light blue, blemished only by a few tattered clouds drifting by as if they had all the time in the world to get where they were going. This made me feel better for a moment, a drowning victim breaking the surface and getting a lungful of precious oxygen, but it didn't last. My head slipped back beneath the water, the freedom only a tease.

I was struck at first by the silence. I didn't live next to a highway or a school, so the neighborhood had always been pretty quiet, but this kind of quiet was next level. Usually the road hummed with some traffic, neighbors could be heard in their yards, even the shrill laughter of children from a public park several blocks over would sometimes drift this way if the wind was right.

But now the silence was so total it was like going deaf. Not entirely, I heard birds chirping and leaves rustling but nothing manmade. It wasn't that people had entirely stopped going out. There were still "essential workers", as they were being called. Medical professionals, police, grocery store workers. However, for the most part the streets were deserted as they were now. People were sequester-ing themselves away.

The only time I had ever experienced anything like this was during a rare southern ice storm several years earlier. The city of Greenville had shut down, the roads too slick to traverse because we didn't have the infrastructure in place to handle that kind of wintery weather like they did up north. I had stepped out onto my apartment balcony and marveled at the silence, the kind of silence one never heard unless they went deep into the country. Then it had seemed peaceful.

Now it did not. Now it felt like the silence of a post-apocalyptic world. As if I were Vincent Price in that old movie, *The Last Man on Earth*.

The longer I stood outside, the more the claustrophobia returned. As if the sky were lowering and the air solidifying. I longed to see the redneck guy across the street barbequing so I could wave at him, hear the kids from the house next door shouting as they played some game with rules incomprehensible to adults. Just to remind me I wasn't alone, that other people still inhabited this planet with me.

I felt a pressure in my chest, starting to rise up my throat, and I realized how close I was to screaming. A wordless, mindless scream of frustration and loneliness.

I hurried back inside before I could give voice to this scream. What was wrong with me? Was I losing my mind, on the verge of a breakdown?

In the kitchen, I poured a glass of water, downed it in a couple of gulps then filled a second. This did not quench my thirst. What I needed to sate my desire was in the trash out back. A sudsy panacea that could soothe my mind and my nerves.

"No!" I said out loud, slamming the glass down on the countertop so hard I was surprised it didn't crack. The beer wasn't the solution, it was the problem. My brain knew this, but my body was not convinced.

I considered getting online and finding another AA meeting, maybe researching how to get a Sponsor, someone I could call when I felt myself getting weak. However, I felt more than weak. I felt unstable. Perhaps I needed something stronger than a Sponsor.

Therapy.

The word sounded dirty to me, like an admission of defeat. I knew this came from my father, who had considered all psychiatrists quacks and people who couldn't handle their problems on their own as losers. However, knowing my father the way I had, I wasn't sure why I still put any stock in the opinions he had held.

Of course, I had my own experience with counseling. Only one session when I was in middle school, but it had left an indelible impression on me.

The boy hesitates in the office doorway. The counselor has not yet spotted him so the boy considers turning around and leaving. Perhaps this whole thing is a stupid idea, he thinks. He actually has just decided to slink away when the counselor looks up.

"Oh hello," she says with a bright smile that seems too big to be sincere. What the boy's father calls a plastic smile. "How can I help you, young man?"

The boy freezes, the quintessential deer in headlights. Finally he turns his head to gaze down the hall, as if seeking an escape route, but all he sees are a group of cool kids. Cool kids that scare him, even though they don't pick on him like they do the ones in the chess club or the honor roll geeks. Middle school can be a jungle out there for anyone who doesn't fit in.

And the boy doesn't feel like he fits in anywhere. The popular kids would have him if he made even a little bit of an effort. After all, his father is rich and famous which gives him an almost automatic "in". But does he want to be "in" is the question. The kids don't really know him, and they don't really want to know him. They want him to be something he's not, and he isn't sure if the effort is worth it.

All of which has led him here, to the guidance counselor's office.

"Don't be scared, I don't bite," the counselor says, her smile becoming more natural.

Still he hesitates, lingering in the doorway, unable to commit to coming in or going out. Something like that weird thing Mr. Mets talked about in science class, the cat in the box that might be alive or dead as long as you don't open the box and commit to one or the other. In this situation, the boy is the cat and the threshold is the box.

Then, biting his lower lip so his words are slightly distorted, he says, "Can I talk to you for a minute?"

"Of course. That's what I'm here for. Come on in and have a seat. Oh, and shut the door."

He does shut the door, though it seems like a moot point. The halls are emptying, everyone rushing out now that school is done for the day. The boy is going to miss his bus, but he doesn't mind. He'll walk home. It will take him longer, but he doubts his father will notice. The old man is almost at the end of a new book so he spends hours and hours each day locked in his office. Some days he doesn't even talk to the boy, which the boy finds preferable.

After he takes a seat, the counselor leans forward on her elbows and points toward the name plate on the front of the desk. "I'm Miss Collins, but you probably already know that. What's your name?"

The boy tells her, but only his first name. The last name is too recognizable and comes with far too many preconceived notions. He keeps that to himself for now.

At first the counselor doesn't say anything, and the boy wonders if he is supposed to start things off. He isn't entirely sure how this works. From the movies and TV, he knows that a counselor usually asks you probing questions regarding how you feel about things, but those scenes usually start after the session is underway. He doesn't ever remember seeing how the ball gets rolling. If he were in a confessional that would be easier. He would start with, "Bless me Father for I have sinned." He is tempted to say that now just to end the silence and break the ice.

The counselor saves him from the lame joke by finally speaking. "So, what brings you to my office? Girl trouble?"

The boy laughs and shakes his head.

"Are you being bullied?"

Again, he shakes his head. "No, more like the opposite. Everyone is way too nice to me."

This elicits a small frown from the counselor. "Too nice? Can there be such a thing?"

"If it's phony, yeah. I think so."

Now the counselor leans back in her chair, her eyebrows raised. He seems to have intrigued her. He muses this probably isn't the kind of problem she's used to hearing. "Why do you think the people being nice to you are phony? Maybe they really like you."

"They don't even know me. They don't know what my favorite TV show is or what kind of music I listen to or what kind of food I like. If you asked them to describe me when I wasn't around, some of them probably wouldn't be able to tell you the color of my hair. No, they don't like me."

"Then why do you think they are nice to you?"

"They are nice to me because my father has money and some prestige. People want to be close to that. I may be a kid, but even I know that."

"I'm not going to tell you that you're wrong. It is human nature, not one of our best features as a species but there it is nonetheless."

"When people are around me, all talking about my father and asking me questions about him, I feel more alone than if no one was talking to me. I almost think I'd like that better anyway. Even my father who is constantly in the spotlight doesn't like it. He'd much rather be alone in a dark room with a word processor."

"So sounds like you and your father have a lot in common?"

The boy shifts uncomfortably in his seat, as if a spring is poking up from the leather cushion. "Not really. See, that's part of the problem. My father doesn't know me anymore than any of the kids at this school. He acts like he doesn't even want to know me, and everything I do upsets or disappoints him. To be fair, I don't know him any better but again that's because he keeps me at a distance. We've never had a heart to heart, he never taught me to ride a bike or throw a ball. I'm just some piece of property to him, but not like one he bought for himself but one someone gave him and he hasn't figured out how to re-gift yet."

"You have a sophisticated grasp of metaphor for someone in middle school," the counselor says and sounds genuinely impressed.

"I guess you could say it runs in the family. You know, last year I got kind of friendly with a girl and I tried explaining to her about my relationship with my father, but she couldn't see past my dad's books. She assumed he based the father/son relationship off our relationship and I couldn't—"

"Wait a minute!" the counselor exclaims so abruptly it causes the boy to jump. "Your father… He's *a writer? Did he write those Young Adult ghost hunting books?"*

Reluctantly the boy nods.

"Oh my god, I love those. I started buying them for my daughter but I ended up trying them to see what the fuss was about, and now I'm more into them than she is. It must be wonderful to have a father who writes such gripping and entertaining books."

"Well, that's what I'm trying to tell you. It's not all it's cracked up to be, and it's certainly not what people imagine it is. If I try to tell them the reality, they don't listen."

"Yes, that must be tough. It's sort of like the one book where the father and son went to the haunted amusement park, Wendy's World. The son thought they were going for a fun vacation and was so hurt when he discovered it was business. Was that based on any real trips you went on with your father?"

"My father has never taken me to any amusement parks."

"Does he discuss his work with you? I know he has one coming out next month that isn't part of the series, but I read he might currently be working on the next installment. I'm not asking you to tell me anything about the plot, but the end of the last one suggested that a ghost from the prison followed them home. Do you know if that factors into the next one?"

"I don't know," the boy says, dejected. "My father doesn't talk to me about what he's writing. He doesn't talk to me about much of anything."

The counselor tips him an inexplicable wink. "I understand. Top secret stuff I know. This is so exciting. I mean, I knew we had the son of a famous author at this school, but to have you sitting across my desk is amazing. You know, I have actually used things from your father's books as examples when counseling students on certain issues they face. In fact, I would love to speak with your father sometime if it wouldn't be much of an inconvenience. If he is too busy, I understand, but maybe I could give you a couple of copies of his books to take home and have him sign for me. Would that be inappropriate?"

The boy sits in silence for a moment, pinpointing the moment this went off the rails. And of course it was the moment the counselor figured out who the boy's father is. As usual his father has ruined everything.

Without a word, the boy gets up and walks out of the office. The counselor calls his name, repeatedly, but he ignores her and continues down the hall and out the door. The day is overcast but humid, the gray clouds suggesting a storm on the horizon. Would the boy make it home before the heavens opened up and shot water and fire down on him?

He didn't care. With his eyes cast down at the sidewalk in front of him, he started the trek from one place where he felt unwelcome (school) to another (home).

No, I thought, leaving the kitchen and heading back toward the office. *I'll skip the therapy. At least the traditional kind.*

I could do a little retail therapy. Going to the mall was certainly out of the question, but the mall had become an antiquated idea ever since the advent of the internet anyway. Amazon was the new mall. In that one digital location were countless bookstores, music shops, clothing venders, hardware, kitchen appliances. Anything and everything, all at your fingertips.

Yes, perhaps what I needed was some extravagant spending on items I didn't need. A Capitalist form of therapy.

I walked into my office thinking I might finally order that first edition of Robert Louis Stevenson's *Strange Case of Dr. Jekyll and Mr. Hyde* that I had seen on an online auction site. It had always been my favorite classic horror novel. I had never been able to justify the expense before, but now I had a lot more expendable cash than I used to.

However, as I sat at the computer, I noticed something was amiss. It took my brain a moment to catch up with what that something was.

The computer screen was still up, but my manuscript wasn't displayed. Instead, my father's notes. His typed summary for the way he had planned for the novel to go. I hadn't looked at this since I decided to go in my own direction. I closed the document and found my manuscript beneath it. It had not been deleted again, which was a relief, but I realized with horror that it had been expanded. Several pages had been added from where I had left off.

Several pages but only three words. Three words repeated over and over and over. I felt like helpless Shelley Duvall in *The Shining*, slowly approaching her deranged husband's typewriter. Only in this scenario, wasn't I also Jack Nicholson?

I scrolled through the new pages, reading the message. What chilled me even more than the words was that I believed them.

I'm a fraud. I'm a fraud. I'm a fraud. I'mafraudI'mafraudI'mafraudI'mafruadI'mafraud I'mafraudI'mafraud...

That night I lay in bed but could not sleep. I checked the time: 11:45 p.m. I felt exhausted yet I could not calm my brain enough to approach anything resembling rest. My thoughts tumbled around in my head like laundry in a dryer, twisting and turning and tangling.

What the fuck was going on in my house? That was the through-line of all my jumbled thoughts, the question that kept repeating, haunting me because I couldn't come up with a suitable answer.

Who could be doing these things if not myself? It seemed implausible someone could get in and out of my house so easily and undetected, and even if they could, who? I didn't know anyone who would want to mess with me in this way. I wouldn't go so far as to say I was universally loved, but I couldn't think of anyone who reviled me, anyone who would call me an enemy. Life wasn't a soap opera, after all, with elaborate schemes and dastardly villains. In real life, if someone had a problem with you they would just troll you online.

So that only left me. I had to be doing these things without remembering. Yet that also seemed a plot device out of some melodrama. Localized amnesia or something. But I was prone to black outs so it still seemed the most likely scenario. Most likely but not least disturbing.

I had written nothing all day. I couldn't concentrate after finding the "I'm a fraud" message. A message that cut to the bone because deep down I believed it to be true. My subconscious making me face what I wanted to deny.

Something was very wrong with me, that much was clear. Something retail therapy wasn't going to fix. Despite my trepidation I knew I needed serious help, a real professional with degrees hanging on the wall and letters after their name. First thing in the morning I would get up and find a good therapist.

Although, why wait? The internet didn't adhere to any certain hours. It wasn't like television in my youth when the channels all played the National Anthem then went off the air after midnight. I could at least do a little research and find some names, send out some inquiries. I still had my insurance through Furman which I was pretty sure covered therapy.

I found myself already feeling better now that I had a proactive plan. The power of persuasion, a psychosomatic placebo of sorts, but a step in any direction was better than standing still, lost and confused. I sat up in bed and started to reach for the bedside lamp, but I came to an immediate halt when my gaze drifted down to the foot of my bed.

The room was dark, but an even deeper darkness seemed to coalesce at the end of the bed. A shadow that almost seemed to have substance, standing over my bed. Of course, it had to have been just a trick of my eyes, but then shifting clouds outside allowed moonlight to filter through my window. Instead of dissipating the shape, it only further solidified it. Gave it contours and features. Features I recognized.

"Pop?" I said, wondering if I were dreaming. Certain I must be dreaming, yet I could feel the bed beneath me, smell the stale odor of the sheets that were a few days past needing to be laundered. My left eye twitched. These details were too convincing to be a dream.

The form at the end of my bed remained still for a moment then raised an arm, one finger pointed upward and then wagged back and forth. The universal symbol for "Shame on you!" Then the entire thing dissipated, or collapsed in on itself.

I clicked on the light, banishing all the shadows. I scurried to the foot of my bed and looked over at the floor. I wasn't sure what I expected to find. Maybe a puddle of black oozing slime? But there was nothing. Everything seemed normal.

But it wasn't. Things were pretty fucking far from normal. And yet things started to make sense, pieces clicking into place to complete a puzzle that was clear yet frightening.

My life hadn't become a soap opera or a melodrama. No, my life had become a ghost story.

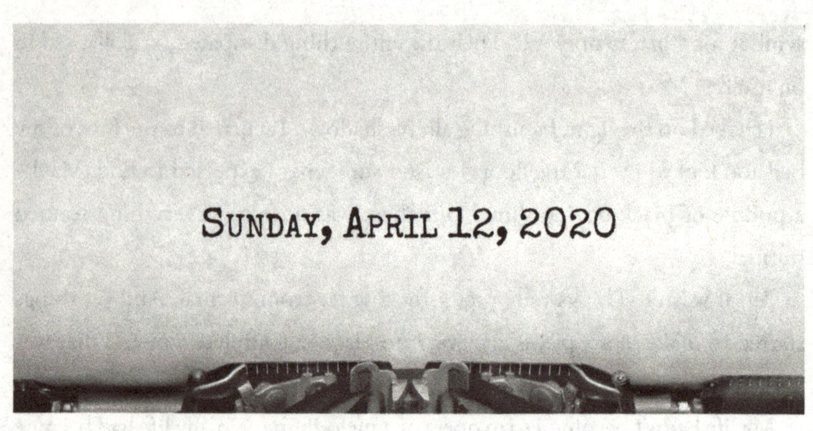

Sunday, April 12, 2020

Rain beat hard on the roof with a sound like tiny stampeding horses. I sat in the living room with the lights off, staring at the carnage on the floor. My books, the New Blood novels from the top shelf, lay scattered on the carpet, pages ripped out and torn into small strips like confetti. One some of the pages that had been spared, a single word was scrawled with such intensity that it tore through the thin paper. *Fraud.*

I had managed to fall asleep the night before after seeing my father's apparition. Instead of keeping me up in fright, shaking under the covers in cartoon fashion, I had found some comfort in having a clear idea what had been going on inside this house. So when I got up this morning and found the book shrapnel in the living room, I had been disturbed but not exactly surprised.

Was I really sitting here, seriously contemplating the fact that my father's ghost lingered in this house haunting me? Perhaps if it had been another sunny day, I would have found the notion easier to dismiss. Instead, the gray day and unrelenting rain only made the impossible seem all the more plausible.

I had never been an ardent unbeliever. While I had never had anything approaching a paranormal encounter, I did find myself intrigued by stories people had to tell on the subject. Having grown up the son of a writer famous for writing about ghosts, people had always felt free to share with me their own ghostly experiences, figuring in me they would find a kindred spirit and a believer. In actuality, I neither believed nor disbelieved.

Okay, some of them I did disbelieve outright. Too preposterous or ripped right out of popular horror movies, or in some instances an obvious case of sleep paralysis misinterpreted as something else. In other instances, I suspected drugs had created these experiences, and in others a touch of mental illness seemed the likely culprit.

And yet... As Brooke Simpson would have said. And yet some of the stories I found compelling, with a ring of authenticity. I at least believed that they believed these things had happened to them. I couldn't say I was a total Mulder because the Scully in me kept reminding that I had never had any verifiable experiences of my own.

Until now.

I had intended to contact a therapist today, and now I found that what I really needed was a ghostbuster. Too bad I didn't know one of those.

I jerked upright in my chair, realizing that maybe I did. Or at least someone who knew more on the subject than I did. An expert, even of the amateur variety. In the age of the internet, anyone could become an expert on almost any subject. Too bad most used that opportunity to yell at each other about politics and troll celebrities on social media.

I pulled out my phone and called Michael Franklin, my former student. He had talked to me on more than one occasion about his interests in the paranormal. He was from Savannah, which he often called "the most haunted city in America," making it sound like something off a tourist brochure. Which it very well may have been. If I remembered correctly, he had a cousin who ran a business where he investigated so-called haunted places, had even written a few books about his experiences. Michael had once entertained the idea of starting a paranormal club at Furman, asking if I would be the faculty sponsor, but when I declined and he couldn't secure any other sponsor, he let the idea drop.

But if anyone might believe what I had to say and maybe even offer some insight, it would be Michael.

He answered on the first ring, almost as if he had been waiting by the phone. Maybe his delving into the paranormal had helped him develop a psychic twinge. "Hey Prof, long time no hear. I was beginning to think you had forgotten all about me."

"I could never forget you," I said, then realized how flirtatious that sounded. I tried never to cross that line with a student, current or former. "You wrote some of the best essays I ever read."

"Flatterer, but I know the drill. You're a famous writer now, so you don't have time for us little guys."

"I think you seriously overestimate my standing in the literary community. I'm basically a gun-for-hire. I'm not exactly on the fast-track to become a household name."

"Just wait. You've got the talent. Remember, I've read your books."

As if I could forget. I never mentioned to my students that I published novels back in the 90s, and I wasn't entirely sure how Michael had managed to find out. In any case, he located used copies of my New Blood books and read all four. He delivered what amounted to dissertations on each of them in my office, making them sound like philosophical explorations of societal ills instead of what they were, entertaining fluff with little literary value. Still, hearing him talk about my work this way had been a nice stroke to the ego.

"Believe it or not, I didn't call you to talk about my writing."

"What, planning to ask me to run away with you? Sorry, I want to finish college first."

I grunted a polite laugh but felt uncomfortable. I knew I should have nipped Michael's crush in the bud ages ago.

"I want to talk about ghosts," I said.

"Oh. I wasn't expecting that one. In the past, I always worried I was being a little annoying when I'd go off on a tangent about ghosts."

"Not at all. It's a fascinating subject, but one I admit I don't know a lot about. And I have a few questions, things that could help me with the book."

Michael let loose with a wordless exclamation so loud and high-pitched I had to take the phone away from my ear.

"Sorry," he said, "but this is so exciting. Basically I'll be your research assistant."

"I hadn't really thought about it in those terms, but I guess so. I know I could look up anything I wanted to know on the internet, but I've always found it's better to talk to someone who knows person-to-person. And you're the only person in my life who knows about this sort of thing."

"Well, my cousin Ryan knows a lot more than me, but any question I can't answer, I'll consult him and get back to you."

"Sounds good. I'll be sure to mention you in the acknowledgments."

"Holy fuck! Sorry, but this is so exciting. Feels like I'm a real part of the literary community, and a part of one of the most anticipated books coming out this year."

"Next year," I said without thinking.

"What?"

"Oh shit, I shouldn't have said that. You have to promise that anything I tell you about this project will stay between us. I don't think Doubleday is ready to release the information I'm about to share with you."

"My lips are sealed. You can trust me."

"Okay, so the book is no longer coming out this December. It's going to be autumn of next year instead."

"Am I allowed to ask why?"

I took a moment to ponder how much I should tell Michael. Truth be told, I wanted to tell him *everything*. Not only about the book but about everything going on in this house, my suspicions, but I was afraid he'd think I was crazy. Maybe he believed in ghosts in an abstract sense, but that was different from hearing someone say their dead father was haunting them and ordering beer in the middle of the night to sabotage them. Hell, just thinking it now made me feel sort of crazy.

Sort of.

It would be better to let Michael think all my questions had to do with the book, but I had to fight against this overwhelming urge to confess all, no matter the consequences. I knew this had to do with my feelings of isolation, my sense of claustrophobia. In a way Michael was a link to the outside world, a reminder of when my life had consisted of more than one location twenty-four hours a day seven days a week. It made me want to throw caution to the wind, but throwing caution to the wind was for people in their teens and twenties. And rarely was it the right decision even then, the young are too inexperienced to know it.

"Let's just say the book is changing direction," I answered after a moment. "I'm taking my father's concept but veering off down a different path with it. Which means it'll take longer to finish."

"So it's not even like you're just finishing your father's book anymore but actually collaborating with him. That's exciting."

He doesn't seem to agree, I thought but said, "Yes, exciting but also stressful. A lot of pressure on me to not screw this up."

"Please, you couldn't screw this up. You're a hell of a writer."

"I'm a writer who hasn't written anything substantial in decades. Trust me, there is much potential for disaster here."

"You just need to get the creative juices flowing again. Plus you've got help now. So hit me with the questions. I'm here to serve. Need to earn my place in those acknowledgments."

I laughed, surprising myself that it wasn't forced. With everything going on, I hadn't thought myself capable of genuine laughter. "I appreciate you taking the time to help an old man out."

"I was always taught to respect my elders," Michael said, and I could almost hear the wink in his tone.

"Okay, so, where do I start? First of all, most everything I know about ghosts comes from either fiction or those ghost hunting shows which are basically—"

"Fiction," he finished for me.

"Precisely. Yet I seem to remember hearing somewhere that there were actually different types of hauntings, different categories. Three different ones I think."

"Ryan would say there are four, actually. Possibly even five."

"What's the difference between all the categories?"

"Let's see. I guess I'll start with a poltergeist haunting, because it's not really a haunting at all."

"Poltergeist? You mean, like the movie?"

"Not remotely. Great flick, but it doesn't represent the reality of a poltergeist."

"Which is?"

"Poltergeists hauntings typically involve things moving around on their own, almost always revolve around a young person, most often girls going through puberty but also older women going through menopause. And like I said, they aren't really hauntings at all but the result of latent psychic abilities, heightened by hormonal changes and stress. Psychokinesis, I think Ryan called it. Without being conscious of it, the person is actually causing the phenomenon."

That didn't sound like what was happening here. Stress I had aplenty, but puberty was long in my rearview and men didn't go through menopause the way women did. Sure, there was the mid-life crisis but that was more mental than hormonal. So mark that one off the list.

"Got it, poltergeists are not ghosts. What's next?"

"You have the residual haunting," Michael said. "These are sort of like materialized memories. Impressions left behind. The spirits in these hauntings are stuck in a loop. Someone might see their deceased grandmother in the kitchen every morning, standing at the stove like she's making breakfast, or their father sitting in his favorite chair smoking a pipe like he always did in life. The spirits don't interact with the living, and some theorize they don't even know they're dead. They merely repeat the same actions over and over, reenacting moments from their lives."

Another one marked off the list, I thought as I glanced at the ripped pages carpeting the floor like monochromatic leaves. My father was definitely interacting with me.

"So residual hauntings are basically just reruns," I said then wondered if a kid Michael's age who grew up in the era of streaming would even know what a "rerun" was. "Got it."

"Very different from a true haunting, what is usually referred to as an intelligent haunting."

I perked up at this. "Intelligent how?"

"An intelligent haunting is what you most often see portrayed in the media. This would be a spirit with a certain amount of consciousness and autonomy. A spirit that actually interacts directly with the living and can cause physical manifestations."

"Physical manifestations like, for instance, knocking books off a shelf and shredding the pages?"

"Is that something that's going to happen in the book?" Michael asked with an eagerness that was almost frightening. His enthusiasm was only a mere representation of the anticipation of millions of readers out there. The very thought of that settled a pressure on my chest like a bolder.

"Let's just call it a hypothetical. So could a spirit manifest itself by causing that kind of damage?"

"*Hypothetically*, sure," Michael said with a teasing lilt to his voice. This was all a game to him, a bit of fun to break up the monotony of the pandemic world, and that was what I wanted him to think. Yet it left me feeling lonely, talking to someone but unable to truly connect because I was hiding behind a wall of deception.

I realized Michael had continued talking, but lost in my own thoughts I had missed it. "I'm sorry, what was that?"

"I said intelligent hauntings typically result from people who died with unfinished business, people with some mission they feel like they have to accomplish before they move on. That kind of purpose gives them a certain power to manipulate the corporeal world."

Mission? Purpose? Like perhaps stopping your queer son from ruining your literary legacy?

"What could a person do to get rid of a spirit in the case of an intelligent haunting?"

"They could always help the spirit complete its mission, I suppose."

"You mean give up?" I said, my voice rising to just shy of a shout.

A pause on the line then, "Give what up?"

"Nothing, just... Let's say for the sake of the story, helping the spirit complete its mission was out of the question, what then? Could they have the house blessed, or maybe some kind of exorcism?"

Michael chuckled. "Doesn't really work on your average spirit. You're more getting into the fourth category of haunting."

"Which is?"

"Demonic."

"You mean like the kind of stuff in those *Conjuring* movies?"

"More or less. A demonic spirit was never a living person but an entity from Hell. They have no real purpose or mission other than to cause chaos and destruction. Usually if you hear reports of a spirit causing physical harm to someone—scratches or bites, that sort of thing—that is the work of a demonic entity."

I mentally scratched that one off the list as well. I'd suffered no physical attacks, not yet at least. Besides, while the idea of a person's energy lingering after the body's death was at least somewhat plausible to me, demons stretched my suspension of disbelief a bit too thin. I didn't believe in guardian angels and all that crap, so I found it almost impossible to believe in their wicked counterparts.

"What about the fifth category? You said there were possibly five."

"The fifth category is the most *out there* of them all. Aliens."

An incredulous laugh shot from me almost like a bark. "Are you just messing with me right now?"

"Hey, I'm just telling you what some believe. I'm not saying I personally believe it."

Aliens I found almost as hard to take seriously as demons. Not that I didn't think it possible, even probable, that life existed in some form out there in the vastness of space, but the idea that little green men visited us regularly on the down low, shoving metal probes up the asses of random people, seemed highly unlikely to me. Science fiction like *The X-Files* felt much more fiction than science.

"Okay," I said, "so I think I'm looking at an intelligent haunting. For the story, you know. But there's no way to get rid of that kind of spirit?"

"Sometimes they fade on their own. If they cannot complete the mission they have, eventually it's like their will is broken and they dissipate."

"So ignore it and it'll go away?"

"Something like that," Michael said with another chuckle.

"And what if a person wanted to do an investigation on their own? Would they need any special equipment?"

"I know Ryan would caution them to be careful. Sometimes an investigation increases the activity. If it's a friendly spirit and you acknowledge it, that may make it want to communicate further. However, if it's a malevolent entity that could open a whole other can of worms."

I thought about this for a moment. I wouldn't call my father *friendly*, not before his death or after, but was he *malevolent*? Was there nothing in between?

Then I thought of my pills being thrown in the trash and reassessed the situation.

"Could you put me in contact with your cousin?" I asked. "I really want to have this stuff be as accurate as possible, maybe even test it all out before I write about it. Maybe you could give him my email and ask him to contact me with any information for a DIY investigation."

"Okay, but on one condition."

"What's that?"

"That my name come before Ryan's in the acknowledgments."

I laughed again, another genuine one. "You got it."

After the phone call, I set out to clean up the mess. Gathering up the ripped remains of my books hurt more than I anticipated. Of course, I still had my own copies in a box in the crawlspace attic, but that didn't do anything to dull the pain of seeing my work, words I had sweated over in my youth, decimated this way. I figured I'd feel similar pain watching my books thrown into a fire. Bad reviews were one thing, and I'd gotten my share of those during my abbreviated tenure as a professional author, but the hate someone must harbor toward a book to actually physically destroy it had to be profound.

The kind of hate my father had always had for my books, a hatred that apparently lingered even after his death.

And yet if he hated the books so much, why had he displayed them on the bookcase in the first place?

So many questions.

I deposited all the torn pages and tattered covers into a trash bag and took them outside. At the trashcan I stared down at the beer for a few seconds, or possibly minutes, at one point licking my lips like some kind of cliché come to life. City garbage pickup for my street wasn't until Tuesday, but I was so eager to get the booze away from my property. The trashcan was too close, too accessible. I recited the Serenity Prayer in my head then upended the bag in my hands, the torn pages fluttering in to cover the beer cans.

Back inside, I gulped down two glasses of water, leaning against the counter and feeling violent shivers pass through my body. *Someone walking over your grave*, I had always heard growing up, but this must have been an army marching over, stomping up and down with their combat boots. I locked the back door as if afraid the alcohol would try to get in after me. I could too easily picture the beer cans out there laughing, digging their way up through the refuse, flipping open the trashcan lid and making a devious trek to the back door.

Of course, this kind of thinking took responsibility for my weakness away from me, putting it onto something outside myself, something beyond my control. I may have only attended one virtual AA meeting so far, but I knew true recovery hinged on taking responsibility for my own behavior and not looking for other sources on which to place the blame.

As I wandered back into the living room, I glanced up at the empty space on the top shelf of the bookcase and wondered if that was what I was doing here. Was I inventing a ghostly presence as an enemy instead of looking inward at my own internalized doubt and fear?

But last night, I had seen his shape at the foot of my bed. True, I hadn't seen his face, but I *felt* him. It was my father, I knew it.

And he didn't want me writing this book. That point had made abundantly clear. And according to Michael, perhaps the only way to get rid of him was to give him what he wanted.

Which wasn't an option. What was I supposed to do, call up Edwin and tell him I had to back out of the deal because my father's ghost was messing with me? I couldn't return the advance even if I wanted to because I'd spent a good portion of it already.

Besides, all my life I had always found that my father's disapproval of something only made me more determined to do it. This was no different at fifty-five than it was at fifteen. I probably wasn't the only child of a distant and critical parent who lived their entire life just to prove that parent wrong.

If my father wanted me to abandon the book, he had another thing coming. If he thought I couldn't pull off the ambitious story I had in mind, I would show him differently. If he felt I was ruining his legacy, I would prove him wrong. His Casper act may end up having the exact opposite effect than he intended.

I remembered something else Michael had said, about how the spirit might dissipate in time if it couldn't achieve its purpose.

Well, Pop, I thought, *get ready to dissipate because I'm not giving you what you want.*

Tuesday, April 14, 2020

I stood by the front door at just past nine a.m., watching through one of the sidelights as the garbage truck rumbled away after the man in the jumpsuit fed my trash into the beast's belly. The beer had been consumed, just not by me, and I felt relief wash over me like a cold shower as the truck rounded the curve and disappeared from sight. Taking the temptation with it.

I had managed to resist the call of the alcohol, but yesterday I had found myself more than once standing outside by the trashcan, only semi-aware of walking out there. I had attended two different virtual AA meetings, but I had feared my strength wouldn't hold out much longer.

And yet now that the beer was gone from my property, I felt good. I felt proud. Sure, a few days sober wasn't much in the grand scheme of things, but small victories could be profound victories. One day at a time wasn't only a sitcom but the AA motto. Any day without a drink was a day you could celebrate a victory.

I may have been only a few day sober, but that was a few more days than I'd been without alcohol in my system in more years than I wanted to contemplate. It gave me a sense of confidence and accomplishment that I needed, and I grabbed onto that like a life raft, letting it spread through my veins until that confidence affected other aspects of my life as well.

Pushing away from the door, I headed back to my office. It had taken some time, but I thought I was now beginning to think of it as *my* office instead of my father's office. Beginning to think of this as *my* home instead of my father's home. Even beginning to think of the new *Senior & Junior* as *my* book instead of my father's book. Part of this may have been defiance, a determination to show my father's spirit who was in charge, but that small semantic change felt empowering.

I sat at the desk, the manuscript already open on the laptop. Without hesitation, wanting to ride this high and not give my doubt time to creep back in, my fingers attacked the keys. Yes, overthinking was a Rick Justice trademark, but I wanted to overcome it. At least for this book. I wanted to be one of those writers who dove in, relying solely on instinct. Allow the story to play out organically without planning and plotting every little moment and exchange.

And it seemed to be working. The past two days, the writing had developed a flow that felt good. In a short period of time, I had gotten through several chapters, and that feeling of productivity fed itself, increasing my motivation. A snowball effect, or maybe a domino effect. In any case, it seemed self-sustaining and instead of trying to stand in its way, I just allowed myself to be swept along.

I was in the middle of a tense and disturbing chapter where the ghost of Senior visited the little boy—soon to be Junior's step-son—in the middle of the night, telling him that Junior didn't love him, didn't love his father, with the intention of turning the boy against Junior and driving a wedge between Junior and his fiancé. For a scene with no overt violence, it was darker than any of the horror novels I wrote in my youth.

My writing session lasted until just on eleven, when my stomach began growling to let me know that I had skipped breakfast and an early lunch was in order. I saved my work and emailed it to Edwin. That had become a new habit, emailing after every writing session. Not only was it a contractual obligation, but if my father's spirit decided to erase my work again, Edwin would already have it. He had emailed yesterday evening to let me know that wasn't necessary to send my work daily, that I could wait until I had completed chapters, so I told him I found this a great way to keep myself accountable. No way was I going to tell him the real reason.

When I opened Gmail to send him that morning's work, I noticed I had a new email from a name I didn't recognize. Ryan Dunn. I almost deleted the message unread, assuming it was spam, but then I remembered Ryan was the name of Michael's cousin. The one who had his own paranormal investigation company in Savannah, the one who Michael had said he'd put me in touch with. I opened the email with some interest. Ryan's message had a tone of familiarity, like we were old friends picking up on an old conversation as opposed to two strangers.

Hey man, Ryan here.

Michael tells me you're interested in setting up a little investigation to research your new novel. I have to admit I've never read any of your father's work, but I did read your vampire novel The Freaks Come Out at Night *back in the day. It was when I was a teenager so I can't say I remember much about it, but I do remember liking it and the way you had the cool kids of a high school as bloodsuckers feeding on the nerds and losers who wouldn't be missed. Thought it was a pretty cool satire of the bullying culture in American high schools.*

Anyway, regarding a do-it-yourself investigation, in this day and age such a thing is easier than ever. Really you can do so much with just your smart phone. You have a camera, video recorder, and audio recorder right at your fingertips. EVP recordings are a great way to find out what a spirit wants. If you aren't familiar with the term, it stands for Electronic Voice Phenomenon and it's when you record the voice of a spirit that can't always be heard by the human ear. You could also order a temperature/emf reader which measures cold spots and electromagnetic fields. DVR systems are much cheaper than they used to be, and they hold a lot of memory, can record constantly, and have night-vision capabilities. Those are all good places to start.

Michael also said you had asked about how to get rid of a haunting, and simple as it sounds, just talking to a spirit can help because often spirits are confused and don't even realize they're dead. A soothing voice letting them know it's okay to move on can really help. As long as you're not dealing with something demonic. In that case, the acknowledgment and engagement can make things worse. So make sure you (or your characters in this case) know what they are dealing with before they start anything.

If you have any follow-up questions or need any further information, feel free to shoot me a message. When we get through to the other side of this COVID stuff, if you ever decide to take a trip to Savannah, hit me up.

Maybe I can arrange for you to go on an investigation with my team.

Ryan

A lot of information in that email, but at first I found myself fixated on Ryan's assertion that he'd never read my father's work but enjoyed *The Freaks Come Out at Night*. Not only enjoyed it, but he actually seemed to *get it*. I had in fact written that novel to discuss the barbaric nature of high school, how it operated almost on a caste system, those at the top terrorizing those on the bottom. A system that was actually fostered by adults who threw out dismissive lines like "Kids will be kids" and "It's just part of growing up." I wanted to explore all that without getting preachy, so I turned it into a vampire story, supernatural elements standing in as metaphor for the real life horrors. Only a couple of years after the book's release, *Buffy the Vampire Slayer* came along and did something similar to great acclaim. I, however, must have been ahead of my time and didn't receive the same kind of reception, critics by and large misunderstanding or overlooking my intent. *The Freaks Come Out at Night* was dismissed as "derivative vampire trash" and "a pathetic attempt to copy Skipp and Spector," referencing the splatterpunk vampire novel *The Light at the End* from a decade before. At the time the criticism had hit hard, because I considered the book the best work I'd ever done, but it felt good to know now that someone out there understood what I was doing and appreciated it. Only took twenty-five years to get the feedback I'd been craving.

The rest of the information was useful, but I wasn't sure if I needed it anymore. Over the last couple of days, there hadn't been much activity to speak of. Yesterday I had found the wastepaper basket in my bedroom overturned, and at one point while writing I heard the shower running and had to go turn off the hot water. This morning I had gotten up to discover the oven turned on even though everything I had made the day before had been in the microwave. It seemed my father still wanted me to know he was here, but he'd scaled down his campaign considerably. I thought about what Michael had said, how some spirits can fade away if they see they are not going to be able to accomplish whatever mission has gotten them stuck on this plane. Perhaps my father was beginning to understand that I would not back down from this challenge, that I was determined to finish this book no matter what he thought about it. In light of my refusal to give in to his wishes and abandon the project, maybe he was losing steam. In another week, he might be gone.

Feeling buoyed by the thought, even though most people wanted to cling to their deceased loved ones instead of wishing them away, I pushed back from the desk and went into the kitchen to fix something to eat. The oven was still off, a good sign, and I pulled out a loaf of bread, some mayo, and a package of sliced turkey breast. As I began assembling my sandwich, I caught sight of something in the sink. A pink pill, one of my Biktarvy, perched on the edge of the drain.

I gasped then held my breath, my entire body going cold as if dunked in a vat of ice water. I had flashbacks to the finding all my pills in the trash. Turning to the cabinet, I opened it and saw my prescription bottle sitting right where it was supposed to be. Only with the top off. I grabbed the bottle and could tell even before I looked inside that it was empty.

"No, no, no, not again," I said, turning to the trashcan. I upended it and sent all the garbage spilling onto the floor. On my hands and knees, I weeded through it all but did not find a single pill. If I hadn't thrown them away here, where could they be? The bathroom trash? Shit, what if they had been placed in the big trash can outside, the one that had only recently been emptied into the garbage truck?

Yet through all this speculation, I suspected I knew exactly where the pills were. The one pill sat in the sink, hanging over the lip of the drain like a boat about to be sucked into a whirlpool. That suggested the pills had been poured down the drain.

I stood at the sink, staring into the black hole, at one point even opening the flashlight app on my phone and shining the light down at the drain. I could see nothing, as if the drain were a bottomless well that went from my kitchen all the way to some kitchen on the other side of the world. Of course, I thought the other side of the world from South Carolina might be the middle of the Indian Ocean. So my pills would be floating around there, where some HIV positive shark might luck out.

For the second time in only a week, I tore through the house like a tornado. This time I was so much more thorough and destructive than the last time. I wrenched drawers out and left them and their contents on the bedroom floor. Everything under the kitchen and bathroom sinks lay scattered like shrapnel after a bomb detonation. I even threw everything out of the refrigerator and freezer, just to be sure. Broken eggs and puddles of milk slicked the tile, but I didn't have time to cry over it.

And yet hot tears burned my eyes as I flipped up the sofa cushions and swiped the books from the bookcase. By the time I was done, sinking to my knees in the middle of the living room, surrounded by the carnage I'd left in my wake, I was weeping, tears and snot streaking my face, panting through my sobs. And empty-handed. Other than the one pill in the sink, I had found no others.

Down the drain. They could be no other place but down the drain. Which suggested my father wasn't merely trying to dissuade me from writing this book.

He was trying to kill me.

I disconnected the call sitting in the armchair. The one remaining pill was clutched tightly in my left fist which I had pressed against my chest, as if guarding something precious that I feared would be taken from me. Which wasn't that far off the mark.

I felt drained and dehydrated, and I knew that was from all the crying. When I first called Dr. Lundy, I had tried to keep my voice calm and steady, planning to explain that I had accidentally knocked over my pill bottle and dumped the contents down the sink. However, all the panic and fear and desperation twisted around my neck and squeezed the tears out of me. I broke down and began sobbing again with such force that I could barely get the words out. I kept apologizing, promising it would never happen again, begging him to help me.

Dr. Lundy ended up having to comfort me, assuring that it was okay and we'd fix it. He did chastise me for being so careless with something to vital to my health, but there were no barbs in his admonishment. I suspected the profundity of my outburst frightened him a bit. He promised to send in an order for an early refill to the CVS a few blocks from my house. They wouldn't deliver, but I could pick them up at their drive-through window later this afternoon. The question remained how my insurance was going to react to this, but I decided for my own sanity I had to make that another worry for another day. I was going to get my Biktarvy, and that was the important thing. There may be times when the pink pill felt like nothing more than a vitamin, but this whole fiasco brought home how much I needed it.

I continued to sit for a few minutes, not trusting my legs to have enough strength to hold me up. The house was a disaster area, but like the insurance, I pushed that away as a lesser worry to deal with at a later date. When my shaking subsided, at least somewhat, I made my way to the kitchen and drank some water to replace all the fluids I'd cried out. It wasn't quite noon yet, but close enough for horseshoes so I downed the one pill I had left.

I actually hesitated, as it was the last one in the house and once it was down the hatch, that left none. I hadn't been in a house without any Biktarvy in years, and the prospect was terrifying even though I knew a new prescription had been called in to the pharmacy. I found myself trembling again and clutched the edge of the sink. The monstrous sink that had gobbled up all my medication.

Again with the anthropomorphizing of inanimate objects, only the sink hadn't just eaten my medication. It had been *fed*.

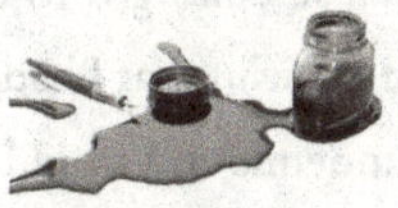

I sat behind the wheel of my car, had in fact been sitting there in the driveway for nearly ten minutes. I had received a text notification that my prescription was ready to be picked up, but I hadn't even gotten as far as turning the key in the ignition.

Everything felt odd. Even an act as simple as placing my hands on the steering wheel felt unnatural, like I didn't really know what I was doing. I found myself reminded of being a child, sitting behind the wheel of my father's Chrysler, stubby legs far too short to reach the pedals, unable to really see out the windshield, gripping the steering wheel and turning it back and forth, playing at driving. I felt as ill equipped to man this vehicle now as I did then.

Which seemed exceedingly silly, but I had to remind myself I hadn't left this house in almost a month. The car had been parked here in the drive all that time, the gas gauge sitting on half a tank as it had been the last time I went anywhere. The very idea of pulling the car out onto the street and going anywhere felt surreal, almost dangerous. As if I were about to embark on a journey through the darkest unexplored rainforests full of untold beasts and perils.

"Stop being ridiculous," I muttered to myself and cranked the car. The vibration was almost startling. I edged backward out of the driveway, feeling like some kid newly behind the wheel taking his driver's test for the first time. I glanced back at the house, fighting the insane urge to just abandon the car in the middle of the street and rush back inside the safety of those walls. I realized that in some ways my experience was not unique. For the most part, everyone in the country—hell, the *world*—was probably experiencing similar fears and neuroses. We were living in unprecedented times, and how fast we had all become agoraphobic shut-ins.

Except most people longed to get back out into the world and resume the norm of crowded sidewalks, close-talking into each other's faces, hugs and handshakes. I supposed I was unique in that I had wanted to avoid that kind of socialization even before the pandemic and would happily have stayed a shut-in for the rest of my life given the choice.

Glancing at the house across the street, I wondered if the good-ol'-boy who lived there, whom I had nicknamed Bubba in my mind even though I wasn't sure his real name, was watching from a window, wondering why his weirdo neighbor had pulled the car into the street only to sit there. I put the car into gear and coasted up to the stop sign at the intersection, turning on my blinker though there was no traffic to care.

In fact, on the five-minute drive to the pharmacy, I encountered not a single other car, didn't see any pedestrians on the sidewalks, no children playing outside. I began to get the eerie feeling I had wound up somehow in an episode of *The Twilight Zone*, finding myself in a world where everyone had disappeared but me. I could almost hear that unsettling theme music playing in the back of my mind.

That illusion was somewhat shattered as I pulled into the CVS parking lot. A few cars rushed down Wade Hampton Boulevard, and across the street I saw a woman in a face mask pumping gas into her oversized SUV. So not the last man on earth, after all. Was I relieved or disappointed?

I pulled into a parking space long enough to suit up. An N95 mask, which according to my research was the most effective and the type used in hospitals, and a pair of white vinyl gloves. I made sure I had my bottle of hand sanitizer at the ready, resting in the cup holder between the driver and passenger seats. All my armor, preparing for battle.

I drove around to the side of the building with the drive-through window. No other cars, no waiting. I pulled up and a young woman with her own mask and gloves sat at the window. Even though we were separated by thick glass, I still recoiled a little in my seat. I tried to see her as a person, a fellow human being sharing the planet, but in the moment I saw her as only a big bag of bacteria, an incubator for millions of fat little oblong sacs of mucus with squirming tails, and I imagined they all perked up when they smelled me, driven by an urge to penetrate my skin and impregnate my body with disease and rot.

"How can I help you, sir?" she asked through the speaker after I rolled down my window, removing one barrier between us.

When I answered, I raised my voice to be heard through the mask. "I'm here to pick up a prescription for Justice. Rick Justice."

She checked her computer then said, "Place your ID and insurance card on the tray."

A metal drawer beneath the window slid out. I placed my cards inside and watched the drawer slide back inside like the jaws of some monstrous robot closing. While the pharmacy tech (pharmer, as one of my exes use to call them) turned her attention to her computer, I gripped the steering wheel like a life preserver, afraid I'd soon be washed out to sea.

Just the day before I had been feeling claustrophobic and hungry for human contact, but now that I was out in the world, I felt exposed and vulnerable and wanted only to hide away behind my closed doors, locking the world away from me. I supposed I was truly learning the meaning of the phrase, damned if you do and damned if you don't.

"Here you go, Mr. Justice," the woman's voice came through the speaker, startling me. The robot opened its mouth again, as if puking up my cards and a white bag stapled shut. I hesitated before reaching out, as if afraid the mouth would snap closed again, biting off my hand at the wrist. Although what I really feared was that despite the young woman's PPE, she had left microscopic bacteria on the items.

Holding my breath, I snatched up the cards and tossed them on the passenger's seat then repeated the process with the bag. I drove away without so much as a "thank you" to the pharmacist. Once I got home I would scrub everything down with hand sanitizer, throw my clothes directly into the washing machine, then take a shower.

Overkill? I would have thought so a few months ago, but now an excess of caution was seen as the responsible course of action. In a weird way, the new world was one that those suffering from OCD had been preparing for their entire lives.

Considering the severe case of agoraphobia I seemed to be suffering, I might have expected my tension and stress to diminish the closer I got to home, and yet it did not. Of course, home couldn't actually be considered a sanctuary when it contained a vengeful spirit that wanted to kill you.

But did my father truly want me dead, or did he just want to scare me to the point I'd stop ruining his legacy? I still felt that adolescent stubbornness, the desire to prove my father wrong, to do something simply because he didn't think I could do it. I understood on some level that wasn't necessarily a bad thing, that it could be used as a motivation for success. Yet when one's life was in danger, it became almost insane to stay the course. Was it worth my health just to try to prove a point to a dead man?

Perhaps, I thought as I rolled down Brushy Creek Road, I didn't have to abandon the book. Maybe all I needed to do was abandon the house. It was where my father died, which no doubt connected his spirit to the property. If I simply went somewhere else, might it not stand to reason that he would not be able to follow me?

But where could I go? With the current state of the world, I wouldn't be able to find a house or apartment to rent, and hotels were actually closed "until further notice." I couldn't even spend my days writing in cafes or libraries because they were all closed as well.

No, for a while at least I was trapped in that house. So if I wanted to write the book, I would have to try to make peace with my father.

Hopefully with more success than the last time.

The young man sits in the car. In fact, he has been sitting in his car for fifteen minutes, ever since he pulled into the driveway. He stares through the windshield, out toward the front door. He knows he needs to get out of the car, cross the manicured lawn, and go through that door. His father is in the house. The two haven't seen each other in several months, and they've barely spoken in that time as well. There has been so much tension between them, even more so than usual, that even across many miles and a stalemate of silence the young man can still feel it.

With a sigh, he finally opens the door and steps out of the car. He retrieves his bags from the back and makes his way down the paved walk to the front porch, the whole time repeating to himself, You're an adult, not a child, you're an adult, not a child, you're an adult, not a child. A mantra he'd been repeating in his head all during the four-hour drive. It had given him strength and confidence then, but the closer he gets to the door, the more he feels he has regressed back into childhood, cowering at his father's feet, begging for approval and validation.

He hesitates at the door, key in his hand, but he stiffens his resolve and lets himself into the house that no longer feels like home to him. His dorm room back at college feels more like home than anywhere he has ever lived with his father, and the friends he has made on campus more like family than his own flesh and blood.

The house is quiet, the kind of quiet of deserted places, ghost towns and abandoned villages and vast deserts. Yet his father's car is outside in the driveway, the young man parked behind it. Perhaps his father is having a little mid-day nap. When one has a job outside the normal nine-to-five framework, the young man supposes you can make your schedule any way you wish, one of the perks of being independently wealthy.

The young man goes upstairs to his bedroom to drop off his bags, thinks maybe a nap for himself wouldn't hurt. Might be best to approach his father rested and recharged. However, when he gets to the second floor, he realizes the house isn't as silent as he first thought. He can hear a soft clack-clack-clacking sound coming from behind the closed door at the end of the hallway. His father's office.

So not napping but working. Not surprising, as his father tends to be working most hours he is awake. His writing, the young man muses, seems less a vocation and more an obsession. Most people didn't understand that, but the young man had grown to understand it intimately. Not just because he has grown up with it, but because he has started to experience that obsession himself.

He stands in the hallway, bags still in his hands, and debates with himself. Interrupting his father was always a cardinal sin growing up, worse than even murder. But the young man isn't a boy anymore, and he fears that if he procrastinates on having this conversation with his father then he may lose his nerve and never have it.

After taking a moment to go into his room—noting the dust that coats all the surfaces and how nothing has been moved since his last visit to the house—and dropping his bags on the bed, he walks down the hall and stands in front of the door to his father's office. Today is a day for hesitating outside doors, he thinks, then forces himself to raise his hand and knock.

There is no response other than the clacking from inside. He knocks again, this time calling for his father, but again his father does not answer. He doesn't believe it is because his father doesn't hear him but because his father is choosing to ignore him. His passive-aggressive way of saying he does not wish to be disturbed.

In the past the young man would have taken the hint and slunk away, waiting for his father to come to him later. But now the young man finds himself becoming angered by how his father expects everything in life to run according to his own timetable. The young man has something to say, words burning in his chest and throat, and he is an adult now, not some child helpless before his father's moods and whims.

The young man twists the doorknob and lets himself into his father's office. The inner sanctum, the Fortress of Solitude, the place where the young man is never allowed unless invited. And he is never invited. Considering what the young man has to tell his father, he figures it is best to establish right away that he is a grown-up, full of confidence and autonomy and a will that cannot be broken.

The office is paneled in faux-wood, decorated sparsely. The carpet is blue shag, the windows blocked out by drawn shades. The young man's father has never been one inspired by seeing the world outside. Instead, the man once said in a television interview that he preferred to shut out the real world entirely while working so he could focus on building his own worlds. Of course, the young man is part of that real world his father shuts out, whether he is working or not.

Even after barging into the office, full of bluff and bluster, the young man still isn't acknowledged. His father sits across the room at his scuffed metal office desk, back to his son, fingers skittering across the keyboard, slightly hunched over as if at any moment he may crawl into the word processor screen.

The young man takes a moment to marvel at the machine, a pang of envy stabbing into his gut. He himself is still using his clunky typewriter, his dorm room always stinking of liquid paper to correct all his mistakes and changes, but his father has this modern machine that seems like it would make editing and revision a snap. The latest Brothers word processor, the keyboard and printer were a single unit that looked similar to the young man's own typewriter, the monitor sitting next to it, the black screen filling up with toxic yellow type. The young man had asked for one last Christmas, but instead he got a Rolex watch he never wears because it doesn't match the bohemian persona he tries to adopt at college. Most everyone there knows his father is rich and famous, but he tries to underplay that and appear approachable and down-to-earth. An expensive gold watch wouldn't help.

After he passes a moment staring at his father's back, starting to feel foolish as the confidence he has tried to manifest slips, he clears his throat and says loudly, "Dad, I'm home."

Finally his father stops typing, and his back heaves with a sigh. Without turning around he says, "Why aren't you at school?"

"It's spring break. I have a week off from classes."

"Then shouldn't you be at some Florida beach with your friends, drinking and making a fool of yourself?"

"That's not my style," the young man says though that is only half true. While the beach isn't his style (he finds sand to be nothing but an insidious irritant, and the vastness of the ocean inspires in him a vague disquiet), drinking and making a fool of himself has become something of a hobby for him of late. Some of his new friends at school have started taking him to a gay nightclub not far from campus called Asylum, and with the help of his fake ID he has spent many weekends intoxicated on booze but also on the dancing and acceptance and half-naked men and multi-colored lights and cartoonish drag queens. Intoxicated on a freedom he had previously only dreamed of but started to doubt existed. Of course, none of that he is what he is here to tell his father.

The two enter some kind of stalemate staring contest for a moment, the young man standing and his father still seated and facing the monitor. Finally his father swiveled around and said, "Well, there's some leftover chicken in the fridge if you're hungry. I'm trying to finish this chapter, so if you don't mind…"

Without awaiting a response, his father turns back to the word processor and starts to type. The young man feels dismissed, an unimportant nuisance that has been vanquished for the moment. His resolve starts to weaken, as he thinks maybe it's not the right time, the conversation he wants to have with his father can wait. It might be best if he just slinks away like always and—

"No," the young man says, resolute.

His father turns back to him. "What?"

"I need to talk to you," the young man says, squaring his shoulders. "It really can't wait."

"If this is about the lifestyle you have chosen to adopt, I've told you I don't want to hear about it. Do whatever you want to do in private, but don't flaunt it in front of me."

This stings, but the young man pushes forward through the pain. "That's not what I want to talk to you about. It's about school."

His father casts one last longing look at the glowing words on the monitor then motions toward the love seat that sits against the wall under one of the windows. The young man chooses to remain standing, thinking it is some kind of power play, keeping him on the higher ground so to speak.

Yet at first the young man finds he can't say anything. His mind is a chaotic whirlpool, and in the mental maelstrom he cannot seem to organize his thoughts. Plus so much of his energy is focused on keeping himself from shaking, thus exposing the confidence he is trying so hard to project as a flimsy façade.

"Well?" his father asks with an impatient sigh. "Are you flunking out?"

"No. I'm doing well in all my classes."

"Then what's so important that you thought it was okay to interrupt me while I'm working?"

"You're always working."

"Yes, real writers never really turn it off, you know."

The young man doesn't miss the emphasis placed on the word real, and it feels like a slap across his face. "All writers do it differently. There's no one right way to be a writer."

"How would you know?"

His father is baiting him, and worse, the young man realizes he is taking the bait. "I am a writer, Dad. In fact, that's the main reason I want to talk to you. I didn't change my major."

The young man expects some kind of reaction, but his father merely stares at him, his face an impassive mask. This lack of a response throws the young man off and he starts to stammer over his words.

"Um, I mean, I know you think, I mean you said you thought me majoring in Creative Writing wasn't practical, but—"

"Waste of time," his father interrupts. "I believe my exact words were that you majoring in Creative Writing would be a total waste of time."

"Look, just because you think writing can't be taught—"

"Again, you aren't being accurate in what I said. I think writing can be enhanced and developed in those who have the natural gift. You, son, do not have the natural gift. I'm sorry, I know you think I'm being cruel, but I'm simply trying to save you a lifetime full of heartache. Publishing is a rough business even for those of us with talent. I know you want to follow in my footsteps, but to be brutally honest you don't have what it takes."

The young man feels the tears behind his eyes building up, the pressure ready to burst the damn, but he holds them back. However, when he speaks his voice has a querulous tremble to it. "Other people think I have what it takes, Dad. Dr. Princeton, for example. He runs the Creative Writing department, and he's a well-respected writer who has published several books of poetry and short fiction."

"Well-respected, huh?" his father says, his lips twisting into a smirk. "Funny, I've never heard of him. What publisher is he with?"

"Um, I think his last book was with Phoenix Press."

"Ah, small press. I see."

His father's snobbery is legendary and incendiary, but the young man can't let himself get sidetracked again. "He's won some prestigious awards for his poetry, and he thinks I have talent. In fact, he's putting up one of my short stories for the college's Excellence in Prose award this semester."

With another sigh (the young man has never known anyone who sighs as much as his father), the man turns around fully, swiveling around the chair so he is facing forward. "All I'm saying is that this Dr. Princeton is an academic. He's not down in the trenches like me."

The young man laughs. "Trenches? You just signed a multi-million dollar contract with Doubleday. I'd hardly say you were 'down in the trenches.'"

"Touché," his father says with a slight smile. "Be that as it may, doesn't change the fact that the world of academia is vastly different from the world of actual publishing. If you want to get a teaching degree and teach English lit, I've no doubt you'll be good at it. But, son, I'm trying to give you some tough love here, and you don't have the spark. If I thought you did, I'd be the first one singing your praises. You don't. You just don't."

This isn't the first time his father has given him such "tough love", and usually at this point the young man scurries away to lick his wounds, but this time is going to be different. This time has to be different. "Look, I don't want to fight. I know how you feel, you know how I feel. Neither of us is going to change our minds, so let's stop going around and around in circles. I'm not soliciting your advice on this. I'm telling you this is what I'm going to do. I'm majoring in Creative Writing, I'm going to pursue a career as a writer. My plan is to use a pseudonym so that no one offers me a contract based on your name. Maybe I'll fall flat on my face, maybe I won't. Either way, I'm going to do it based on whatever talent I have and the passion I bring to my work. I'm not asking you to celebrate that, because I know you won't, but I'm asking you to accept it. I'm an adult now, old enough to make my own decisions about my future, and this is the decision I've made. I'm resolute, so if you can't support me, at least don't fight me."

The young man had planned out his whole speech on the drive home, but of course in the moment he forgot it all and he knows he stumbled over his words and wasn't as eloquent as he had wanted to be, but he got out the cliffs notes of everything he'd wanted to say. Now he waits with a knot in his stomach for his father's response.

Silence fills the room, broken only by the soft humming of the word processor, and then his father shrugs and says, "Whatever, it's your life."

Then his father turns back around and resumes typing, as if he'd never broken off.

The young man stands there stunned for a moment while his brain tries to catch up with what just happened. He has imagined this moment for a while, and in his imaginings one of two things resulted. Either his father would continue to argue, or his father would be so impressed by his son's determination and passion that he would be won over and give his blessing. The latter seemed unlikely, so he had steeled himself for the former.

However, he is not prepared to be met with such…indifference. Apathy. As if the young man's future was inconsequential to his father.

"So, we're good then?" his son asks.

His father does not pause in his typing, the black screen continuing to fill up with that yellow text. "You're going to do what you're going to do, so have at it. Just don't expect me to bail you out when you fail."

The young man continues to hesitate in the room. In the reflection of the screen, he sees the outline of his father's face. It has taken on that dreamy quality it gets when he's lost in his work. He probably no longer even realizes his son is in the room. He has gone off to spend time with the people he really loves, the characters he can control and manipulate.

The young man leaves the room, closing the door behind him. He retreats to his bedroom but doesn't start to unpack. After a few moments of standing in the middle of the room, he grabs his bags and goes back downstairs and outside to his car. He will return to his dorm, which feels like his real home anyway. His father won't even notice he has gone.

He starts the car but sits in the driveway for a while and gives in to his tears. He has gotten what he wanted, more or less. His father isn't going to fight him anymore on the young man's decision to follow his writing dream, so why does the victory feel empty? Why does it feel like a loss?

He hadn't expected his father to jump for joy, but he also hadn't expected to be dismissed as a lost cause, a write-off. The young man realizes the reason he feels so hollow is that his father's lack of a reaction has confirmed what he feared to be true.

His father does not care about him one way or the other.

Deep in my thoughts, I almost missed my turn. Of course, my father had been right. After a promising start, my writing career tanked and I had to go back to school for teaching. Then again, my father played a pivotal role in the disillusionment of my dreams. He may have seemed apathetic that day, but that hadn't stopped him from throwing a little sabotage my way.

Of course, a therapist would probably tell me to stop blaming other people for my failures. And the hardest thing to accept was that they would be right. My father had thrown a huge obstacle in my path, but I was the one who decided not to try to find a way through it. I had given up when things got too hard.

Which made me even more determined not to make the same mistakes again.

I pulled into the driveway and got out of the car, clutching the bag with the prescription against my chest. I was halfway to the door when I paused, a gasp escaping my lips. The glass storm door was closed, but behind it the front door was standing wide open.

I couldn't have walked out of the house without closing and locking the door. Could I? I thought back to see if I could conjure up the memory of me pulling the door closed behind me, but I had been so frantic and distracted when I left that I couldn't remember. It was at least possible I had been so unaware and thoughtless that I'd neglected to close the door. And yet it was also possible someone had broken in and was now lying in wait inside the house.

Behind me, I heard a door opening. I turned to see Bubba coming out of his house, crossing his lawn to retrieve the trash can that still sat at the curb. He didn't wear a mask, and the sight of his uncovered bearded face seemed sinister to me. In this Bizzaro world, people not hiding their faces behind masks felt villainous. I backed up a step even though we were more than the recommended six feet apart.

"Howdy," Bubba said, raising a hand in a wave.

I retuned the wave, started to turn away, then thought about how earlier I'd wondered if he saw me pull out into the street from his window. "You didn't happen to see anyone around my house while I was out, did you?"

He had started to pull the trash can away but stopped and said, "Can't say I did. Why, something wrong?"

"Probably not. I was in such a hurry, I must have left my front door open."

"Think you had a break in?" he asked and started across the street.

I reacted as if he were advancing on me with a baseball bat. I backed up so fast I almost tripped over my own tangled feet. "No, no, nothing like that. They don't call me the absent-minded professor at work for nothing. I'm sure I left it open. It's embarrassing. It's a wonder I haven't burned the whole place down by leaving the stove on or something."

I knew I was babbling, but I was also desperate for him to stop crossing the street. The idea of him standing in front of me, breathing on me, flecks of spittle flying from his mouth to land on my cheeks like little wet bombs, had me all but hyperventilating with panic.

My outburst did have the desired result. Bubba stopped just shy of halfway across the street, and his expression changed from one of concern *for* me to one of concern *of* me. Now he eyed me as if I might advance on him with a baseball bat.

"You sure everything's all right?" he asked.

"Yes, really. I've been stressed out lately, like everyone else in the world. Making me a little bit crazy, I guess."

At first he didn't say anything, just continued to look at me as if trying to decide if I were eccentric-crazy or psychotic-crazy. Or both. After a moment he nodded and said, "Well, I know you're relatively new to the neighborhood and if things were different, I'd have welcomed you by now. It's a pretty good place to live, but last year I did have somebody break into my work truck and steal my tools. I mean, they didn't really break in because I was stupid enough to leave the doors unlocked. So that means you aren't the only absent-minded one on the street. Anyway, I try to keep an eye out for anything suspicious. Sort of a one-man neighborhood watch. If you have any trouble, feel free to give me a holler. I've got a pistol and I know how to use it."

I know he meant that last bit to be comforting, but it also felt menacing. Especially to a gay man in the South. Of course, Bubba had no way of knowing I was gay. Except for my voice and my walk and the rainbow sticker on the back of my car. However, I chose to take his comment as the gesture of friendliness in which it was intended, a Good Ol' Boy's version of a fruit basket.

"Thanks, and I'll try to keep an eye out myself. I'm Rick, by the way."

"Name's Hanson."

"Mmm-Bop," I said without thinking.

He gave me another of those I-think-my-neighbor-might-be-cuck-oo-for-Cocoa-Puffs looks. I realized he was probably in his early-thirties at the most and probably wasn't well versed on 90s pop one-hit-wonders.

"It was nice meeting you," he said with another wave then retreated to his property and pulled his trash can the rest of the way to the side of his house. It felt a little as if he were running from me, not unlike the way I had wanted to run from him only moments before.

Deep in my mortification, I hurried into the house, closing the door behind me and feeling the comfort of once again being secure in these walls wash over me.

Then I remembered that the door had been opened when I got here, and the comfort dissipated as my entire body tensed like a squeezed fist. I had lied to Bubba out there (I was unlikely to ever think of him as anything but Bubba); I wasn't at all sure I had left the door open when I left the house earlier. Of course, that didn't necessarily mean an intruder of the cat-burglar variety. There was another option in this situation.

If I had told him I thought my house might be haunted, would that have solidified his suspicions that I was a looney?

Still, just to be safe, I did a quick sweep of the house, checking all the closets, behind the shower curtain, under my bed. The place was empty and nothing was missing. The combination of the two suggested my absent-mindedness as the culprit for the open door, but somehow that wasn't as consoling as I would have liked. It didn't change the fact that the reason I had left the house in such a flurry of worry and anxiety was because my father had dumped all my pills down the sink.

I went back to my bedroom closet and opened the small fire-proof safe that sat on the self. I didn't know how difficult it might be for a spirit to open a locked safe, but putting my pills in there at least made me feel a little bit better.

That done, I went into my office and sat down at my desk. Not to work, not to write, but to go on Amazon and order a DVR system.

Wednesday, April 15, 2020

I figured midnight would be the appropriate time to try to communicate with the dead. At least, that always seemed to be the case in movies and novels. Of course, as a creator of fictions, I knew that often the fiction didn't reflect reality. Still, it felt right.

I sat in the living room, all the lights off except for a small lamp in the far corner. I had lit a few candles and placed them on the coffee table in the center of the room. Sitting on the floor, I felt a little silly but also not. I didn't have a Ouija board or anything, nothing so cliché or trite, but I downloaded a recording app on my phone so I could do some kind of half-ass amateur EVP session.

I had also retrieved the copies of my old horror novels from the attic and had them spread out on the table as well. After the copies from the bookshelf got demolished, I figured fresh copies may trigger some kind of response. The DVR system I ordered wouldn't be here for two days, but my plan was to stay up for several hours, trying to get my father to communicate directly with me.

The house was quiet except for the refrigerator's soft hum from the kitchen. The candlelight flickered, casting eldritch shadows throughout the room. Definitely the proper atmosphere. All that was missing was a black cat and an old crone.

I started the recorder and said to the room, my voice sounding as loud as a gunshot in the silence, "Hello, Dad. Seems like you've been trying to get my attention. Well, you got it. I'm here, I'm listening. Why don't you talk to me now?"

I paused, waiting, ears straining, but I heard nothing. Of course, from what I knew of EVP, you often couldn't hear the spirit with the human ear. Only when the recording was played back would the message come through.

"Why are you so angry with me?" I asked. "Why can't you just let me live my life? Is it because of the new book? You realize that this isn't really your book at all. Whether the book is a triumph or a failure, it won't do anything to your legacy. It'll be a judgement against me, not you. Why don't you give me the space and freedom I need to see if I can make this work?"

Still I listened, on the off chance my father's response was so strong that it came through loud and clear. Nothing.

Letting the app continue to record in case my father was feeling chatty unbeknownst to me, I picked up the copy of *The Freaks Come Out at Night* and began flipping through it. The dedication was a mere two words—"For Cliff"—but two words that felt like a one-two knockout punch. Cliff was the first man I had ever said "I love you" to. We had been dating only a week when I had to turn in the dedication for this book, and by the time it was published, that relationship had gone down in flames. In retrospect it was obvious he had never been as into me as I was him, but I had been blinded by first love and convinced that despite his aloofness and noncommittal attitude we were going to last forever with a little house and a Shih Tzu and a joint bank account. Instead I ended up with only a broken heart and this dedication to serve as a painful reminder. That was the last time I dedicated a book to someone I was dating, but not the last time I got my heart broken.

My love life, such as it were, had consisted of nothing but a string of romances with emotionally unavailable men who never returned the affection I threw their way. A definite pattern, doomed relationships another Rick Justice trademark. I could see in this pattern a disturbing pathology. Always going after the men who were distant and treated me at best like a tolerable nuisance. In the end, creating constant carbon copy facsimiles of the relationship I had with my father.

A midnight séance was not the setting for this kind of uncomfortable self-analysis. Personal demons weren't the ghosts I was hoping to draw out.

To distract myself, I turned to the first chapter of the book. I recalled that originally this was the prologue but Greta had said readers didn't like prologues, considered them old fashioned and would often skip them. She suggested I retitle it "Chapter One". I had pointed out that whether I called it a prologue or Chapter One, it was the exact same text so it would seem it wasn't the actual prologue readers didn't like but the term itself. Greta had shrugged and said something I never forgot: "Readers are a weird, unpredictable animal."

Smiling at the memory, I began reading by candlelight. The chapter (prologue) plays out in a high school parking lot after a football game. A freshman who is one of the team's towel boys is making his way to his car when he is beset by several members of the team who start taunting him, calling him "pussy" and "faggot." A scene that begins like a typical bullying sequence you'd find in almost any 80s movie devolves into something more frightening when the football players reveal their fangs and pounce on the poor boy inside his own car. When I wrote that part I had in mind the scene in *Jurassic Park* where the little Dilophosaurus attacked Newman from *Seinfeld* in his jeep.

Ryan's email had reminded me of how much I had liked *The Freaks Come Out at Night* at the time I wrote it. My second of the four New Blood novels, I had always considered it my best, the most fully realized and executed. This was the first time I had looked at it in over a decade at least, maybe more. While I found the prose a bit sloppy, it held up quite well. Something I could still be proud of.

"Did you ever read this one, Dad?" I asked. "Did you ever read any of them? I've never been sure, not even about *Skeleton Bones*. Were you just making assumptions based on the titles and subject matter you considered trashy?"

I closed the book and tossed it on the table, causing the candles to tremble and the scant illumination to waver like sunlight on water. I felt an odd disappointment burning in my chest like indigestion, but at first I couldn't discern the source of the feeling. With a dawning consternation, I realized I was disappointed that I found the book decent. Part of me had been hoping all my insecurities would be confirmed, that I would read my prose and discover I in fact had no talent, that my father had been right all along, and I could pack it up and forget the new book for Doubleday, and go back to my quiet fulfilling life as an academic.

Was my life really all that fulfilling, though? It was quiet, that much was true, and it wasn't without its joys and comforts. But fulfilling?

The question was moot in this instance, anyway, because I did find skill in the book. Which meant there was skill in me. Which meant my father had been wrong, either due to snobbery clouding his judgement or because he had wanted to intentionally hurt me for reasons I could not comprehend.

Which meant that if I gave up now I would be turning my back on something not because I didn't want it, not because I thought I couldn't attain it, but because I was too much of a chickenshit to push past the pain to get it.

Of course, a homicidal ghost was a lot to push past.

I got up, trying not to focus on how hard it was to stand up from the floor or how loud my knees popped, and made my way to the kitchen. I had cleaned the house earlier so it no longer resembled a disaster area. I opened the fridge and stared inside for several minutes, finding nothing to satiate the craving I felt, trying to ignore that what I really wanted was a six pack of beer. Back in the living room, I sat down on the sofa because I knew if I got back down on the floor I might not be able to get up again.

"I'm not going away," I said, partly to my father's spirit but mostly to myself. "I'm going to see this through, finish this book. I'm going to be the writer I always knew I could be, even if you didn't. I don't need your support, I don't need your blessing. All I need is for you to get out of my way."

Ice clunked in the ice maker from the kitchen, and if that was my father's attempt to communicate, I couldn't decipher the message he wanted to send. It looked like I might be in for a long night. The gazillion ghost hunting programs and YouTube channels didn't show you this part, the long hours of sitting around in the dark waiting for something to happen. If you believed them, every investigation was a constant string of strange noises and furtive shadows and men running down halls with shaky cameras yelling, "Dude, what the *fuck* was that?"

The stress of the past week started to settle on me like a weighted blanket. Hell, not just the past week. Ever since I got the offer from Doubleday, ever since COVID made its presence known and changed the world into little pockets of isolation. No man is an island, unless there is a virulent pandemic going on.

I thought about going back to the kitchen and making myself a pot of black coffee, but I couldn't muster the strength. Instead, I leaned back and stared up at the ceiling. I found my mind drifting to the other big pandemic in my life.

AIDS.

Funny how differently the two were handled. Not *ha-ha* funny, but more *I-want-to-stab-myself-in-the-throat* funny. Even with a moron in the White House who underplayed the virus and still refused to wear a mask, the government jumped on COVID with record speed. Meanwhile, while AIDS ravaged the queer communities, the government of the time refused to even acknowledge it for years. Over twenty thousand people had died before President Reagan even mentioned the disease. If COVID had originally manifested in gay men, maybe the response wouldn't have been so swift and decisive. True, a lot of progress had been made in the last decade or so, but the hate was still there, bubbling beneath the surface. And since the 2016 election, a lot of that hate was finding its way back to the surface, rearing its ugly head into the sunlight once again.

I felt myself teetering on the precipice of a dangerous and unhealthy thought spiral, so I closed my eyes and tried to think of more pleasant things. Instead my brain turned back to the book which of course brought my thoughts back to my father and his campaign even from beyond the grave to decimate my dreams and leave my life in ruins. If he left me with a life at all.

With my brain such a jumble of negative contemplations, I figured I wouldn't need the coffee to keep me awake through the night. Yet even as this thought played in my head, I drifted off.

I dreamed of my father's funeral.

Not the way it had played out in reality. That had taken place in a large cathedral with hundreds of people in attendance. In the dream, the funeral took place here in the living room of the house he'd died in. As is the way of dreams, it was both this house and not this house. The living room was larger and had a few trees growing right out of the floor. In the center of the room lay the coffin, an extravagant white chrome box with silver trim, nothing like the simple black casket in which he'd really been buried.

At the head of the coffin stood a priest who looked more like the cartoon figure of death, his body shrouded in a moldy brown robe with a hood that hid his face in shadow. He read not from the Bible but from a copy of *Alice's Adventures in Wonderland*. In this version, however, Alice was beaten and raped by the Mad Hatter during the tea party. Curiouser and curiouser.

The coffin's lid was open, and my father's face even in death was pinched, his lips pulled down in a bitter frown, brows pulled together as if having a secret conversation between his eyes. Gazing down at him, I saw no peace in death. Instead, he seemed frozen in an eternal state of anger and disappointment.

As I stood there, a breeze blowing through the house and causing the leaves on the trees to rattle, the priest stopped reading and threw the book at me, quite literally. I leaned down to dodge it and that was when my father's eyes snapped open. Before I had time to react, he reached up and wrapped his hands around my throat, dragging me down into the coffin with him.

The space should have been narrow and confined, barely enough room for the two of us, and yet in the dream it was vast, a cavern in which I scrambled and fought and tried to crawl away. My father fought with the strength of a dozen men, his grip like steel, his growls like those of wild animals.

Then the fighting stopped and I lay still, staring up at the world outside the coffin as my father leaned over it, smiling down at me. We had traded places, and when I tried to sit up, I found I couldn't. It was as if I were paralyzed. Now the coffin seemed smaller than normal, brushing up against the sides of my body as if I didn't fit and had been squeezed in. Claustrophobia took hold of me, and inside I screamed and thrashed, but my body only remained motionless.

Above me, my father reached to close the lid of the coffin but then he paused as if reconsidering. He looked down at me and the smile that twisted his lips terrified me even beyond what I already felt. He held up a lit match that seemed to materialize in his hand and said, "I always thought cremation was more tasteful."

Then he tossed the match into the coffin with me.

I awoke to the smell of smoke.

It wasn't the acrid stench in my nostrils that pulled me out of sleep, though; it was the high-pitched screaming.

At first I fought the dream fog that shrouded my brain, trying to untangle myself from disorientation, noting the milky moonlight filtering through the sidelights. I actually looked around for the coffin, but that had only been a dream. The smoke and the screaming, on the other hand, were very real.

I realized as the sleep fog dissipated that it wasn't screaming I heard but the blaring of the smoke detector.

I followed the sound and the smoke to the kitchen and stood in the doorway, questioning if I were truly awake as the sight before me seemed something out of a nightmare. All four burners on the stove were on, glowing a deep red, and on top of one a paperback book lay in flames.

Snapping into action, I grabbed two potholders from a hook next to the stove and in one quick fluid motion snapped up the book and tossed it into the sink. I turned on the water to douse the flames. I turned off all four burners, remembering what I had said to Bubba yesterday, about being so absentminded I might burn the house down by leaving the stove on.

After flipping on the overhead light, I turned back to the sink, examining the charred and smoldering pages as the water saturated them. I found myself unsurprised as I recognized the book. *The Freaks Come Out at Night.*

I tried waving the smoke away from the smoke detector with a dish towel, but in the end I had to remove the batteries to stop its wailing. I left the soggy remains of the novel in the sink, not quite ready to deal with the cleanup.

In the living room, I found my cell on the tabletop, and the app was still recording. The phone's battery was almost drained, down to only twelve percent charge, so I plugged it up so I could scan through the file. There would be a lot to go through. It was almost four a.m., which meant the app had been recording for several hours.

I started at the beginning, listening to myself talk to the empty room, asking questions no one answered. I increased the volume and played that part again but still heard nothing that could even be construed as a spectral voice. After a few minutes the tape went silent and I knew this was the point where I had fallen asleep. I held the phone close to my ear and strained to hear something, anything.

I sat there for half an hour, listening to nothing but silence. Every so often, there would be the sound of me snorting or farting in my sleep, but nothing to indicate the presence of my father. I realized I couldn't just sit here for hours.

Bringing the phone with me into the kitchen, I plugged it up there and connected my Bluetooth earbuds, and let the recording play while I cleaned up the mess from the pyrotechnics. I deposited the blackened, waterlogged book in a trash bag and took it outside, tossing it in the trash can. Not a very dignified burial for a piece of myself, but I did take a moment before I closed the lid (*my father reached to close the lid of the coffin but then he paused as if reconsidering*). This had been my only copy of the book and it was long out of print, not even a digital version available. Of course, I would be able to find a second-hand copy online, probably for no more than fifty cents.

That thought only depressed me further, so I let the lid dropped closed with finality and went back inside.

I got to work cleaning the sink and the stovetop. This kick-started my "spring cleaning" instinct, and I ended up scrubbing the kitchen from top to bottom. I cleaned out the fridge, took a Brillo pad to all the dried, hardened, stuck-on bits in the microwave, swept and mopped the tiled floor. I even pulled both the fridge and the stove out of their respective alcoves and cleaned behind them. I found a fork and a straw hiding underneath the fridge.

From there, I took my cleaning jag into the living room. Everything needed a good dusting. When you live with it daily, you don't realize just how much dust accumulates on every surface, but taking a damp washcloth brought up so much I wondered when this room had last been dusted. Certainly long before my father had died.

I thought of something I'd once read, that dust is just dead skin cells that we have shed. That would mean some of this dust I was wiping up had come from my father, in essence was a part of my father. Perhaps the last physical part of him that existed. I entertained the silly notion that this could be the source of the haunting, these old, discarded cells that still connected him to the house, to the corporeal plane, and perhaps by cleaning them away I could rid myself of his spiritual presence. In spite of everything going on, I tucked that idea away in the corner of my mind because I thought it might make a good story. The imagination of a writer never shuts down, not really, always wanting to take the messiness of life and organize it into a coherent string of events with a resolution at the end.

From the living room, I moved into the bedroom. Changed the sheets, made the bed, re-organized the drawers in the dresser. I also checked the safe in the closet, confirming my pills were still there and had not been tampered with. Next came the bathroom. I used bleach to scour the toilet and the shower. I was aware that the shower was where my father died, but all the more reason to scour it. I flashed back to a line from the original *Poltergeist*. "This house is clean." Of course, not fifteen minutes after that line was uttered, corpses were bursting through the floorboards and a portal in the closet tried to eat the children.

The cleaning turned out to be therapeutic for me in a weird way. It emptied my mind, gave me something to focus on outside of myself. In that respect, it was almost Zen. Especially combined with the white noise coming through my earbuds as I let the recording continue to play out.

However, that white noise was interrupted just as I started to clean the bathroom mirror. The voice in my ear came so suddenly that I dropped the bottle of Windex into the sink and spun around, thinking someone must be standing at my shoulder. But no, the voice came through the earbuds.

I rushed to the kitchen and snatched up my phone, taking it into the living room. I rewound thirty seconds on the recording. I waited, not daring to breathe, to see if I had heard what I thought I had heard.

And there it came again, a deep scratchy voice that uttered a single word. There was darkness in that voice, thick and distorted with rage, but the word was clear: "Trash!"

My father's voice? It was hard to tell, the voice was almost a hiss but also partly a growl. The voice of an animal learning to speak human language.

I let the recording continue to play, and I could detect some kind of rustling and a thud. Nearly a minute passed with no other sounds on the recording, then that animal voice spoke again, this time sounding distant as if it were traveling away from the phone. Part of what it said was indistinguishable, but I caught the last of it and it froze me as if ice water had been pumped into my veins.

"*...cremation was more tasteful...*"

I sank onto the sofa, shivering against the full-body chill that engulfed me. Had the dream been more than a dream? Had my father began haunting my dreams as well as my waking life?

On the recording, silence stretched out again until the blare of the smoke detector cut through. I stopped the recording and tossed the phone back onto the table. It slid across and thudded onto the rug. I stared at the extinguished candles, wondering if trying to contact my father had been a mistake. Had I only provoked him, making matters worse?

Then I thought about all my medication being poured down the sink and realized matters had already been worse before this. The DVR system would be arriving from Amazon later today, and I knew I would set it all up. I didn't know what good it could do me, but now that I had the soundtrack I wanted the visuals to go along with it. If nothing else, to prove to myself I wasn't crazy and this was really happening.

I stood and began to pace, wringing my hands and trying to think this through. I needed help, but who could I call since ghostbusters didn't actually exist? Not the police, they would just laugh at me. A psychiatrist would try to have me locked away in a nuthouse. There was Ryan, but he was all the way in Savannah, GA. Still, perhaps he could offer some more detailed advice if he knew how dire the situation had become.

By this point, the sun was up and streaming through the windows, but it didn't dispel the gloom of the house or my mood. I stopped by the door and looked out one of the sidelights, feeling like that part in *The Wizard of Oz* when everything went from black-and-white to Technicolor. And everything went from banally predictable to insanely unpredictable. I had my own Wicked Witch hell-bent on destroying me; I simply had to figure out what I could use to melt him.

My earbuds began beeping in my ears. At first I thought their batteries were dying, but then I realized I was getting a call. Picking up my phone from the floor, I saw Edwin was calling. I frowned. The man had never called me this early. Like with a ringing phone in the middle of the night, my stomach began churning and I felt a dread akin to premonition. He was calling with bad news, had to be.

I almost didn't answer. However, I knew enough about Edwin's tenacity to know he would keep calling until I picked up.

"Hey Edwin, I didn't realize big shot New York editors rolled out of bed before brunch." I tried to keep my voice light, but I could hear the strain and tension in it.

Even worse, I could hear the strain and tension in Edwin's voice when he responded, "Don't worry, Rick. Our PR department is all over damage control. We're going to put the best possible spin on this that we can. In the meantime, if you are contacted by any reporters, tell them you have no comment. At least until the PR guys craft the perfect statement. And I wouldn't make any social media posts right now."

He was talking a mile a minute, and it took my brain a bit to catch up with everything he said. Even when I caught up, I was still behind. "Edwin, slow down. What are you talking about?"

"Have you not been online this morning?"

"Actually, no. I've been cleaning since I got up."

"Then you don't know. Jesus, okay, so, here's the thing. Don't freak out. We both know your father had no filter, and he could sometimes say things without thinking. I'm not sure he even meant half the things he said."

"I'm still not following you," I said, my dread mixing with frustration and leaving behind a muddy feeling that felt worse than either emotion on their own.

"There's a video that surfaced. Who even knew such a video existed? Anyway, it was shot many years ago at one of the rare convention appearances your father made. He says some...*things* about your writing. Some unflattering things. Someone uploaded it to YouTube last night, and it kind of went viral. A lot of fans are up in arms about you taking over the *Senior & Junior* series now that they know how your father felt about you as a writer."

I found myself running through the house to the office, where I opened the laptop and pulled up YouTube. I did a quick search for "Bentley Justice convention interview" and hit ENTER. Not many hits because my father made very few personal appearances, but the video in question was at the top of what did come up. The thumbnail picture was a split screen; on the left was a close up of my father's face, his nose wrinkled in disgust, and on the right the cover of my last New Blood book *Skeleton Bones*, the one with an embossed skeleton holding a bloody knife. The title of the video was, "Bentley Justice Tells Us How He Really Feels About Son's Work." The poster's name was Justice4Justice, and the video had been uploaded after ten last night and already had more than two hundred and fifty thousand views.

"Rick, you there?" Edwin said. "Say something."

"I'm about to watch the video."

"You really don't have to, man. I'm serious, let us handle it and you just hunker down."

"I'll call you back," I said, then disconnected the call.

Edwin's advice was sound. I could imagine the things my father had said. After all, I knew what the man had thought of my skill as a storyteller. I could simply stand up and walk away, not subjecting myself to this humiliation.

And yet I couldn't. Morbid curiosity would eat at me like acid, and with my dark overactive imagination I would likely conjure up all kinds of possibilities that were probably much worse than the reality. Yes, I convinced myself, I should watch it so I could see it probably wasn't as bad as I was imagining.

As I reached my hand toward the touchpad, I saw that my hand was shaking. I clicked onto the video, maximized it to fill the screen, then hit PLAY.

The first thing I noted was the footage was shaky and of low resolution, a bit grainy and fuzzy. The camera panned a large crowd in what seemed to be a hotel meeting room, finally finding its way to the front where my father sat at a table on a raised platform. Next to him sat a young woman with glasses. They both held microphones. Judging by my father's fuzzy sideburns and the woman's baggy overalls and platform sneakers, this interview had been recorded sometime in the late 90s.

Which explained the shitty look of the video. This would have been before cellphone cameras. This had been recorded on an actual camcorder and somehow digitally transferred.

The video started with the crowd applauding as my father sat up there looking uncomfortable with the adulation but also as if he were drinking it in. The clapping and wolf-whistling continued for nearly two minutes before it finally died down.

"Quite a reception," the woman, the interviewer, said. "That must make you feel wonderful."

My father either smiled or grimaced, it was hard to tell. Because of the video quality but also because of the unreadable nature of his face. "I do appreciate having my work appreciated."

"So modest," the interviewer said with a giggle and a toss of her hair. Was she flirting with my father? He had to be at least twenty years older than her. "I am curious, how does it feel to be one of the most successful writer's in America? I mean, you did come in at number nine on the *Forbes* list of the highest-paid authors last year."

"I'm happy that my work has reached so many, but my focus really is on the work itself. Everything else is gravy."

I recognized that as one of my father's standard lines. *Everything else is gravy.* That might have been true, but the man certainly loved gravy.

"We certainly know you are used to praise," the interviewer said, leaning forward and I suspected giving my father a peek down the gaping front of her overalls. "But what about criticism? Does it really hurt someone of your stature?"

"I assume you are speaking of the recent article in that cheap little horror rag?" my father said with a flap of his hand, as if shooing away a pesky fly.

"Yes. For those in the audience who may not know, *Fangoria* magazine recently published an article about your work and accused you of stealing elements from the horror genre for what they described as 'disposable children's stories.' They called it a form of cultural appropriation and said you were watering down the genre by domesticating it into something safe. How do you respond to that?"

My father sat in silence for half a minute then heaved a great sigh that blew into the microphone and sounded like hurricane winds tearing toward the audience. "I don't necessarily think such drivel requires a response, but since I keep getting asked about it, let me go on the record. That article was laughable, because it attempted to make the horror genre seem like it was something respectable and laudable. What a joke. This is a genre that routinely churns out the lowest form of sub-literate garbage, and yet they suggest that I am impugning on their reputation?"

Laughter from the audience, and the interviewer joined in. "So it's safe to say you are no fan of horror then?"

A definite grimace from my father this time as the camera zoomed in on his face, taking a second to focus, and I recognized this as the shot used for the thumbnail. "It's a trash genre, a ghetto market. Even at its best, it's nothing but a funhouse ride. That's fine for the masses, but there's nothing intellectually challenging or even particularly interesting about it. I mean, it's easy to throw buckets of blood at the reader and call it entertainment, but it's all shadows and smoke. I'd say style with no substance, but honestly most of the work in the genre lacks style as well."

"Please, don't hold back," the interviewer said with another laugh. "Tell us how you really feel."

My father leaned forward a little, his hands balling into fists on the table, and I recognized this posture. He was about to go on a rant. Growing up, I had been subjected to many of his rants. Most of them on literature and writers he felt were not deserving of the success they attained, but he could rant about anything. The rising cost of gasoline, the neighbor who insisted on mowing his lawn at seven a.m. on Sunday mornings, people who thought Disney World was a bucket list vacation destination, restaurants that added an automatic tip to your bill. He could have gotten a gold medal if ranting had been an Olympic sport.

"Let's take as a for instance New Blood. Are you familiar with this Simon & Schuster imprint? It is touted as 'intellectual horror,' an oxymoron right up there with 'devout atheist.' In fact, their tagline is 'Where Horror Meets Literature.' Trying to make out as if what they are producing is somehow better, more sophisticated than the average horror offering. Well, you can pour as much cheap perfume on a corpse as you want, but that doesn't cover the stink of rot."

I felt my entire body tense, and my stomach cramped like I might throw up. Even if I didn't know from Edwin what to expect, I would have been able to see where this was going. I wanted to pause the video but I couldn't move. I had to see this through to the end, like it or not.

My father turned to the audience and continued, "Have you seen the crap New Blood is pedaling? Their latest release is this utter piece of rubbish by someone named Rick Henry called *Skeleton Bones*. Yup, you heard me right. *Skeleton Bones*. Take a minute and really let that sink in. The title alone is so mind-numbingly stupid that it makes you want to scratch your own eyes out. A skeleton is comprised of bones, so they might as well have called the book *Bones Bones*."

This one really hit home, because I had always hated that title. My original name for the book when I wrote it was *The Skin We Wear is Not Our Own*, but the folks at New Blood felt it was too abstract and would confuse readers. Their market research, I was told, suggested readers liked short punchy titles, no more than two words, three if the title contained a "the" or "of." *Dark Dance, Personal Darkness, Lost Souls, Drawing Blood, Bad Brains, The Darker Saints, Dark Advent, Wet Work, Making Love, Shadow Twin, The Wilding.* All examples used to bolster their argument. Some marketing person I had never met came up with the title *Skeleton Bones*.

I had fought against it, and to her credit so had Greta, but in the end it had seemed like a battle not worth fighting. It was the last book in my contract, and I had wanted desperately to do nothing that might upset getting a new contract so I had gone along both with the ridiculous title as well as the cavorting skeleton cover. I thought of it as a stepping-stone, having no idea at the time of my acquiescence that it was going to be a dead-end instead.

"And books like this aren't singular in the horror field," my father continued. "In fact, you could hold *Skeleton Bones* up as a poster child for all the dreck which saturates that particular market. Rick Henry may be a perfectly nice person, but a writer he is not. So if he is an example of what horror has to offer readers then *Fangoria* should be ashamed of themselves for daring to try to come after me. False modesty aside, I think I'll be remembered long after my death, whereas Rick Henry likely won't be remembered next month. They dismiss my work as being for children, as if that is a pejorative, but horror as a genre is that one that is truly juvenile, even puerile. I guess I'll sum up by saying that *Fangoria* is simply jealous that I take elements associated with horror and use them in ways that are memorable and intellectual."

The audience broke into applause, and the camera panned the crowd to see several getting to their feet for a standing ovation. Then the video cut to a snippet from my recent appearance on *The Brooke Simpson Show*.

Me: "Yes, between 1991 and 1997 I published four novels with New Blood Press."

Brooke: "Not a lot of people know that because you wrote under a pseudonym."

Me: "Sort of. I dropped my last name and used part of my first and my middle name. I published those books under Rick Henry."

With that, the video ended.

Jesus! I had tried to convince myself that the video probably wouldn't be as bad as I imagined, but in many ways it was even worse. He had come for me specifically. He could have picked any book to hold up as a condemnation of the horror genre. In fact, I remembered that he had particularly hated the work of Stephen King, which he called sloppy and crude and full of humor and gross-out that appealed to the lowest common denominator reader. Now if he really had wanted to use an example that the audience would know about, King would have been the perfect target.

But his rant hadn't been aimed just at the horror genre; it had been aimed at me. He had kept my secret and not revealed Rick Henry was really Maverick Justice, but he knew it and I was sure had taken great pleasure in taking a jab at me in a public forum like that. It must have given him a special thrill. He hadn't bothered to mention anything specific about the plot of *Skeleton Bones*, probably because he hadn't bother to read it, but that hadn't stopped him from throwing me to the wolves.

Although this had to be the speech that started the domino effect that ended my writing career, I had never seen it before. In the late 90s, the internet had been a fledgling thing people were still figuring out, and not every aspect of life was documented then immortalized on the web. This particular video had been buried for twenty-three years, and now it had been resurrected. Which gave my father's rant a second chance to ruin my career.

I felt sucker punched, as if the air had been knocked right out of me. And yet I still began to scroll down to read the comments. I knew I shouldn't. In general, it was a good rule of thumb never to read the comments on anything when it came to the internet. The comments section was where all the nastiest trolls and ogres lived, just waiting for you to cross their bridge.

The very first comment on the video set the tone for what was to follow. "Doubleday should be ashamed! Bentley Justice must be turning over in his grave knowing they've turned his work over to someone they know he thought was a shitty writer. I hope the book is a huge flop for them. That would serve them right."

The next comment wasn't any better: "So disappointing. I was actually excited for this book, but I won't be getting it now. For a son to betray his own father this way, I just can't! An obvious cash grab, but they won't be getting my cash."

There were nearly a hundred comments already, and as I scrolled down, I saw that most of them were variations on the same theme. I was an evil, ungrateful, untalented, spoiled brat who was intentionally ruining his father's legacy to get back at him for not buying me a pony when I was ten years old, and Simon & Schuster was a greedy, corrupt organization who worshiped the almighty dollar and cared nothing for the integrity of art. We were accused of trying to destroy people's childhoods, and there were calls for petitions to have me replaced or to boycott the book, a few to boycott all Simon & Schuster titles.

Not one comment saying, "Hey guys, let's give him a chance. Let's reserve our judgement until the book is out." Nope, nothing but vitriol and anger that snowballed, each subsequent commenter feeding off the ones before, things escalating quickly. I was fast becoming the Antichrist of the literary world. Pretty soon they would be calling for my crucifixion.

Edwin called again but I did not answer, and I did not listen to the voicemail he left. I wasn't ready to talk to him about this yet. I needed time to think, to process, but I didn't know if that was possible. I felt as sideswiped as the last time my father had sent a wrecking ball into the building where my dreams of being a writer lived.

The young man sits in his editor's office, thinking back wistfully to the very first time he ever sat in this office a few years ago. That had been a much happier time, the tension that filled the room then born from anticipation and excitement. This time around the tension comes from fear and dread. So much has changed.

One thing that has changed is that the editor can barely fit behind her desk now. Eight months pregnant, she looks as if she has swallowed a beach ball. She has to sit so far back from the desk the young man can't imagine how she actually gets any work done. The sight might have been amusing under other circumstances, but today he can find no amusement. The editor's discomfort is stamped on her face, and he knows that at least for the moment, the discomfort is less about her physical situation and focused instead on the bad news she is delivering.

"So that's it then?" the young man says.

The editor looks pained, and her fingers tap nervously on her extended belly, giving her unborn child a little drum solo. "I'm sorry, I really am. I fought for you, I want you to know that. I was prepared to offer you another three-book contract before that article came out."

On top of the editor's desk is the latest issue of *Fangoria* magazine, opened to page twenty-two. The headline of the article screams up at the young man in bold print: **WHAT THE HELL HAPPENED TO HORROR?**

The young man hasn't read the article all the way through, but he has read enough to get the gist. The writer of the article goes on at length about the classic tradition of horror literature, from Shelley to Stoker, M.R. James to Shirley Jackson, and suggests too many working in the field today lack the ambition to create great works like their literary ancestors, instead churning out cheap, quick "shock-tomes" that entertain through titillation and clichéd scare tactics but aim for nothing more substantial. The article singles out a few names, but the majority of the examples come from the young man's own work. His pen name appears in the article so many times that if he took a shot for every mention he would be flat-on-his-ass drunk. Which might not be a bad idea after this meeting.

"And all this is because of my father?" he asks.

The editor hesitates before she responds. "We can't know that for sure, but what I've heard is that the magazine was flooded with hate mail regarding the article they published about your father's work. And he apparently said some unkind things about the quality of the genre at a convention appearance, mentioning New Blood specifically."

"Mentioning me, you mean?"

The editor doesn't answer this time, which is in and of itself an answer.

"And just like that, my contract goes poof? Tell me, did the other writers mentioned in the article lose their contracts?"

The editor shrugs. "I don't know."

"Bullshit. Two of the other writers mentioned publish with Simon & Schuster so you have to know about them."

The editor takes a deep breath and meets the young man's gaze. "No, they haven't lost their contracts."

"Then how is that fair? What makes them so special?"

"Because their books sell better than yours."

The young writer's head snaps back, and when he tries to speak all that comes out is a thin whistling. He feels as if he has been stabbed in the windpipe with an icepick. It isn't as if he doesn't know his sales figures, on average each title has sold less than three thousand copies, but he finds he doesn't like hearing it put so bluntly from his editor.

Correction, his ex-editor. The young man is being given the boot, shown the door, handed his pink slip, sent packing. He figures if he will no longer be writing for New Blood, he may as well cash in all the cliché expressions he can.

"I don't mean to hurt your feelings," the editor says, and the pity in her face hurts almost as much as the brutal honesty. "That's the simple reality. With this kind of bad publicity, my bosses don't feel it's practical to keep you on in light of the revenue your books generate for the company."

"You always said I was part of the New Blood family, but turns out I'm no more than revenue. Or in my case, a lack thereof."

"You know that's not how I feel, but yes, this is a business and those at the top are concerned with the bottom line. I tried to convince them otherwise, but ultimately I was overruled. I hate this more than you know, but I can't do anything to change it."

The young man feels tears threatening but he holds them back, not wanting to become a blubbering mess in the office of a woman he once respected. Hell, he still respects her, and he knows everything she says is the truth. She has always believed in him and fought for him. But she is the bearer of the bad news, and there is that saying about shooting the messenger. He can't help but direct some of his anger and disappointment at her even though he knows none of this is her fault.

Ultimately, he realizes if anyone is to blame it is his father. His fucking hateful father who always wants to knock him to the floor then kick him when he's down.

"So this is the end? New Blood is flushing me like a used condom? You know, you could have told me all this over the phone. No need to go to the expense of flying me all the way up here to New York. Your bosses must consider this a terrible waste of resources."

The way the editor cuts her eyes and blushes tells the young man that he hit the proverbial nail on the head there. "I wanted to do this in person, because I do care about you. Not only as a client, but as a friend. Telling you face to face was the least I could do."

"So this is my consolation prize?" he asks. "One last hoorah in the Big Apple for the poor prince deposed by the wicked king?"

A few tears dribble down the editor's cheeks, and she reaches for a tissue. "I'm not going to tell you how hard this is for me because I know it's even harder for you."

"Thank you for not telling me that."

"Go ahead, use me as an emotional punching bag if you need to. You have every right to be upset, and I want you to get it all out."

The young man feels his anger begin to deflate. It isn't as cathartic to rage at someone when they've given you permission. What replaces the anger is a black void which he thinks represents his future as a writer. Nothing but an empty expanse. "Are we done?" he asks in a soft voice.

The editor blows her nose discreetly into the tissue then tosses it in a wastepaper basket. "I know you aren't asking for my advice, but I'm giving it anyway. Take some time, let the dust settle on this, but don't give up."

"I don't have to give up; I've been fired."

"Don't give up writing," the editor says with vehemence, leaning forward over her stomach. "I know all this press is disheartening, but you are a talented storyteller. I'll be honest, maybe New Blood was never the right fit for you. A paperback original horror line, no matter the pedigree, predisposes people to think lower quality. And frankly, the metaphorical aspects of your work I think are being overlooked because of that prejudice. You're ahead of your time, if you want my honest opinion. The literary world needs to catch up with you, that's all."

The young man feels a pressure in his gut like a bubble that travels up through his chest and lodges in his throat. The editor probably has no idea, but her praise only makes all of this harder, more painful.

"I know you are halfway through your new novel," she continues. "Keep working on it. And once this brouhaha has died down and is a bit in the rearview, start submitting it to agents under your real name."

The bubble in the young man's throat bursts and spews from his mouth in the form of harsh laughter. "You're kidding, right? I've just been roasted in a popular magazine considered one of the leading authorities on the horror genre, my publisher has kicked me to the curb, and you think I should just dust myself off and start over? I can't go through all this again. I'm not that much of a masochist."

"I wish I could tell you success was a guarantee, but unfortunately the world doesn't work that way. Sometimes extremely talented people don't get the success they deserve, and things happen like this that aren't fair, but I don't want this to make you doubt yourself. You have so much potential to—"

The young man stands abruptly, sending his chair toppling over. "Thanks for the pep talk, coach, but I'm going to go. This will probably be my last trip to New York on someone else's dime, so I'm going to make the most of it before I have to head back tomorrow."

The editor plants her hands on the desk and with some effort leverages herself to her feet. "Don't lose my number, okay? Keep in touch, and if you do feel at some point in the future like you want to try again, call me. I'll give you some names of agents I think might respond positively to your work."

"It's been real," the young man says and hurries from the office. He has the elevator to himself and spends the trip from the tenth floor to the first *giving in to the tears that patiently bided their time.*

This feels worse than all the years of rejection that came before the deal with New Blood. Then he hadn't had anything to lose, still struggling for any little crumb of success. Now that he has had a taste, having it snatched away from him feels like losing a limb. And his editor thinks he should give it another shot. What would be the point in that? His father would still be there, ready to shoot out the tires of his ambitions as soon as he got any momentum going.

As the young man stumbles onto the busy street, wiping furiously at his eyes, he thinks that what is even worse than the fact his father has never believed in him and feels his son has no talent is that the young man suspects his father might be right. All of this is only confirmation of his deepest insecurities.

"Fuck it," the young man grumbles and heads off to a bar he spotted earlier on his way to the editor's office. Time to start taking those shots. After all, he is in pain and shots are medicinal.

As if the memory acted as a summoning spell, my phone buzzed with an email notification, and when I glanced at the screen I saw it is from Greta. I swiped the notification away. I was no more in the mood to talk with her than I was with Edwin. Now was not a time for editors and their consolations.

I had the eerie sensation of time folding in on itself like a piece of paper, some sort of nightmarish origami creation that crashed me right back into one of the darkest periods of my life. I had been devastated when New Blood dropped me, and my drinking—which had already been extensive—started to spiral out of control. That in turn lowered my inhibitions and I ended up being a bit too indiscriminate in my sexual practices, thus becoming infected with HIV.

I would have to admit I took some small, schadenfreudian consolation when New Blood imploded a little over a year later. It turned out distancing themselves from me did not help salvage their reputation after the vicious takedown from *Fangoria*, and sales for all their titles suffered. After Greta, probably seeing the writing on the wall, stepped down as HBIC, Simon & Schuster shelved the imprint altogether. So my father's casual cruelty had not only ruined my writing career but an entire publishing line.

He'd also killed an entire fictional world. At the time of my last meeting with Greta, mere weeks before the birth of her daughter Aurora, I had been halfway through a novel I had considered my best work to date. The working title was *Tainted Blood* and dealt with a parasitic organism that spread from body to body, draining healthy young men in New Orleans of their strength and vitality, sucking them dry then moving on to a new host, leaving the old host a withered shell. I had seen the whole thing as a metaphoric exploration of how the AIDS epidemic had decimated the homosexual population. Almost prescient, considering the turn my own life was soon to take.

Yet after being dismissed by New Blood, I never wrote another word on the novel. In fact, the work's very existence offended me, a constant rubbing of salt in an open wound. My solution, come to after copious amounts of alcohol and participation in an orgy in the back room of a seedy club, had been to wipe the book from existence. I erased it from my computer, destroyed the floppy disk on which I'd saved it, and burned the samples I had printed out.

Over the years at various times I had regretted that rash decision, often mourning the loss of the story, but other times—like now—I felt I had done the world a favor. Who needed another hack story from a hack writer?

I had told Greta back then I didn't want to try again, that I couldn't take the disappointment if it all went sour a second time. After all the intervening years, one might think I had developed a thicker skin, a suit of armor to protect me from life's nasty twists and turns, but I found this no less devastating. The repeating of history was as atrocious as it was suggested to be.

Of course, I reminded myself that Doubleday had not yet dropped me, but surely that outcome was inevitable. In only a few hours I had become an object of scorn and ridicule online, a laughing stock and no doubt an embarrassment to Doubleday.

When my phone rang, I expected it to be Edwin, calling to deliver the bad news. No trip to New York this time, not with most airline travel prohibited during the pandemic. However, when I glanced at the screen I saw the call was not from my editor but from Michael.

I almost let the call go to voicemail but then reconsidered. I wasn't in the mood to talk to my editors, current or former, but perhaps I could use a friendly voice. The weeks of isolation came crashing down on me like an avalanche.

"Hello, Michael."

"Hey, Prof. Are you okay?"

The genuine concern in his voice almost brought me to tears. It made me feel even more alone somehow, realizing that the closest thing I had to a best friend was someone half my age who barely knew me. I had never been what anyone would call a social butterfly, but in my youth I had friends and went to parties and even hosted a few. However, as I got older I began to withdraw into myself, my world becoming an insular bubble I rarely allowed anyone to penetrate. I told myself I liked being alone, it was easier that way, I was my own best company, but now in my state of emotional rawness I could admit I had only ever been scared. Scared of rejection, betrayal, being disappointed or being the cause of disappointment.

And I was so very lonely.

I cleared my throat and tried to make sure my voice didn't crack when I answered. "As well as can be expected when every troll on the internet has come out from under their bridge."

I meant for it to come off as a joke, but Michael wasn't laughing. "Man, I can't believe how nasty the human race can be. I mean, I can believe it because this isn't the first time I've seen evidence of it, but I don't want to believe it. I want to believe people are more empathetic and compassionate than that."

"Ah, so you want to believe in fairytales," I said. "No, the anonymity of the internet just makes it easier for people to dehumanize others and say things to people they'd never say to them face to face. Well hell, even that's not true anymore. I think the internet has trained people that it's okay to say the most vile things to others. I know I sound like an old codger, screaming that the internet is bad. I mean in so many ways it has been a wonderful tool, but it definitely has had some unfortunate consequences. I apologize for the dissertation; my mind is more than a little scattered at the moment."

"You have nothing to apologize for. I hate that you're having to go through this. I've spent the morning pushing back online, telling people how great your writing is, because it's obvious all these people piling on you haven't even read your work."

"In this day and age, informed opinions aren't exactly in fashion. We're in the era of people getting all their news from headlines without ever reading the actual articles."

"Is there anything I can do for you?" Michael asked.

"Merely knowing I have someone in my corner is a big help," I said, pacing through the house to work off some of the nervous energy that thrummed through my body like an electrical current. "Promise me you won't waste too much time defending me online. That's a losing battle and I wouldn't want you to get sucked down the vortex."

"I know, but it pisses me off so royally. I'm sure this isn't the way you wanted to end up trending on Twitter."

I closed my eyes and let out a shuddering breath, standing before the open closet in my bedroom. "So I'm trending on Twitter already?"

"You didn't know?"

"I saw the clip on YouTube and the comments there, but I didn't realize I'd crossed social media platforms already. What are they saying over on the little blue bird? More of the same?"

"Pretty much. There's a hashtag going around."

I thought of the YouTube video, and the name of the account that had shared it. "Let me guess, #Justice4Justice?"

"Yeah, how'd you know?"

"Has the kind of ring to it that would catch on," I said, walking into the kitchen.

"I still can't believe your own father would have said such nasty and vicious things about you."

"I wish I could claim to be surprised," I said as I unscrewed the lid off the bottle.

"It's all such bullshit. You have mad skills, and you're going to do a fabulous job with this book. I know it."

"You're awfully sweet, Michael. If only everyone—"

My words cut off as if severed with a scalpel when I looked down and saw the prescription bottle in my hand, tilting over the sink, and I watched in horror as two of my Biktarvy spilled out. One went straight down the drain while the other bounced off the edge and landed in a puddle of water collected in the basin.

I cried out, dropping the phone so it clattered on the tiled floor, only its sturdy case keeping it from shattering. I slung the bottle away from the sink. It landed on the counter, the pills scattering across the faux-marble surface but at least they weren't lost down the drain.

Again.

I could hear Michael's distant, tinny voice shouting my name. I retrieved the phone, said, "Sorry, I stubbed my toe, let me call you back," then disconnected the call. My legs felt rubbery, and I put my back to the refrigerator and sank down until I was sitting on the floor.

What the fuck was wrong with me? I had almost dumped my newly acquired medication down the drain without any conscious thought or will. I had a vague awareness that I had gone into the bedroom and opened the closet, but I didn't remember opening the safe and taking out the bottle. It all felt surreal and removed, as if it hadn't been me at all. Like I had been in some kind of trance or altered state. A puppet whose moves and actions were controlled by some force outside myself.

With fumbling, trembling fingers, I opened my email on my phone and shot off a quick message to Ryan. A single question. No preamble or greeting, no salutations or valedictions, just the one line. "Is it possible for a ghost to possess a living person and make him do things he isn't consciously aware of?"

I began to shiver, a full body chill as if I were caught out in a blizzard wearing only a speedo. I pulled my knees up to my chest and wrapped my arms around myself, a sense of violation overwhelming me. My father had gotten behind the steering wheel for a bit and started gunning the car directly toward a cliff with no guardrail.

Had this been the first time?

I thought of the other instances of my pills being tossed, the book burning on the stove. Had my father used my body to do those things? Was that the only way he could cause physical manifestations, by putting me on like a suit?

I checked the status of my DVR system order, the tracking indicated it would arrive by five p.m. Then I thought, *Fuck it*, and opened the grocery store app, putting in an order for a case of beer to be delivered.

In this situation, Biktarvy wasn't the only medicine I needed.

I was two and a half beers in, sitting out back in one of the Adirondacks that circled the fire pit, when Edwin called again. With everything going on, I didn't feel crushed with guilt about my tumble off the wagon, but instead only a sense of relief as the alcohol hit my bloodstream. In fact, it gave me the courage I needed to talk with Edwin once more.

"Hey ET, what's shaking?"

This enthusiastic greeting was no doubt unexpected, and Edwin hesitated a second before saying, "How you holding up, Rick?"

"That remains to be seen, depends a lot on how this conversation goes. How are you and DD doing?"

"DD?"

"Yup, Doubleday. Hey, I just came up with that. ET works for DD. Pretty funny when you think about it."

"Are you drunk?"

"I'm on the road to drunk, but I haven't quite reached my destination yet," I said, then took a swig from the can. I hadn't bothered to refrigerate the case when it got here, just took it with me to the back yard, but warm beer was better than no beer.

"I guess you're entitled," Edwin said with a weary sigh. "I could use a stiff one myself."

"I'd make a lewd joke right here, but I'm afraid that would violate our strict professional relationship."

This elicited a chuckle from Edwin, but the mirth was short-lived. "It's quite the shit storm on social media, and it keeps building."

"I know, I'm still trending with the twits on Twitter. I've managed to beat out coronavirus and J.K. Rowling's raging transphobia for people's attention."

"If only it stopped there. Bloody-Digusting.com has posted up on their website an old *Fangoria* article that was a reaction to what your father said at that convention, and it only makes matters worse. And then there's the budding TikTok challenge, but I'm hoping it doesn't take off."

I drained the third beer and immediately opened a fourth. I had a feeling I would need a hell of a buzz to get through the rest of this phone call. "What TikTok challenge?"

"Somebody posted a TikTok of them ripping up an old copy of one of your books and feeding it into a shredder and called for other Bentley Justice fans to do the same. So far there have only been two other similar videos."

"Give them time. Probably not too many people out there with copies of my books, so they'll have to get them off eBay or scour thrift stores. There's still time for me to become the next eating Tide pods."

"It's not all doom and gloom," Edwin said. "There have been some on social media coming to your defense, and a hashtag has immerged in the last couple of hours. #GiveJusticeAChance."

I held up my beer can in a silent salute to Michael. That had him written all over it.

"In the meantime," Edwin continued, "Doubleday has issued an official statement saying we hired you because we believed in your ability as a story-teller."

"But that's not true, right?"

"What?"

I took another fortifying swig. Alcohol often gave you the courage to go places you would never dream of going sober. Often there were good reasons not to go there, but that kind of regret was for mornings-after.

"We've never really talked about this, ET, but I'm curious. Did anyone at the publisher ever even read any of my work before they hired me?"

Edwin sputtered a bit before answering. "I can't be expecting to know what everyone at Doubleday has or hasn't read."

"Had you ever read my work?"

"Yes, I've read all the chapters you've sent me," he said. "And they are terrific."

"But had you read my work before I was hired? Tell me the truth, everyone at DD thought it would be a clever publicity stunt to get the son to finish the father's work. Had nothing to do with me personally or any talent I may or may not have. Optics, that was behind the decision."

Edwin's answer was to not answer, which spoke volumes.

"Bet you all must be kicking yourselves now," I said with a laugh. "I mean, you guys never would have offered me the gig if you'd known my father had said all those nasty things and lost me my original publishing contract."

Silence for a moment then Edwin said, "Is that true? Did you already know about all this?"

I could hear a petulant sense of betrayal in Edwin's voice, but I didn't feel sorry for him. What did he expect, that someone would be offered a huge amount of money then say, "Before I cash the check, fellas, let me enumerate all the reasons you shouldn't give it to me."

"You guys should have done your homework," I said then belched. "If you don't take a good look under the hood before buying a used car, sometimes you end up with a real lemon. Then there's nothing you can do but junk it."

"We're not junking you," Edwin said, but I thought we could both hear the *yet* implicit in the statement.

"So then what's the strategy, ET? What do you want me to do?"

"Nothing. No statements, no response. We want you to stay off social media as well."

I stood up, walked around the fire pit as if playing musical chairs, than sat in one of the other Adirondacks. "You don't think I should at least try to defend myself at all?"

"You've got nothing to defend," Edwin said. "And that's the impression we want to send to the reading public. Like you think all this is beneath your concern, so ludicrous that it doesn't even warrant a reaction."

"Ignore it and it'll go away, huh? Seems I'm getting that advice from all sides lately. Hasn't worked with my father."

"Your father? What are you talking about?"

I waved a hand as if shooing a fly. "Never mind. If radio silence is what you want from me, radio silence is what you'll get. It'll be like I'm the dead one."

"I know this is hard, Rick, but don't let it make you doubt yourself. You're doing great work, and I've been telling everybody at Doubleday how fantastic the chapters you've sent me are. I'm in your corner, and I'm going to go to bat for you."

I could have told him he was mixing his metaphors, but that would have been a dick move so I held my tongue. In truth, I found myself moved by his belief in me, to the point that I had to blink away the blurriness that came to my vision. Of course, Great had believed in me too, she'd been in my corner and always went to bat for me, but that hadn't stopped New Blood from kicking me right out on my ass.

When I didn't say anything right away, Edwin cleared his throat and said, "Would you mind if I offered you a little personal advice, not as an editor but as one man to another?"

I was glad he didn't say *not as an editor but as a friend*, because though our relationship had thawed as of late, we weren't anything close to resembling friends. The fact that he didn't try to pretend otherwise made me feel an even deeper tenderness toward him. "Advise away."

"When I say stay off social media, I'm not just talking about you not posting. Don't go on there at all. At the best of times, social media is a cesspool, but since everyone has gone into lockdown, it really has brought out the worst dregs of humanity. People have too much time on their hands, they are angry and scared and turning to the internet to unleash all that. I say this is the perfect time for you to take a social media break. Think of it as a spiritual cleanse."

"A colonic for my soul?"

Edwin laughed. "Exactly."

I wanted to laugh with him but couldn't find it in me. I stared up at the sky, a perfect crystalline blue today. A flock of birds flew over in perfect formation, not having to worry about social distancing or masking, enjoying the camaraderie of a synchronized group, likeminded and connected. I envied them.

"So what you're telling me," I said as I watched the flock bank and disappear off toward Main Street, "is that while I'm trapped here all alone in this house, I should cut off the only access I have to the rest of the world. That kind of deprivation goes beyond cabin fever, don't you think?"

"Email and text friends, call me anytime you want to chat about the book or anything else, but avoid social media like it's the plague. No good can come of it. Focus on the work instead. Your father always said his characters were better company than most people in the real world."

"My father said a lot of things, including that I'm a shitty writer. Are we picking and choosing which Bentley Justice nuggets of wisdom we should believe the way people do the Bible?"

"Christ," Edwin said. "I'm sorry. I wasn't thinking. My foot permanently lives in my mouth."

Feeling generous, I decided to let Edwin off the hook. I knew he meant well, and that was something. "Don't worry about it, ET. I'll get back to work on the book pronto. I have a household project I'm working on right now, but I won't neglect Senior and Junior."

A pause on the line before he responded. "My bosses would have a shit-fit if they knew I was about to say this, but the book isn't as important as your mental health. We're all feeling on the edge of breakdown these days, but you have so much more pressure on you than most of us. And now on top of that you have this social media pile-on. I meant it when I said you could call me if you ever wanted to chat."

Earlier I had appreciated that Edwin hadn't put up the pretense that our relationship was anything but professional, but now I wondered if he wanted it to be more. I didn't delude myself into thinking he was angling for anything romantic, but did he want to be my friend?

"I appreciate that, ET," I said, uncomfortable. "I really should go now. Thanks for the advice."

I hung up before he could respond and took another drink. Could anyone have a better friend than beer?

I stretched out my legs and slid further down in the chair. The day was warm without being hot, a nice breeze carrying the scent of early-blooming flowers. Purple wisteria climbed a scraggly tree in the corner of the property, dressing it up in the color of royalty.

Out on Brushy Creek Road, I saw an Amazon Prime van coasting along then slowing and turning onto my street. It moved out of view but I heard it stop on the other side of the house. My package had arrived. I waited until the driver dropped it at the front door and drove off again before pushing myself up and walking (staggering? maybe just slightly) around the house. The box wasn't super large, but I had my DVR system. Whatever havoc my father created in the house tonight, this time I would capture it all on video.

I had three small cameras for the DVR system, and I placed them strategically. One in the living room, pointing toward the bookcase. One in my bedroom, aimed at the foot of the bed. The last in the kitchen, with a good view of both the stove and the sink. All areas where manifestations had occurred. Whether I got any evidence or not, it felt good to be doing something proactive.

I had received an email response from Ryan earlier.

There have been reports of demonic entities possessing people, but simple spirits not really. There are mediums who can channel these spirits, allowing the dead to talk through them, but in those cases the medium actually courts that connection. I have never heard of a ghost forcibly taking control of an unwilling person. The spirit would have to be invited.

I certainly had never invited my father, at least not on a conscious level. However, I had taken over his home, taken over his work, so in some weird way did that give him permission to take over my body? Tit for tat, turnabout's fair play, all that sort of thing. Had I left the door open without even realizing it?

As I finished setting up the final camera, my phone rang. Michael calling. I almost answered but then let it go to voicemail. I was not quite drunk enough to ignore the fact that I was far too drunk to talk to him. In my state of inebriation, I feared I would tell him what was really going on and he would think I had lost my mind. Of course, Michael was a believer, so if anyone might take me seriously, he was the one. No, my real fear was that I might respond to his flirtatiousness in kind. Not because I was interested in him, a twenty year old was too much like a kid to me, but because I was in a vulnerable condition, the kind of condition that leads to bad choices and regrettable actions.

Instead I grabbed my laptop from the office and took it into living room. No chance would I be writing. Edwin had suggested I focus on the work, but I couldn't see myself focusing on anything of substance today. I pulled up YouTube and started bingeing a cooking channel hosted by a once-famous TV chef whose career had crashed and burned when she said something racist. Seemed she was using the lockdown to try to reinvigorate her brand. Not a bad time to do it; the current administration had made blatant bigotry fashionable again.

I couldn't say why I was watching as I had never been a fan even before her downfall, but there seemed something hilarious about watching her fumble her way around the kitchen, suggesting her expertise had been more a creation of

TV production than skill. And with a few drinks in me (or maybe more than a few), it all seemed even more hilarious. At any rate, it was a distraction that took me out of myself for a while and I sorely needed that.

Outside, the sun was setting and I realized I hadn't eaten much of anything today, and yet I didn't even feel hungry. As I glanced at the beer can in my hand, I realized I was keeping my stomach pretty full even if not with food. Besides, wasn't beer made with barley and hops? So a vegetarian diet, and wasn't that healthier?

I laughed louder than necessary as on the screen the racist chef tried to turn a cake out of a pan and ended up sending half of it flopping right onto the counter.

THURSDAY, APRIL 16, 2020

I WOKE UP WITH a throbbing headache and a grotesque taste in my mouth, like I'd been gnawing on a dead rat. I was lying on the sofa at a weird angle, my neck bent awkwardly on the arm. I pushed myself up and the pain in my head intensified, a rock slide inside my skull, beating my brains to a pulp. I feared for a moment I might throw up on my lap, but I remained still until the pain ebbed to a dull ache, a much more manageable level.

The room was pitch dark except for one candle, its flame fluttering as if it knew the futility of its fight against the darkness. Beer cans were strewn all around me, and the familiarity of the sight sent depression crashing down. I was a failure. At writing, at sobriety.

At life.

I searched around for my phone, finally locating it stuck between the sofa cushions, and checked the time. 3:42 a.m. I looked around the room, what I could see in the paltry glow of the candle and my phone. The normal carnage one could expect from a night of drinking, but nothing more than that. No burning books, no displaced objects, no threatening messages scrawled on the walls in ectoplasm.

Of course. Now that I was ready with cameras, no otherworldly activity. I shouldn't have been surprised. If I had learned anything from all those ghost hunting shows on TV, it was that ghosts were infamous for being camera shy and suffered performance anxiety when being recorded. When no one had a camera out, spirits could appear in full body manifestations, throw shit all around the room, but the second you hit record you were lucky to catch a fleeting shadow or creaking door. They were a lot like that damn frog from the Warner Brother's cartoons that way.

My disappointment, in both myself and my lack of concrete evidence, was eclipsed by the overdriving need to piss. I had countless cans of beer sloshing around inside me and they wanted to be released into the world again. I stood up too fast, causing a detonation of explosives in my head. Putting a hand to the back of my head as if trying to keep my skull from splintering apart, I moved with the shuffling gait of an octogenarian. I noticed a second case of beer under the glass-topped table. I didn't even remember ordering it.

In the bathroom, I leaned forward and rested my forehead against the wall as I let the urine stream out of me. The spray didn't always hit the bowl but I was beyond caring at this point. I was hoping the voiding of my bladder would also take the headache with it, but it hung on like a beast with claws sunk deep into my gray matter.

I wanted to blame my father for this lapse, but he hadn't put the beer in my hand. He hadn't even possessed me to place the order. I had done that of my own free will. The most disappointing part wasn't the fact I'd returned to drinking in such a splendidly messy fashion; it was the fact that none of this was surprising in the least.

All my life I'd been a giver-upper, perhaps the ultimate Rick Justice trademark. In many ways, I could define myself by my inability to persevere when things got hard. Sometimes it seemed I expected life to simply hand me things, and when I realized I'd have to work for them, I turned tail and ran off. One could say my philosophy had always been, "You can't lose if you don't play." However, now I was beginning to see that if you didn't play, you were guaranteed to always lose. In sports, if one team refused to take the field, it wasn't that team that won by default.

I knew all of this, and the prevailing wisdom was that the first step to recovery was admitting you had a problem. Yet admitting you had a problem wasn't a magical solution that suddenly made everything better. That was the easy part then you had to move on to step two then three then four, etc. No, after admitting you had a problem was when the real hard work began. And when I usually gave up.

I stumbled out of the bathroom, not bothering to flush or clean up the doused toilet seat and floor, and into the bedroom. All I wanted to do was crash on the bed and lose myself in unconsciousness for several hours. I needed to do something—about my drinking, about the book, about my father—but I couldn't think past the pounding in my skull.

I tried to kick off my shoes, but I lost my balance and fell against the dresser. Leaving my shoes half on, I stumbled to the bed, scuffing and dragging my feet. This wouldn't be the first time I'd slept fully clothed after a night of drinking. Would it be the last?

Halfway across the room, I paused, a chill spreading along my spine as if someone ran an ice cube down my back. I squinted into the darkness, rubbed my eyes, and looked again. On the opposite side of the bed, by the window, I saw my father.

What I actually saw was a deeper shadow among the shadows, a solid-looking form in the shape of a man. It stood as still as death but then inched an arm up, pointing toward me. An accusation, an admonishment, a warning?

"Why won't you leave me alone?" I yelled, wishing my voice didn't crack, wishing I didn't hear the desperation and fear in my words. Wishing I wasn't crying.

The shadow figure did not answer, just stood pointing at me.

"You fucked up my life enough while you were alive. Can't you give it a rest now that you're in your goddamn grave?"

Still no answer. The taciturn nature of the spirit began to turn my fear into frustration. "Go toward the fucking light!" I screamed. "With any luck, it's the fires of Hell waiting to consume your hateful ass!"

When the spirit still did not respond, I launched myself over the bed, wanting to throttle my father. Of course, I passed right through the shadow as if nothing were there. I didn't even feel a cold spot. I banged my head against the edge of the windowsill, making my headache even worse.

I lay there for a moment, shook my head, then sat up, raising a hand against the glare of the sun through the window.

At first I couldn't comprehend where all the light was coming from. I hadn't thought I'd lost consciousness, but I must have. Otherwise, it couldn't have gone from pitch black to sun-shiny in the course of seconds.

I touched my fingers to my left temple and they came away tacky with blood. I also noticed drying blood on the windowsill. I considered going to the emergency room to be checked for a concussion or to see if the gash needed stitches, but I dismissed the idea. Ironically, in a global pandemic the last place I wanted to be was a hospital. At the best of times, they were crawling with germs. How many people went in for a procedure only to end up with an infection that turned septic and killed them?

In reality, that number was probably quite small, but my fear of hospitals had been born at a young age watching *Halloween II*, and the time spent in one after the suicide attempt had only compounded that. Fears that lacked rationality were called phobias, and I clung to mine like a tree branch on the side of a cliff.

Looking around, I found my phone on the floor. In my tumble, the screen had been cracked, a spider web pattern in the lower right corner, but it still seemed to be working. I saw that I had several missed calls, texts, and emails but chose to ignore them, instead opening the DVR app I'd installed yesterday. I had been so inebriated, I was surprised I'd managed to do it right, but it seemed I had in fact done it. The footage the cameras shot were sent directly to my phone.

I pulled myself up and sat on the side of the bed. I recalled it had been about a quarter to four when I had woken up on the sofa and gone to the bathroom. I pulled up the camera in the living room and found that moment, watching myself stagger around like some kind of Romero zombie. I felt shame seeing myself like that. The sight was quite sobering, I thought, even as I cringed at the bad pun. It was like watching one of the homeless drunks that wandered around downtown Greenville, begging for spare change.

Once my image on the screen staggered out of frame, I switched over to the bedroom camera. And instantly saw my mistake. I'd had the candle in the living room providing some illumination, but I had forgotten to turn on any lights in the living room and the cameras were not equipped with night vision or anything of the sort. Therefore the footage was nothing but solid darkness. I didn't even realize I had entered the room until I heard on the audio, "Why won't you leave me alone?" There could have been an army of vengeful spirits in the room, but there would be no way to tell.

Another failure.

Not surprising. Failure was the only thing in my entire life I'd ever consistently succeeded at.

Tossing the phone onto the bed, I went into the bathroom and looked at my reflection in the mirror. After cleaning the blood from my temple with a washcloth, I was relieved to find the cut wasn't as bad as I feared. There was a knot there with some purple-black bruising around it, but I didn't think I required stitches.

However, the rest of me was a mess. My hair seemed to have sprouted so much more gray in the past week, and it stuck up in tangled tufts and corkscrews, giving me the appearance of someone who had just received an electrical shock. The bags under my eyes were so deep and dark that it looked like makeup, very stark against the sickly paleness of my skin. My lips were dry and cracked, my eyes red and haunted. I had thought on the footage that I looked like a zombie, and this view of myself up close only reinforced that impression.

I turned away and sat on the edge of the tub, feeling so much exhaustion and despondency that for a moment I didn't think I could move. I didn't think I could even muster the motivation to draw my next breath. I'd of course heard people talk about despair before, but I felt most didn't really understand the meaning of that word. It was used to describe a simple case of the blues, but true despair went beyond sadness, beyond depression. In fact, it was almost a lack of feeling altogether. Not exactly numbness, because that suggested feeling right below the surface of perception. No, true despair was a hollowness and emptiness, a sense that your body was a shell with nothing inside but a sucking vortex, a housing for a black hole that siphoned away all joy and love and enthusiasm but replaced these things with nothing. Not even unhappiness or hate or apathy. There was just *nothing*. You didn't even feel like a person, more a wraith going through the motions every day but affecting nothing around you. Nothing you did seemed to matter, every action and word pointless. That was the quintessence of despair, that your very existence seemed pointless and of no consequence to anyone, least of all yourself.

I had pondered the nature of despair before, because this wasn't the first time I had experienced it. Considering where it had led me last time, I would have been scared if I was capable of feeling anything at all.

Leaning over, I plugged the drain and turned on the water. I'd take a long soak in the tub and either relax or drown myself. I would decide in the moment. Even I was curious to discover which way it would go.

I knew the living room was a mess, but the idea of cleaning it filled me with dread. Which was at least something, some kind of emotion. If I cleaned then the dread would be gone and I would be emotionless again. No, better to leave the dread lingering there, some reminder I was alive. It may be the thing that kept me from sinking beneath the water and taking a deep inhale.

As I stripped out of my clothes, repelled by the stench of booze and sweat and bleakness that wafted from my skin, I walked back into the bedroom to retrieve my phone. I wanted to check through the messages and see if there was any new news from Edwin. It wasn't too late for Doubleday to drop me.

Part of me fervently wished that would happen. Then I could walk away from this whole mess without feeling like I had quit. I could give up by proxy.

I found myself disappointed, this time by news that a week before would have elated me. I had a rather lengthy text from Edwin:

EDWIN

You're not answering your calls or emails, but I want to assure you that DD (now you've got me thinking of the company that way) is not going to break the contract. I won't lie and say they are happy about this turn of events, but they have placed an investment in this book and they aren't going to throw that away. They aren't going to throw you away. Our marketing department even thinks this has the potential to be the success story of next year. People love a whipping boy, yes, but they also love an underdog that comes out on top.

So Doubleday was going to stick with me, hoping I could prove the naysayers wrong by delivering a book that impressed the world. That kind of pressure felt like hands wrapped around my throat, squeezing until I couldn't breathe. There had already been so much interest and focus on this book; the latest turn of events only increased that tenfold. How could anyone expect me to perform under such an expectation? I felt a sort of creative impotence coming on. I had only been able to get my imagination semi-rigid to begin with; now it felt as flaccid as a deflated balloon.

I saw I also had messages waiting from Greta and Michael as well. My personal little cheerleaders, and I found myself picturing the two of them in short skirts shaking pompoms above their heads and surprised myself with a genuine chuckle. That little bit of mirth almost made me feel human again, spreading a bit of warmth through my body.

But then I felt an icy breath caress the back of my neck. I spun around and found myself staring into the open freezer. I frowned at the frozen meals and half-empty tub of ice cream. When had I walked into the kitchen? I had no memory of that at all. The last I remembered I had been in the bedroom after...

After starting a bath.

I ran to the bathroom, splashing through the water that waterfalled over the side of the tub. I reached quickly over and twisted the faucet to turn off the flow, then splashing my hand down to unplug the tub. For a second I thought I saw the wavering face of my father beneath the water, but then I realized it was only my own distorted reflection.

Or had it been an overlay? My face over his? Were we becoming one and the same?

As the water began to drain from the tub, I looked around at the mess in the bathroom floor. It wasn't as bad as it could have been. Apparently I hadn't been zoned out long enough for a complete flood. I went to the linen closet and grabbed an armful of towels and spread them over the tile, sopping up the large puddle that had been created.

More lost time. It was beginning to happen so often that I couldn't say it was even surprising at this point. Disturbing, yes, but not surprising. Becoming rather old hat, if I were to be honest. A regular part of my day.

I checked the closet safe again, relieved to find the pill bottle safely tucked away. I shook it to make sure the pills were still inside. Only then did I return to the kitchen to close the freezer door. However, I noticed something I hadn't before, an object stuck behind the tub of ice cream. I reached in and pulled out my copy of *Wind in the Canyon*. It had been in the freezer long enough to have already formed a thin layer of frost on the cover.

I nixed the bath and had a quick shower instead. Afterwards, I sat in my bathrobe in the living room, staring down at *Wind in the Canyon*. It had always been my least favorite of the quartet of the New Blood releases. A rather uninspired ghost story about a young man who returns to his hometown and childhood home after the death of his parents, only to find spirits waiting for him. Nothing much going on beneath the surface with that one, no metaphor or deeper meaning. Just a string of haunted house clichés and horror tropes. Some writers talk about the sophomore slump, but I'd had a junior slump.

Then again, that kind of thing only applied to writers who had ever achieved any real success. You couldn't slump if you'd never been upright to begin with.

So one book burned, one book frozen. What was in store for the other two? And was there some kind of symbolism in these acts I was missing?

I found it hard to think past the throbbing headache that made me feel like some kind of Greek god about to give birth through my cranium. I knew I should take something for the pain, but instead of the medicine cabinet, my mind and gaze turned to the beer under the coffee table. A bit of hair of the dog, yes, that might be just the thing. Everyone had their ideas for hangover cures—water, sports drinks, vitamin B, chamomile—but in my rather extensive experience I had found the most surefire cure for a hangover was to get drunk again right away.

The beer began to call to me. Not a shout, but a soft intimate whisper. Seductive and enticing. I felt myself weakening, melting before the sweet nothings being murmured by the drink. I leaned forward to put the book on the table and actually reached for the case beneath.

Then I stopped myself. I pulled my hand back as if I'd had an electrical shock. Making a decision, I snatched up the case, holding it away from my body as if it were a bomb, and carried it into the kitchen. It took me the better part of fifteen minutes to pour the contents of each can down the drain, and the smell itself was nearly intoxicating, actually helping to lessen my headache. However, I didn't stop until they were all empty.

After that, I commenced cleaning the living room, depositing all the trash into the bin outside. *The garbage men are likely to think me an alcoholic*, I thought then began to laugh. There was an edge of hysteria to the sound that disturbed me, but at least I was laughing.

I told myself not to judge my behavior too harshly. In my short time in AA, I had learned that a common part of recovery was the backslide. Some people had to fall off the wagon several times before they secured their seating up there. One step forward, two steps back, but that didn't mean I couldn't start forward once again.

And I needed to be sober if I was going to fight my father. Only a while ago I was contemplating whether I should dunk my head beneath the waters of the tub and die in the same spot as the man, but that was nothing but self-pity and fear talking. I was stronger than that. Or if I wasn't, I needed to become stronger than that. I had learned that I didn't have to be drunk for my father to influence me, but the drink lowered my inhibitions and senses enough to make it easier for him. Plus it was a distraction from doing what needed to be done in this house.

Not to mention, if my father was trying to destroy me, I shouldn't be helping him along.

Once the room was put back to rights, I looked down at the damp copy of *Wind in the Canyon*. The book always made me think of Don Hapner, a man who had worked for a few months in the Furman library a couple of years ago. I had harbored a crush on him for months before he surprised me by asking me on a date. I had been flattered and flabbergasted, thinking him far out of my league, but I had said yes without reservation. I figured it would be a good time, even if he lost interest after one date.

And we did have only one date, but he wasn't the one who lost interest. He asked me out again—several times—but I always found an excuse to put him off. He eventually left Furman to go work at the Spartanburg County Public Library. He asked me to keep in touch, and I said I would. But I didn't. I hadn't talked to him since. I knew he never really understood what had soured me on him, because I never told him.

But it was *Wind in the Canyon*. The book was the nail in the coffin of our relationship.

The professor stares through the windshield from his place in the passenger's seat, a puzzled smile gently curling his lips. "Is this some kind of joke?"

The librarian pulled into a parking spot and cut the engine. His own smile had a teasing edge to it. "What? You've never been here before?"

"Never on a date."

"That just goes to show that even at your age, there's a first time for everything."

With a wink, the librarian pops open his door and steps out of the car. Amused and bemused at the same time, the professor follows.

They walk across the parking lot, side by side. They do not hold hands, but several times their hands brush one another and the professor finds the contact electrifying. He doesn't date much these days, but he has to admit the librarian is magnetic. He keeps his expectations low, best way to keep from experiencing crushing disappointment, but almost against his will he feels a bubble of hope beginning to expand in his chest.

Bubbles have a tendency to burst, he reminds himself.

Once they reach the building, the librarian opens the door and holds it open like a proper gentleman.

The professor pauses, still waiting for the punchline. "So you're serious? This is where you're taking me for our first date?"

The librarian lets the door swing shut again and steps close to him. Close enough that the professor can feel the man's minty breath caress his face. "I could have done something conventional like taking you to a movie or out to dinner, but that doesn't seem very memorable. And I want our first date to be memorable. Admit it, you aren't likely to forget a first date shopping at Goodwill, are you?"

The professor laughs. He can't help but laugh. "You've got a point there."

"I know I do. Now come on and let the fun commence."

This time when the librarian holds open the door, the professor dips in a clumsy curtsy and says, "Thank you, kind sir," before entering.

This particular Goodwill is large, perhaps the largest the professor has ever been in. A secondhand Mecca for thrift-seekers and bargain-hunters. At least a dozen shoppers mill about the aisles, digging through bins of other people's refuse, looking for buried treasure.

Without a word, the librarian takes his hand. Even in the post- *Will and Grace* world, the era of *Ellen*, this draws a few disapproving glances. However, neither the librarian nor the professor care in this moment. They walk into the clothing section, perusing the clothes no one wants.

"Ah, just the thing for you," the librarian says, taking a hideous shirt from the rack and holding it up in front of the professor. The design of the shirt can only be described as "TV test-pattern," a frenzied juxtaposition of contrasting colors that pain the eye.

The professor lets out an exaggerated scoff. "So you think this is the look for me?"

"Why not? It would be sure to neutralize your enemies if they tried to look directly at you."

"Ah, I see. The latest in Medusa fashions."

The two share a laugh then move on further down the aisle. The librarian next plucks an orange T-shirt with a black jack-o'lantern design on the front. "I might seriously get this," he says.

"Halloween is right around the corner."

"Oh no, this shirt would only be cool if you wear it anytime other than around Halloween."

The professor nods, thinking he's beginning to understand. "More of your unconventionality, I take it."

The librarian shrugs, replacing the shirt on the hanger. "Conventional typically equals boring. Has being queer in the south taught you nothing?"

"I guess I've never really thought about it."

"It's sort of like high school. Remember how everybody wanted to sit at the 'cool table' at lunchtime? Well, experience has taught me that the cool table was usually the dullest table in the cafeteria. Things were a lot more colorful and fun if you sat with the book nerds or the artistic weirdos or the band geeks or the theater queers."

"Or the ones who wore jack-o'lantern shirts anytime other than around Halloween."

"Now you're getting it."

"It's an intriguing perspective," the professor concedes with a smile then moves on.

They find a collection of old vinyl records, two for a dollar, and begin to rummage through them. The professor doesn't own a record player; he honestly doesn't understand the new retro revival. Who wouldn't prefer the crisp sound of digital music over these crackling relics that inevitably got scratched and skipped? For some, it is all tied up in the nostalgia of their youth, but nostalgia isn't a pool in which the professor swims very often. He finds the waters are muddy and foul.

"Take a look at her," the librarian says with glee, holding up an album he finds in the middle of the stack.

The professor stares at the image on the cover for a moment then bursts into laughter. It is rather ridiculous.

Linda Ronstadt, a name the professor knows but not an artist he listened to much in his youth. An album called Living in the USA, with a cover that seems to have little to do with patriotism. Ronstadt stands in a pair of roller skates, wearing long athletic socks and kneepads. The photo shoot seems to have taken place in a narrow hallway with unflattering florescent lighting, and the singer clings to the walls on either side of her like she can barely stay up on the skates. Her face bears an expression that conveys the message, "Just take the damn photo already so I can get out of these skates before I bust my ass!"

The professor laughs and takes the album. "This is an interesting choice they went with for the cover."

The librarian leans close, ostensibly to study the album cover as well but the two men's shoulders press against one another. "I'd imagine they must have taken dozens of photos, and this was apparently the best one. Seriously, take a minute and really let that sink in."

They share another laugh, and it feels so good, so comfortable, that for a moment the professor feels a stab of panic. This sense of puzzle pieces fitting together with ease unnerves him, because a lifetime of experience tells him not to trust it. He pulls away from the moment, placing the album on top of the stack then wandering off toward home furnishings.

Nothing here is as humorous as the album, but the librarian continues to crack jokes about the sofa patterns and chintzy lamps. They move on from there to the ample selection of VHS tapes which the professor muses will get no less ample. VCRs haven't caught the attention of nostalgic hipsters the way record players have. Over in electronics, the librarian picks up an old rotary-dial phone and pretends to call Sarah, asking to be connected to Mount Pilot.

The professor can't stop laughing at these jokes. Despite himself, he knows he is falling for the librarian. Hard and fast. Against his better judgement.

Against the back wall of the Goodwill is a large bookcase that contains hundreds of discarded books in various states of disrepair. The librarian stands before the bookcase with his hands on his hips, like a landowner surveying his property. "Saved the best for last," he says then winks at the professor. "Here we are, a librarian and an English Lit professor. It's like we've found our way home."

The professor smiles, still thrilling over that wink. It's funny how profound small gestures can seem, how they affect a person.

The librarian claps his hands and rubs them together. "Okay, a little game. I'll start on one end, you start on the other. We'll meet in the middle and see which of us found the most ridiculously hideous book in the bunch. We will exclude cookbooks and overtly religious tomes, because those are too easy."

"Interesting, but how will we define 'ridiculously hideous'? What are the criteria?"

"It can be a horrible cover, or an absurd title. Or just a really shitty book, something like those teen sparkly vampires."

The professor isn't going to that he doesn't hate that series. He doesn't love it, but doesn't hate it. Instead, he says, "That all sounds very subjective. Who's going to be an objective judge of this?"

The librarian scratches his chin, as if he's taking all of this quite seriously. "We'll discuss and have to come to an agreement or else the game is null and void."

"And what does the winner get?"

"What does the winner want?" the librarian asks with another wink.

The professor feels the heat in his cheeks and knows he is blushing like a schoolboy hearing his first dirty joke.

The librarian claps his hands again. "Okay, so you go down to that end. I'll meet you in the middle."

Despite the silliness of the game, the professor does as instructed, walking to the left end of the bookcase as the librarian goes to the right. Perhaps he needs a little more silliness in his life. In fact, possibly that is the exact thing he has been missing. His life, while a good one, has definitely been stagnating the last few years. A life of repetition to the point that it sometimes feels like Groundhog Day with only the slightest of variation.

Perhaps, he muses as his eyes scan the titles on the top shelf, the secret to remaining youthful even as you get older is injecting a little silliness into your life. In which case, the librarian is providing him with some much-needed medicine. A panacea to stave off old-fogie-itis.

The professor spots a thin children's book titled How to Eat Fried Worms. He remembers this somewhat from his own childhood, but mostly because it more recent years parental groups have decried the book as a bad influence on young readers. The title and premise alone should ensure the professor the win, so he holds the book close to his chest. However, he continues to peruse the titles in case something even more ridiculous calls out to him.

He squats down to see what's on the bottom shelf, and a paperback catches his eye. The spine is cracked, making the title almost illegible, but the professor recognizes it all the same. He takes the book off the shelf, looking at the nondescript but familiar cover. The silhouette of a house on top of a hill, blue lightning forking above it.

Wind in the Canyon by Rick Henry. Years out of print, this is the first copy the professor has seen out in the wild in ages. And of course, it would be *here in Goodwill, with paperbacks two for a dollar. Fifty cents, which some critics would say is still too much.*

"Whoa, I see you're worthy competition."

The professor looks up to find the librarian standing over him. "What?"

The librarian points to the book he holds in his hands. "I see you're taking this game seriously. That's what I call scraping the bottom of the barrel."

"You know this book?" the professor asks with a frown.

The librarian hunkers down next to him. "Back in my youth, I was a real horror hound. I read everything from the front shelf stuff like King and Koontz to the worst vampire drivel with those cheap, tacky covers. I wasn't exactly discerning and I read a lot of substandard crap, but that book right there was by far the worst. Have you read it?"

The professor glances at the nondescript cover again. "It has been years," he says in a thin voice, barely above a whisper.

"And here I thought I had this competition in the bag," the librarian says and holds up two books. One entitled The Man Who Mistook His Wife for a Hat, the other Everything I Know About Women, I Learned from my Tractor. "I was sure one of these two would nab me the trophy for sure, but you're

digging deeper than mere bonkers titles and going for deep existential badness."

"I guess I don't remember it being all that terrible."

"It's not memorable at all," the librarian says. "And in horror fiction, that is the ultimate sin. Being forgettable. Bland prose, bland characters, bland plot. If I remember correctly, I think this author single-handedly brought down a publisher then disappeared completely, like a thief in the night. He's probably flipping burgers somewhere now."

Or teaching English Lit at a southern university, the professor thinks but doesn't say.

Instead, he puts the book back on the shelf and says, "Can't believe I won and I wasn't even trying."

"You're naturally gifted. So what do you want as your prize? Name it."

The professor smiles, knowing the effort is weak. "I'll have to think about it."

The librarian winks again, but this time the gesture doesn't bring the same thrill. In fact, the professor knows this first date will also be their last. Although the librarian isn't yet aware, the date is for all intents and purposes over. The professor will come up with a tactful way of cutting things short. He doesn't want to be rude, but the date has gone off the rails and there is no salvaging the wreck now.

It isn't the librarian's fault. Not exactly. He doesn't realize what he has done, but that ignorance only creates the perfect situation for the man to be brutally honest about his feelings.

Whoever coined the phrases "honestly is the best policy" and "the truth shall set you free" were liars.

Don Hapner. I hadn't thought of the man in ages, but now I found myself wondering how he was weathering the pandemic world. The libraries were closed, after all, so like the majority of us I assumed he was trapped in his own home, sanctuary become prison, constantly scouring the internet to feel a part of humanity.

Which made me wonder if he had seen the online backlash against me and this new book. If so, did he remember our one date and the book he had mercilessly blasted in front of me? And if he made the proper connections and realized what he had done, did he feel bad about it?

Or did he feel relieved, like he'd dodged the proverbial bullet?

Resisting the impulse to grab my phone and scroll through the latest vitriol being directed at me, I went into the office and sat at my desk. Writing was the last thing I wanted to do, but perhaps it could be therapeutic to get lost in another world. Besides, if Doubleday wasn't going to cancel the contract, that meant I still owed them the book. Despite everything going on around me.

How could a person be expected to write under circumstances such as these? I knew there were some who did it, somehow managing to be productive even under the immense pressure, but I had never been made of that sterner stuff. After all, the last time this sort of thing had happened, I ran away with my tail tucked between my legs.

I reminded myself this situation was different. This time my publisher was sticking by me, even if only to protect their investment. All those years ago, if

Greta had been successful and kept me on the New Blood roster, would I have been able to deliver? Or would the criticism have crippled me?

I didn't know the answer, but I supposed I was about to find out. This was my second chance, my do over. Even I was curious to see what I would do with it.

I pulled up the manuscript and put my fingers on the keys, hoping that some ethereal muse would invade my hands and take over. Writing at its best felt sort of that way. The trick was courting the muse, getting them to accept your invitation. Muses could be remarkably fickle and unreliable. They might show up two days in a row then go on sabbatical for a month before making a surprise return for only a day. Muses were notorious teases, sort of like ghosts themselves.

Ghosts were on my mind a lot these days, for obvious reasons. I was writing about ghosts, and I was living with one. I was surrounded by ghosts.

Ghosts of fathers.

I froze at the desk, my hands still poised over the home keys as I had learned taking Typing with Miss Hughes my freshman year of high school. Funny how long it sometimes takes the brain to make certain connections, but once they are made you aren't sure how you ever missed them to begin with.

The similarities between my life and my fiction were undeniable. The spirit of an angry father haunting the son he disapproves of, trying to prevent that son from finding happiness. The specific circumstances weren't exactly the same, but close enough for government work. Was it a case of art imitating life or life imitating art? The lines had become so blurred that fantasy and reality seemed to overlap and intertwine until I couldn't extricate one from the other.

Why not use it? a tiny voice spoke up in the back of my mind. The voice of the muse? It was too soft to say for sure.

Yet the advice was solid. All writers tended to borrow from life to bolster their fiction, and I found myself in a unique position here. If I introduced some of my experience into the narrative, it could lend the whole thing an extra layer of authenticity.

I began a scene where Junior wakes up to find all the books in his house shredded, ripped pages littering the floor like dead birds. I toyed with the idea of the word "Fag" being scrawled on the walls, to mirror my own father's use of the word "Fraud." In the end, I thought that might be a bit too ugly for a YA novel and went with "Queer" instead.

The scene, though it took place in the blinding light of the morning sun, was dark and disturbing, but that was exactly the tone I wanted to strike. Once done, I saved my work, emailed it to Edwin, and logged onto an online AA meeting.

One day at a time, and each day was a new chance to start fresh after all.

I answered the emails from Greta and Michael, thanking them for their support. I also received an email from Edwin in response to what I had sent him. "Painful but powerful," was all he said.

I felt a sort of shaky confidence. Instead of breaking me, my tumble off the wagon had only given me a renewed determination to fight. Fight my own addiction, fight my father's interference, fight to prove all the doubters on the internet wrong. Could I do it? I didn't know, but I meant to try.

I took Edwin's advice and avoided going on social media, seeing all the hate being spewed my way by people who didn't even know me. I realized that my own father fit into that category. He'd never bothered to get to know me, so in a way I was as much a stranger to him as to any anonymous troll on Twitter.

That evening after a light supper, I retired to the office and spent over an hour writing again. I had this idea that the only real way to rid myself of my father's lingering presence was to finish the book. If it was done and to the publisher, good or bad, perhaps that would break my father's will and he would move on. I could use my real life haunting not only as inspiration but also motivation.

I toyed with the idea of making Junior's boyfriend HIV positive, but in the end I didn't know if that would be appropriate in a YA novel. I did include a scene where the spirit of Senior pours the man's "medicine" down the kitchen drain, but I remained vague about what kind of medicine. I worried I was making Senior too irredeemable. After all, unlike my own father, I needed to leave room for redemption at the end.

This led me to doubt everything I was doing, the entire direction of the story. Perhaps this whole thing was a mistake, and I really was ruining my father's legacy. Maybe he had a right to be angry.

Before I could drown in a sea of self-recrimination, I saved and emailed my progress and decided to call it an early night. However, before I turned in, I made sure the lights were on in the living room and kitchen, and even left a lamp on in the bedroom. If my father made an appearance tonight, I wanted to make sure the cameras caught it.

Friday, April 17, 2020

I awoke to the sound of someone beating on the door. The right side of my face stung, feeling inflamed and sore. However, the pain took an immediate backseat when I realized I wasn't lying in bed but standing in the middle of the living room. I didn't have much time to break through the confusion because my muddled thoughts were interrupted by another volley of pounding.

And a voice from outside yelling, "Are you okay in there?"

I didn't know the time, but it was still dark outside. I stumbled to the door and looked through one of the sidelights. The streetlights outside provided just enough illumination for me to make out Bubba from across the street, standing on the porch and banging on the frame of the storm door.

Baffled, I opened the front door and flipped on the porch light. The glass of the storm door separated us, but it felt like a flimsy barrier.

"Can I help you?" I said, realizing that the question sounded absurd. I wasn't awake enough to ferret out exactly what was happening, so everything about this situation was absurd.

Adding to that absurdity was the fact that Bubba stood on the other side of the door wearing nothing but a pair of boxer shorts. His barrel chest was furry, matted in black hair, his legs thick and muscled. I found myself aroused at the site of him.

"What's going on?" he said, his voice sharp and edged with a bit of anger. "Are you okay?"

"Um, yeah, I'm fine. Why wouldn't I be?"

He gave me that wary look again, like he thought I might be dangerous. "What was all the ruckus going on over here?"

I frowned, reaching up to massage my aching cheek. "Ruckus? I'm not sure I know what you're talking about?"

"There was a whole bunch of hollering and shouting coming from over here. Woke me up from a dead sleep. Sounded like World War III."

My frown deepened, as did my confusion, but I said, "I was having a nightmare."

Bubba looked skeptical. "Nightmare? I've had nightmares, but I've never screamed the way you were screaming."

"I used to have night terrors as a kid. I think with all the stress I've been under lately, they've resurfaced. I'm sorry I woke you."

He still didn't look convinced, but I thought I detected a bit of concern in his face. "You sure that's all?"

I realized he wondered if someone might be in here with me, just out of sight and holding a gun on me. A scene out of some melodramatic psychological thriller.

"I'm fine, really. Just embarrassed. I'm so sorry that I disturbed you."

He fidgeted on the porch, first crossing his arms across his chest then lowering them to cup his hands in front of his crotch. I suspected now that the adrenaline of the moment had passed, he felt self-conscious about being at my door in only his underwear. "Don't worry about that. I'm just glad everything's okay. I know you were worried about finding your door open the other day."

"I know, I must seem like a total nut."

"No, it's cool. But if you need help with anything, give me a holler."

He turned and stepped off the porch and headed back across the street. I remembered how he had told me he had a pistol and knew how to use it, and I wondered why he hadn't brought it with him when my screaming woke him up. Unless he had concealed it in his shorts somehow. Under other circumstances, such a thought would have amused me. *Is that a pistol in your boxers are you just happy to see me?*

Alas, these were not other circumstances.

I closed the door, locked it, then put a hand to my stinging cheek. I went over to the mirror that hung on the wall opposite the bookcase and looked at my reflection. The right side of my face was a deep red, the cheek puffy. I felt disoriented, unmoored, unsure what had happened.

But, of course, I could find out.

I went to get my phone. It wasn't on the nightstand where I knew I had left it, but after a short search I located it next to the sink in the bathroom. A minor mystery in light of everything else. Seeing that the time was almost four a.m., I sat on the edge of the tub and pulled up the DVR footage, running it back about half an hour. I started with the camera in the bedroom. I had a decent shot of me lying in bed. I did not toss or turn, did not seem to be in any sort of stress. No signs of a nightmare.

However, fifteen minutes in, I suddenly bolted to an upright sitting position in the bed. My head was out of the shot so I couldn't see my eyes, but I assumed I was awake since in the next moment I threw back the covers, grabbed my phone, and shuffled into the bathroom. I had not placed a camera there so I couldn't track my actions. It was almost ten minutes before I reemerged, moving with an almost robotic gait, going into the living room.

I switched cameras and watched myself walk to the center of the room and freeze. I looked like a statue and began to wonder if the footage had paused until I noticed a slight sway in my stance. So a statue on the verge of toppling.

I felt as if I were watching a scene out of one of those *Paranormal Activity* films, and a full body chill worked its way through me as I viewed myself as if viewing a stranger. I had no memory of this at all. Sleepwalking?

I nearly dropped the phone when the image on the screen abruptly raised its hand and slapped itself in the side of the face. When *I* suddenly raised my hand and slapped *myself* in the side of the face. Then I did it again. And again. And again.

Then I began screaming.

The volume on my phone was turned low, but even if there had been no sound, the bulging veins in my neck would have suggested my screams were loud and booming. Loud enough to wake the neighbors and send one rushing across the street to see if I was being accosted.

Which I was, but by myself.

"YOU CAN'T DO IT!" I screamed on the footage. "YOU RUIN EVERY-THING YOU TOUCH! WHY DON'T YOU GIVE IT UP BEFORE YOU CAUSE ANYMORE DAMAGE!"

On the small screen, I watched in mute horror as I continued to abuse myself. The slapping continued, and yet I didn't seem to react in the moment. I didn't flinch or turn my head, just stood resolute. Between each slap was more screaming.

"YOU'RE WORTHLESS, YOU'RE TALENTLESS, YOU'RE A PA-THETIC HACK! YOU'VE ALREADY PROVEN THIS IN THE PAST, WHY ARE YOU HUMILIATING YOURSELF ALL OVER AGAIN? YOU'RE NOTHING, YOU'VE ALWAYS BEEN NOTHING, YOU'LL ALWAYS BEEN NOTHING!"

There came a pounding on the door, not now but *then*, on the footage. The screaming stopped, my sway even more noticeable, and then I looked around as if I didn't know where I was.

I turned off the footage and stared across at my reflection in the mirror above the sink. The redness in my cheek was fading but not the swelling. Self-inflicted injury. Or was it?

It was my father, continuing his campaign to get me to quit the book. He had never believed in me, his entire life he made that clear in word and action, and he had carried that into death. The man was nothing in if not relentless. One of his defining characteristics. That and cruelty.

I opened my email and sent a message to Ryan Dunn. Sometimes it paid to have a ghost hunter on standby. I knew he felt possession was only possible with demonic forces, but I asked him how a person possessed could get free of the invading spirit. Demon or ghost, the cure had to be similar. I even gave him my phone number and asked him to call. How odd, a month ago I would have laughed if told how soon I transition from a slight Scully to a full-on Mulder. Only difference being that I didn't *want* to believe, but I had no choice but to believe.

I didn't know what to do now. Going back to sleep was definitely not in the cards. Hell, I didn't know how I'd ever manage to sleep again. I walked through the house, turning on every light as if that would somehow protect me. I made some coffee and took it outside to the backyard. At the fire pit, I had a seat and stared up at the stars. The night sky had always had a way of making me feel small, which was a often a good thing. If I was small then my problems were small. The vastness of space put things into perspective.

Usually, but not tonight. My problems felt anything but small. Insurmountable might have been the most appropriate word. I couldn't see a way through or even around this.

The answer is simple, said a voice in my head that sounded so much like my father that I actually turned to see if his spirit knelt next to me. *Give up the book. Sure, Edwin says Doubleday will stand by you, but I'm sure they wouldn't fight too hard if you said you wanted to break the contract. They would probably find it a bit of a relief.*

The voice was annoying because I suspected it spoke truth. The most convincing argument the devil could make would be laced with honesty.

I didn't realize I had started crying until I tasted the saltiness on my lips. I leaned forward, my head touching my knees, and gave in to all the confusion and sadness and fear that enveloped me. I sobbed into my hands with only the stars to witness.

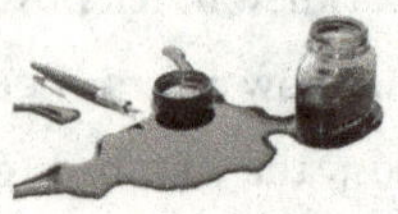

I scrambled some eggs for breakfast and once the sun was up set up shop again out by the fire pit. I brought my laptop and decided to do some work in the fresh air. Honestly I didn't want to be in the house. I felt safer outside, even though I didn't know if that made me safer. I had no evidence my father's influence was confined to the house. After all, the yard was still part of the property. Besides, I didn't even know for sure that it was the house itself that was haunted.

What if it was me? What if I was haunted? Then it didn't matter where I went, I would only drag my father's spirit along with me.

I tried to work on the book, but I found it hard to concentrate. I went back and reread some of what I already had, and I found it all disappointing. The idea was solid, the concept exciting, but my execution was lacking. My prose felt flat, two-dimensional, without the depth of emotion I had hoped to achieve. Without that heart, the whole thing would be empty.

I couldn't do it. That was what I came to realize as I sat out in the warmth of spring, scrolling through the manuscript. My father may be vicious and cruel, but that didn't mean he couldn't also be right. I simply didn't have the talent to pull this off.

I thought of the people in my life who did believe in me. Greta and Michael and Edwin, even the kind things Ryan had said about *The Freaks Come Out at Night*. Were they delusional or did they merely have bad taste? It had to be one or the other, because every word I wrote was trash. That was becoming abundantly clear to me now.

I closed the laptop, feeling near tears again, but wondered if these thoughts were really my own. What if it was my father, getting into my head and planting these doubts into my brain? If he could control my body then surely he could control my thoughts as well. I couldn't trust myself, which made this whole ordeal even more frightening.

When my phone buzzed, I hurriedly dug it out of my pocket, hoping it would be Ryan. He still hadn't responded, but I reminded myself it was still early. However, the Caller ID showed it was Edwin.

"Hey Eddie baby," I said, trying to sound normal but only sounding like an unhinged nut. "What's up? You read what I sent you yesterday?"

"Yes, but that's not all I read. Unfortunately."

His voice was gruff and angry, catching me off guard. We had become so friendly of late, I didn't know what this change of attitude might signify.

"What's wrong?"

"I told you to leave it," he said. "I told you to stay off social media and absolutely not to comment on anything. Were those instructions too complicated for you to follow?"

"I don't know what you're talking about."

"I'm talking about all those belligerent social media posts you made. All it has done is make matter worse. Oil to the fire."

"Social media posts? I didn't—"

My voice cut off, like tape being sliced by scissors, because I realized that while I may not have made any posts, my father may have. I thought of the footage, taking the phone into the bathroom. What was I doing in there before coming out to the living room?

"Were you under the influence last night?" Edwin asked.

I thought about that question. I wasn't under the influence of drugs or alcohol, which was what the editor meant, but I was under the influence of *something*. Yet I doubted I could explain that.

Edwin took my silence as admission. When he spoke again, his voice had softened but still had brittle edges. "I know this is hard for you. I mean, I can't really imagine what it's like to have strangers belittling and ridiculing you on the internet so I guess I don't know how hard it is for you. However, if we're going to get through this, we need to keep our heads, think before we act. I'm trying to help you, honestly. Your posts have caused a lot of damage, and some of the Bigwigs at Doubleday are quite upset with you right now. I'm trying to calm them, but I need you to keep quiet from here on out. Not even an apology. Might not even be a bad idea to disable your social media accounts for the time being. Remove the temptation."

He was scolding me like a child, and I wanted to protest but I realized that would only make me sound like a child. *I didn't do it, my dog ate my homework!* So I took his advice and I kept quiet.

"I won't say I'm not upset and disappointed," Edwin continued. "But I'm also not without sympathy. If you need anything, just reach out. It doesn't have to be about the book. If you just need to talk to someone, I'm here."

"Thank you, I appreciate that," I said.

"Good. Now I suggest today you decompress, don't even worry about working on the book. Take a little time for R&R."

Things must have been bad indeed if he was suggesting I take a day off from working on the book. I could have told him I was thinking of taking *all* the time off from working on the book, but again remained silent.

As soon as we disconnected the call, I started searching my social media apps to see what mischief my father had gotten up to. I found all the real damage on Twitter, which seemed about right. All the trash fires raged out of control on Twitter. That was why the reality star President loved it so much.

I had made a string of Tweets, one after the other. All aggressive, all in caps. The first read, "FUCK ALL YALL HATERS! JEALUSY IS UGLY & SO R U!" The last was a photo of the toilet and the caption, "THIS IS WHERE I PUT UR OPINNIONS OF ME IN THE SHITTER WHERE THEY BELONG!"

I discovered I had also commented on several posts using the #Justice4Justice hashtag. Mostly obscenity-laced insults, misspelled and inarticulate.

No, none of that was helpful to the situation, which of course I was sure my father knew. That was why he'd done it. All part of his campaign to destroy me.

The sun suddenly seemed too bright, blinding me with its unrelenting glare, the light stabbing at my eyes like toothpicks. Before I gathered the laptop and went inside, however, I took a moment to take Edwin's advice.

I deactivated all my social media accounts.

I decided to mow the lawn. Not because I thought it needed it, but because I needed something to occupy my mind. I had the vague notion that if I kept busy, I could keep my father at bay. I wondered if it was easier for him to take control of my body when I was at rest, making an easy target for him. Nothing I had ever read about ghosts or possessions led me to believe this. It was a theory of my own devising, perhaps a bit of magical thinking.

Once I was done, having worked up quite a sweat, I took a shower then began pacing the house, the phone gripped in my hand. By ten o'clock, I had grown quite impatient for a call from Ryan. Of course, I knew nothing about the man's life, his schedule, but I needed to talk to him, get his advice.

I realized I had the world of the internet at my fingertips, full of information. I also realized that not all of that information could be trusted. Anyone could put anything online, no matter how ridiculous or uninformed, and there would be some idiot who took it as fact. Weeding out truth from fallacy could be quite difficult. Better to get information straight from an expert.

If there could be *experts* on a subject as steeped in speculation as the paranormal.

Still, I did a little research. Looked for the less sensational articles, things rooted in real Wicca as opposed to Hollywood's broad interpretation of witchcraft. I found one article that suggested making a circle of salt around a house could keep evil spirits from entering. Only problem was that my spirit was already inside. That would be like locking myself in a room with an ax-wielding psychopath.

I went into the bedroom and began going through the closet, rearranging the clothes, straightening the shoes that lined the floor, mentally bookmarking certain items I never wore much for Goodwill. All in an attempt to keep on the go. Edwin had suggested I rest and relax, but that simply wasn't possible. I felt exhausted, mentally and physically drained, while at the same time buzzing with an unfocused energy like one of those ground spinner fireworks. I felt jacked up on caffeine as if I'd had five pots of coffee, and I wondered if this was how someone felt after a bump of cocaine.

In my youth I had smoked my share of weed, tried acid once, went through a brief period where I did poppers like candy, but I had never done any of the serious drugs. Heroine, meth, cocaine, I'd never been fool enough to get mixed up with any of that. And these days Biktarvy was the only drug I took, but I did take it every day. I had to become a drug addict to survive.

At a little past eleven, my phone rang. I didn't recognize the number but it was a 912 area code. Savannah. Had to be Ryan.

"Hello!" I said, perhaps too eagerly.

"Hey, is this Rick?"

"Speaking."

"This is Ryan Dunn. I got your message."

I wanted to say, *You certainly took your damn time getting back to me*, but instead I took a few breaths and said, "I appreciate you taking the time to get back to me."

"Not a problem, man. I think it's awesome you want to get this right. I read so many books that deal with spirits or demons and laugh at how ridiculous it all is. You know, I once read a novel where the main characters banished a demon by standing in a circle singing 'Kumbaya.' I mean, can you believe that?"

"So I should scratch that method off my list," I said, surprised by how natural I sounded. Maybe if the writing thing didn't work out, I could go into acting.

Ryan laughed. "Definitely. Although if you do it enough, the demons might flee on their own."

"I'll keep that in mind. Seriously though, what would you recommend to someone?"

"Well, if you want the most effective method, I would always go with an exorcism. Possessions are tricky because once a demonic presence has its claws in a person's soul, it doesn't want to let go. You really need the full power of the Church behind you to extract the demon."

"So we're talking the full Linda Blair treatment?"

"Not necessarily. The Catholic Church is what most people think of, for good reason, but almost every world religion believes in demonic entities. Some of these religious date back way before Christianity even existed as a belief system. If the person being effected is a Hindu, for instance, the Catholic rites of exorcism as outlined in the Ritual Romanum might not have much impact. They would need religious leaders in Hinduism to banish the presence."

"What if the person isn't a member of any particular religion?" I asked. Even though the events of late had turned me into more of a Mulder than a Scully, I still didn't know if I bought into all the fairytales surrounding organized religion.

"There are secular demonologists who don't believe in the whole fallen angels origin of demons, and they have their own rites to expel such creatures."

I thought this was all interesting and good to know, but so far everything he mentioned involved close contact with other people.

"I can't have anyone coming over to the house," I said. "Not with the lock-down."

"Oh man, you're setting this during the pandemic!"

I realized that for just a moment I had forgotten I was steeping this conversation in the guise of being about my book, not about my life. "Um yeah, I thought this would be great for the narrative. Sort of trapped inside with the ghost or demon."

"That's perfect. I have been wondering how storytellers were going to deal with the whole COVID nightmare."

"Yes, but that complicates the exorcism thing because he can't have other people right now."

"Interesting. Is he quarantined with anyone else, family member or spouse? Someone who could download the Ritual Romanum and try to perform the rites themselves?"

"No, it's just him. Could he do it himself?"

"If he's the person being possessed then I think not."

"So what? There's nothing he can do? He's screwed?"

The silence from the other end made me realize how strident and angry my voice had become. Maybe acting wasn't in the cards for me after all.

"I'm sorry," I said. "I get caught up in my stories. Especially now with being cooped up with no other outlet, I am probably a little too invested in the fiction."

"I understand. We're all going a little stir-crazy."

It seemed I had sold it, so maybe acting was back on the table. "Is there anything my character could do?"

"He could try a baptism, submerging himself in cleansing waters."

"How would he accomplish that?"

"He would have to start by creating his own holy water. You could look up online a variety of ways to accomplish this. Fill the tub, maybe surround it with images of Saint Benedict who is called upon a lot in exorcisms. The character could then submerge himself in the water to cleanse himself of the spirit. Of course, again if the character isn't religious, this doesn't have to be from a Christian approach. My wife is actually pagan, and I know there could be a baptism with certain herbs and crystals, maybe some iron which is used for protection and purification."

This sounded intriguing and doable. "What kind of herbs and crystals?"

"Let's see, white sage and Verbena are the best herbs. Also burning Palo Santo is good for cleansing. As for crystals, I'd go with quartz, onyx, or obsidian."

"Hold on a sec," I said, rummaging through the long drawer of the entry table until I found an old pad and a pen. I jotted down the names of the herbs and crystals. "This is all good information."

"Of course in real life, before any of this, a person would want to go through psychiatric testing to rule out any mental health causes for his or her behavior."

"Yeah, sure, of course," I said, eager to be off the phone now that I had the answers I was after. "I really appreciate all your help."

"My pleasure. I look forward to reading this when it's done."

"Reading what?"

A pause. "The book."

"Yes, that's right. Absolutely. I'll send you a copy. Thanks again."

I disconnected the call without saying goodbye and opened my laptop to do a little exorcism shopping. The herbs I needed weren't of the everyday variety, like oregano or thyme, nothing I could get delivered today from my local market. It would take time for me to get the crystals anyway, and I ordered a couple of Saint Benedict medals. Yes, that was mixing religious and secular methods, but I figured I could use all the help I could get. Maybe a combination would prove more potent. I ordered everything complete with expedited shipping, but it would still be two days before I had all the materials I needed. A long time to wait, but that wasn't my biggest problem.

My biggest problem came when I researched how to create holy water. Some recitations and salt, seemed simple. The salt had to be natural, like kosher or rock, not iodized table salt with added ingredients like I currently had in the kitchen. I could get that from the grocery store, but the real issue was the water itself. According to what I read, ideally it should be water from a natural source, but if it came from the tap the sources recommended running it through a purifier. I certainly didn't have any natural water sources nearby, and I thought of how many times I'd have to fill a filtered pitcher to get enough purified water to submerge myself in.

I went to the grocery store site and ordered kosher salt, four Britta pitchers, and after a brief hesitation more beer. I felt a bit guilty, but the decision was easier than I might have anticipated. I supposed falling into old habits always felt easier than anticipated. That was the thing about slippery slopes, it didn't take much effort to start the slide and then it felt like a rollercoaster.

Besides, with all the stress I had on me right now, perhaps it was not the best time to try sobriety. I could get sober next month, once I got through all this, once my house was back to normal. Once the world was back to normal. It would be easier then.

Some part of me recognized all these thoughts as rationalizations and excuses, but recognizing them as such didn't make them any less compelling to me. I confirmed the order and marveled at my lack of guilt.

Could that be my father's influence? If so then I didn't really have free will in the matter and therefore couldn't be held entirely responsible. A supernatural get out of jail free card.

That evening, as the sun began to slip toward the horizon, I sat out at the fire pit, sipping beer and staring at the blazing orange and red hues igniting the clouds above. The temperatures were mild but I had started a fire nonetheless. The flames flickered and jumped like dancing imps. My gaze went from the light show in the sky to the one in the pit then back again.

I had been drinking since around lunchtime when my delivery arrived. In fact, I skipped lunch and was in the process of skipping dinner. The beer was all I needed. I hadn't guzzled it all down like a maniac. Even in my tumble from the wagon, I showed a little restraint and self-control. I consumed the alcohol at a leisurely pace, savoring it. I had a pleasant buzz that made me feel almost disconnected from my body. Not a complete out-of-body experience, but more like my spirit was tethered to my body by a short string, bobbing like a balloon just above my head.

This imagery made me laugh, so loud that Bubba could probably hear me across the street. I didn't care. He already thought I was a lunatic. Why not add more fuel to the fire?

Fuel to the fire. The phrase struck me as funny as well, since I was sitting next to a fire, and I laughed even louder until the sound lost all meaning. Just noise that didn't seem connected to me in any way.

My phone buzzed and I read the new text.

MICHAEL

How you holding up?

Without giving it any thought, I sent a lewd response.

ME

I'd be holding up better if you were holding me down.

I stared at the screen, awaiting a response. Not so drunk that I didn't realize how inappropriate this was, but drunk enough that I didn't really care.

The ellipse appeared, indicating he was typing a response. Then it went away, reappeared, went away again. Obviously he was having trouble formulating a response. Finally one came through.

This caused me to lean forward so far that the heat of the fire baked my face, causing the skin to feel like a hard shell. I laughed so hard I had trouble breathing. Michael had my number, figuratively as well as literally.

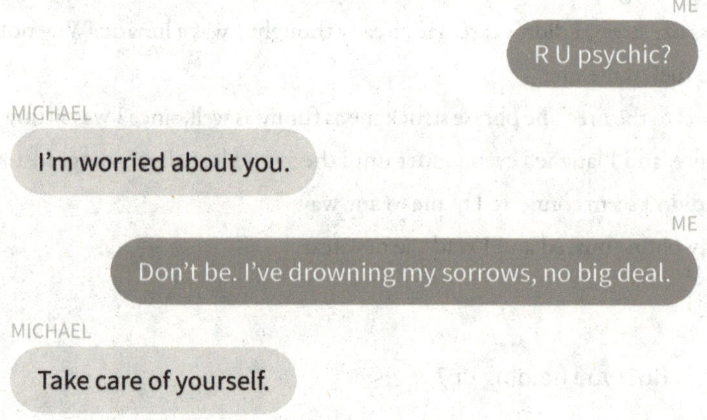

I typed, "Wish you were taking care of me," but stopped myself before hitting send. I deleted that response and instead wrote:

A friend. Michael hadn't really responded to my lecherous come-on at all, which made me wonder if my theory about him having a crush on me had been wrong. Had I mistaken innocent friendliness for some kind of schoolboy lust? Had I only wanted to think he had the hots for me so that I could consider myself the type of man someone like Michael could have the hots for? An ego stroke that existed only in my imagination.

I felt beyond embarrassed, a pathetic old man looking for validation in a fantasy. And now I had embarrassed myself further by my miscalculation. Michael was being magnanimous about it, but I could only imagine what he was thinking about me right now. Had I destroyed the friendship with a single ill-conceived text?

I sent him another message, hoping I could do some course correction.

ME

I really am sorry. You were right, I am drunk and not in a very good place emotionally. I hope I didn't offend you.

I waited a full two and a half minutes for a response, and when it came it was in the form of a thumbs-up emoji.

"Fuck!" I hissed, shoving the phone back in my pocket. I remembered something I had thought about myself soon after the implosion of my writing career with New Blood. After my diagnosis, after my botched suicide attempt. I had thought I had the opposite of the Midas touch. Everything I touched turned to shit.

Apparently I had not lost my touch.

I still had half a can of beer in my hand. I turned it up and downed the rest in two deep swallows then grabbed for another. The stars were starting to come out in the sky, twinkling as if they were winking at me but I was probably imagining it just as I had imagined Michael's supposed flirting.

As I continued to drown myself in alcohol, the stars became blurry dots that blended together and at times seemed to zig-zag through the darkening sky. My legs became sore and I looked down to find myself not sitting in the Adirondack anymore but standing by the fire pit as the flames roared up toward my chin. When had I stood up, and how long had I been standing here?

I looked down into the flames, squinting to focus my vision, and realized something was burning in the fire other than the logs I had put on earlier. Clearly a book, already charring with some of the pages fluttering up like butterfly wings. Enough remained that I recognized it as *With Friends Like These*. I was standing out in the backyard burning one of my own books.

I tightened my grip on the beer can only to realize it was too small to be a beer can. Only then did I realize I held my bottle of Biktarvy, the cap removed, out over the fire, the bottle on a tilt as if I were about to pour the contents into the flames.

With a gasp, I jerked back the pill bottle, clutching it to my chest. This was becoming a regular occurrence, and I thought my father must put a lot of faith in the saying "if at first you don't succeed, try, try again." Somewhere down the block I could hear the boom and pulse of music as well as laughter. Sounded like someone was having a party. At any other time this wouldn't have surprised me. This was Friday night after all. In the pandemic world, though, a party felt not only irresponsible but dangerous.

Yet as I continued to listen, I only heard the one laugh. Perhaps it was a lone lonely soul, cranking up the music and making merry to distract from the isolation. That scenario struck me as incredibly sad but also incredibly possible. The whole planet was on the brink of going insane, and whatever we had to do to make the new normal feel like the old normal was good medicine.

Thinking of medicine reminded me of the pills I held in my hand, seconds away from being tossed into the fire. On shaky legs, I stumbled onto the patio and into the house. All the lights were on even though I didn't remember leaving them that way. I could check the cameras, but I had no doubt all they'd show would be me walking back into the house, turning on all the lights, then grabbing the book and pills and heading outside again.

That was the insidious nature of my father's haunting. If I tried to show anyone the evidence I had, they would see nothing but me. Me doing it all. They would think I was either trying to perpetrate some hoax or simply crazy.

I put the pills on the counter and dug in my pocket for my phone, only it wasn't there. I knew I had put it back in my pocket after making a fool of myself with Michael, but now it was gone. Of course, I had missing time again. I searched the house and found the phone on my desk. The manuscript was open but I didn't pay it much attention. I snatched up the phone because I needed help.

My plan was to call Ryan, come clean with what was happening to me, and beg him for any assistance he could provide. However, when I looked at the phone I was distracted by three missed calls from Edwin, and he had left a voicemail.

I entered my code and listened to his message. The tone of his voice immediately put me on edge. It wasn't angry, but there was a tenseness that made his words feel strained, squeezed through clenched teeth. What I heard was a concern that bordered on fear. I listened to the message twice.

"Rick, I want you to call me back asap. This new chapter you sent me is clearly a cry for help. I'm worried. Please call me and let me know you are okay. I know you've been under so much pressure, and maybe I haven't been as sensitive to that as I could have been. I've been thinking mostly of the book and not how all this is affecting you emotionally. I apologize, but I'm here now. We'll forget the book, forget I'm your editor, and talk like friends. Please call me."

New chapter? What new chapter was he talking about? When I glanced back at the computer screen, I saw text I didn't recognize and sank into the chair. I began to read the unfamiliar chapter, and with each sentence my blood ran a little colder. Unlike the recent format of the manuscript, which was double spaced in Times New Roman, the new chapter was single spaced in Arial. The spelling in the first few paragraphs was also atrocious, containing so many red squiggly lines under the words that it looked like a bloody ocean.

Junior woke up with a revalation. A truth so simple he was embarased it had taken him this long to relize it. He lay in bed starring at the celing for a while, listning to his boyfiend snoring next to him. It was late or early, still dark outsside, the world utterly quite. The kind of silence that alows deep thinking.

The kind of deep thinking that leds to revalation.

He got out of bed and wen tto the bathrom, closing the door behind him. After pluging the tub and turning on the water, he gazed at himsself in the mirror. He didn't look any diferent but he felt differrent, because he finnaly understud something fundimental about himself.

He was a fraud.

His father had been the talented one in the family, the one who had cracked all the cases and helped all the spirits move on. Sure, Junior could see spirits but he had never been able to effectively communicate with them. In his long and storied career as a paranormal investigator, Junior had never once helped a spirit find closure, comforted a ghost, ushered a lost soul to the light.

That had all been Senior.

His father had possessed all the power, all the skill, all the ability. Junior had only been along for the ride, basking in his father's glory, riding his father's coattails. He had never once had to stand on his own.

Until now.

And Junior knew he didn't have what it took to continue his father's legacy. And Senior was the nonliving proof of that. Junior could see his father's spirit, but he couldn't really get through to him, have a meaningful dialogue with him, and that was because Junior had not inherited any of his father's talent and it was time he admitted to that.

Junior was a failure, a loser, a disappointment on all fronts. His father knew it, which was why he lingered even after death. He didn't want his son ruining the reputation Senior had spent his life building.

And if Senior knew Junior was a fraud, and Junior himself knew it, that meant it was only a matter of time before Junior's boyfriend realized it too. Junior had the opposite of the Midas touch; everything he touched turned to shit. This relationship was surely going to prove to be another case of that.

Glancing in the mirror again, he saw the ghostly, slightly translucent form of his father standing behind him. His lips twisted into a frown, his eyes full of judgement.

"I'm the one who should have died," Junior said, the sound of his own voice making him jump.

He hadn't known he was going to say those words, but they came from a well of truth deep at the center of his being.

His father had always been the strong one, the capable one, the one everyone wanted when things got rough. Junior was a pale substitute. Not even a substitute, not really. Substitutes could usually at least fake it, but Junior doubted he could even do that.

The wrong member of the team had died.

"I wish I could trade places with you," Junior said into the mirror, meeting his father's spectral gaze.

Senior turned his head slightly in the reflection, his own gaze moving toward the tub.

The tub that was brimming with water.

Without bothering to get undressed, Junior climbed into the tub, sinking down into the warm water. More than warm, almost scalding. He had thought he had turned on both the hot and cold but apparently not.

Still, the heat felt good, burning some sense into him. Making his path clear. There was only one way to end the trail of disappointment he left in his wake like shrapnel for other people to fall into.

Tears streamed down his cheeks as he let his head slip under the water. He stayed submerged until his lungs began to burn, then he opened his mouth and took a deep breath.

I sat, staring at the screen, my entire body shivering as if I'd been dunked in a tank of ice water. There was definitely a message here, a thinly veiled metaphor. No wonder Edwin had been worried.

I also couldn't help but notice that the first few paragraphs were a mess of typos and misspellings, almost like a very drunk man had attempted to write something coherent. Yet the moment in the story that Junior acknowledged himself as a fraud, the text cleaned up, almost as if someone else took over. A someone who was a better writer and had a point to get across.

And I got the point loud and clear. So did Edwin.

It was past eleven, too late to call Edwin back. Besides, I didn't want to actually talk to him lest my voice betray my fear. I wasn't a good enough actor for that. Instead, I sent him a brief text I hoped would allay his own fears. My hands shook so much that I kept fat-thumbing and having to delete and restart but I got it done after a few minutes of deep breathing through my ineptitude.

I hit SEND then looked back to the laptop. I reached toward the keyboard with the intention of deleting the chapter, but instead I hit enter and typed THE END beneath the text.

SATURDAY, APRIL 18, 2020

I DIDN'T EVEN TRY to sleep. I went back outside to retrieve what beer was left and camped out on the bed. At first I tried to find a movie to fall into, but I ended up on YouTube watching videos of people rhapsodizing about my father's work. How much it meant to them, how much it shaped them during their formative years, etc. I even found a few recent videos talking about the new book I was finishing.

These videos were easily divided into two camps. The ones before the recent controversy, in which people expressed guarded excitement, and the ones that came after, where I was talked about as if I were the literary antichrist. I mostly watched the latter. Glutton for punishment, yet another Rick Justice trademark.

I found one channel where the girl had a whole string of videos in which she read from my father's work then my own work. She wasn't as vicious as some of the others. She didn't call me a hack or anything of the sort, but instead focused on pointing out stylistic differences that she thought made me the wrong choice for the job. She didn't think my style meshed at all with my father's and therefore the project was sure to be a disappointment to fans of Bentley Justice.

It was odd, I found her videos rather comforting. Yes, she was still saying I shouldn't be allowed to write the book, I would likely ruin my father's legacy, but at least she did it without the over-the-top histrionics. She at least acknowl-edged that I had a style, even if it wasn't one she particularly liked. That was something, even if just a straw to grasp at.

The name of the channel was Debbie Does Books, and I started to feel like Debbie was my new best friend, my most staunch supporter. Some part of me knew that wasn't the case, but perception was nine-tenths of the law. Some part of me also knew that wasn't how that saying went, but my inebriated brain told me that maybe that was part of my style. Getting sayings wrong and thus creating new sayings. Yes, "perception is nine-tenths of the law" was going to catch on with the young people, and they would start using it in school hallways and across all social media platforms. In the distant future "perception is nine-tenths of the law" would be as commonplace as "barking up the wrong tree" or "beating around the bush." Like those, no one would know the exact origins of the saying, but I knew that I was the author of that gem, the father of an immortal phrase. That would be my true lasting legacy, not these stupid books.

Feeling magnanimous and grateful, I made a comment under Debbie's video that simply said, "Perception is nine-tenths of the law."

Of course, by the time the sun started to rise, filtering around the edges of the drawn shades of the bedroom, I had long run out of beer and was thus sobering up. With a headache pounding at the inside of my skull, my new phrase no longer seemed to make much sense. In fact, it started to sound like gibberish to me. I went back to Debbie's video and deleted my comment, hoping no one had seen it yet.

I stumbled to the kitchen, realizing that sometime during the night I had stripped down to only my underwear. I also vaguely remembered masturbating at some point to that old Tone Loc song, the one that seemed a thinly veiled endorsement of Ruffies.

I poured a glass of water, drank it all down then poured another and drank it as well. I took two Aleve and then started a pot of coffee. I considered scrambling some eggs or making a bowl of instant grits, but the very idea of food made me want to go kneel before the porcelain god so I vetoed any breakfast that wasn't black coffee.

I was on my second cup when Edwin called. I didn't want to answer, didn't want to talk to him or anyone really, but I knew he was worried about me. If I ducked his call, he would only become more worried. If he thought I was on the verge of drowning myself in the tub where my father died, might he not call local law enforcement to come check on me? I didn't want that.

"I'm so sorry," was how I answered.

"God, Rick, you really scared me last night," Edwin said, and the tense sound of his voice made me believe it.

"I know, but I'm on my second cup of coffee and sobering up. I admit, I was in a bad place last night and made the unfortunate decision to drown my sorrows in massive amounts of alcohol which tends to only increase sorrow as opposed to drive it away."

"So you're… I mean, you aren't thinking of… You're okay, then?"

I could tell he didn't want to come right out and mention the word "suicide," as if the very sound of the word might drive me over the edge and send me running for the razor blades.

"I'm not all rainbows and kittens, but yeah, I'm okay."

"When I read that chapter, I freaked out man."

"Honestly, I don't even remember writing that," I said, which was the truth even if not the whole truth.

"I don't like the idea of you all alone there drinking yourself into a stupor every night," Edwin said, and again the genuine concern in his voice moved me.

"No more drinking for me," I said, which may or may not have been the truth. I suspected not.

"You will call if you need anything, right?"

"Absolutely. And you will call if there's any news from Doubleday about all this mess, right?"

"Absolutely," he said, though I noticed the slight pause. "And keep the faith. Controversy can actually be a great marketing campaign. Maybe all this attention will only drive sales of the book."

"Perception is nine-tenths of the law."

"What?" Edwin said.

"Nothing. I need to run but I'll be in touch soon."

I hung up before Edwin had time to say any more. I felt I had reached the limit of my ability to act "normal" for him, and I hadn't even been doing a good job as it was. It was clear he suspected I was an alcoholic. He hadn't come right out and said that, but it had been implied. Maybe implication was nine-tenths of the law.

No, that one didn't have quite the same ring to it.

I threw on some sweats and went out to the fire pit. The fire had died out, though little embers still flared like fireflies in the blackened ash. I saw remnants of my book and thought about how many had been destroyed in the last couple of weeks in this house alone. Out in the world, apparently even more were being fed into shredders. If this kept up, maybe all copies would be wiped from the face of the earth by the boxful. Which maybe was a good thing, like the eradication of smallpox through vaccination.

Out of print, out of mind, I thought then chastised myself for more of this mangling of familiar phrases. Was I working on another trademark?

I pulled up the grocery store app and ordered another case of beer. Already breaking my promise to Edwin, but I decided moderation was the key. I couldn't go cold turkey; I'd already tried that more than once and failed. I would have to ween myself off the booze. That was how it had to be done with certain drugs, and alcohol was unquestionably a drug. My plan was to avoid binge drinking. I would allow myself one beer every two or so hours. Hopefully that would be enough to satisfy the craving without getting me drunk, just enough so I didn't go off the deep end with my Thirst.

Responsible alcoholism. Yes, I thought I'd go with that. Some would call that rationalization and justification; I called it a working compromise.

Perception was, after all, nine-tenths of the law.

As I waited for my delivery, I sat in the living room, staring down at my phone. Debating whether or not I should call Michael to apologize. Of course, I had already apologized last night, but should I reinforce that apology with a more sober one? Or would that only make matters worse? Sometimes it was best to let sleeping dogs lie until the dust had settled. A mixed metaphor? Possibly, but if I was going to misquote sayings I might as well mix metaphors as well.

How had I been so stupid to think that Michael had a crush on me? Was my ego that desperate for validation? Still, I told myself, it wasn't as if it were unheard of for a student to develop a crush on his teacher. Or young men to be attracted to older men. They wrote books and made movies on the subject.

Of course, I realized my own past history also bore this out. I had lost my virginity (more or less) at seventeen to an older man, one I'd had a crush on for years before I even actually met him. Is it any wonder I had recast that scenario with Michael in my role and me in Gregg's?

The teenager stands at the back of the line, the book he just bought clutched to his chest like something precious and magical. His hands are sweaty, and his skin tingles with excitement and nerves. The line is long, but it is moving rather fast. Up ahead, the teenager can see the writer sitting at the table, his auburn locks strategically disheveled and his plump lips spread in the same bright smile recognizable from the author photo on the back of his books.

The teenager looks down at the book in his hands, a glossy new hardcover. No real cover art, just a black background with the title in deep red letters. Do You Want It? Beneath the question mark, instead of a dot is a dribbling drop of blood. This is the sixth book in the Vampire Feast series, and the teenager has only read the first two so far. However, he'd discovered them only last month so he is tearing through them fast. When he'd learned the author, Greg Nigel, would be doing a talk and signing here at the Barnes & Noble in town, he'd put his plan into motion. He'd told his father he would be spending the night at a friend's house then camped out in front of bookstore overnight to ensure he'd be first in line since seating was limited.

And just as he had strategized to be first in line when the doors opened, he has strategized to be the last in line for the signing. The writer keeps the line moving by only asking the name of the person getting the autograph and then moving on to the next. No time to strike up a real conversation with anyone, but the last person in line might well be able to get a bit more out of him. Much of the time pressure might be lifted, leading to a real interaction.

Of course, the writer could be too tired to talk by time the teenager gets to him, but he will simply have to think of some way to keep him engaged. As he makes his progress through the line, the teenager practices possible scenarios in his head, trying to come up with the perfect conversation starter.

Not "I love your work." That is too trite and something he probably hears every day. Definitely not "I'm your number one fan,"—sounds too much like hyperbole. The teenager can pick something specific about the writer's work, his characterization or his ability to build tension through ambiguity, and focus on that to show he is more than a casual fan. However, after spending an hour and a half talking about his work, maybe he would feel depleted on that subject.

Something personal? The teenager knows from an interview he read in a horror magazine that the writer lives in Asheville up in North Carolina and recently bought and restored an old Victorian mansion. Maybe that could be something to ask about, but will it make the teenager seem a bit stalkerish?

He definitely knows he shouldn't bring up his own fledgling writing, as it will paint him as an opportunist who merely wants to use the writer as a contact.

The teenager begins to fear he is overthinking this, and whatever he says will come out sounding rote and robotic, like a rehearsed speech. Perhaps it will be better if he leaves it to the moment,

allows inspiration to lead him in the right direction.

Except, that hasn't worked out for him in the
past.

He flips the book over and looks at the author photo
on the back. That glorious, sexy author photo. This
is what first drew the teenager to Greg Nigel's work.
Two months ago as he perused the horror section of
this very bookstore, what had made him purchase the
copy of Nigel's first book, Life After Death, hadn't
been the title or even the description; it had been
the author photo. They say not to judge a book by
its cover, but what about its author photo?

Lust at first sight, that is the only way the
teenager can think to describe it. The writer
doesn't look anything like those overly muscular
men in the few porno mags the teenager has hidden in
his closet at home, but in some ways the mischievous
smile of the writer feels more sexually charged and
potent than all those images of naked oily men.

Then when the teenager read the book, he discovered the writer to be not only beautiful but talented as well, which makes him even more desirable. The
teenager quickly bought the rest of the series. He
read that the writer almost never does promotional
tours anymore, so this one for the new novel is
a bit of a surprise. And coming so soon after the
teenager has discovered the writer's work, it feels
more than a coincidence.

It feels fated.

A silly, romantic notion, but at seventeen he hasn't quite outgrown silly, romantic notions.

In what seems like an eternity and no time all at once, he is the next in line. Ahead of him, a middle-aged pudgy woman in a pink tracksuit is blathering on as the writer signs her book. The teenager notices that when she says, "You're my second favorite vampire novelist after Anne Rice," the writer grimaces. He tries to cover, but the young man definitely sees it. A reaction as if the woman has said, "You're my second favorite after a pile of shit."

Even after the book is signed and given back, the woman doesn't seem to want to leave. She just stands there like a human-sized piece of bubblegum, now asking about the writer's influences, saying she sees parallels between his work and that of Stoker. The writer responds, "Everything is an influence," a vague non-answer that even the teenager can tell is meant to be dismissive.

The woman, however, doesn't seem to catch that. She keeps talking until the writer finally says, "It has been a pleasure meeting you, but I do believe there's someone else waiting."

The woman turns back and glares at the teenager like the annoyance she no doubt thinks he is. "Oh, I'm sorry," she says, sounding anything but. "It's just that it's rare I get to talk with a real writer of books I admire."

The teenager nods. "Same here. So if you don't mind, it's my turn."

She blows air forcefully out of her nostrils then takes her book and storms off, as if the young man has done something wrong by merely existing. This doesn't bother him; he is used to it from interactions with his own father.

"Sorry for the delay, young man," the writer said, flashing that alluring grin and reaching for the book. "What's your name?"

The teenager almost tells him but then hesitates. A fellow writer might recognize his name as the son of another famous author, and he doesn't want their entire conversation to become about his overshadowing father. Instead he shortens his first name and adds his middle name. "Rick Henry."

"Okay, Rick, do you want me to write anything in particular in the inscription?"

The teenager shrugs. "No. Whatever you want to write."

"I think I can manage to come up with something memorable," the writer says with a tantalizing wink then bends his head as he scribbles on the title page.

The teenager tries to think of something intelligent to say. Or at least witty. Or at least coherent. His mind feels blank, emptied out. He stands still, mouth hanging slightly open, like some kind of mute.

"*There you go,*" *the writer says, handing the book back.*

The teenager takes it, stares down at the inscription—"To Rick, thank you for your patience. I hope I was worth the wait. Good things come to those who wait."—and still can't come up with a single thing to say. He's going to squander this opportunity, leave here having made no impression on this man who had become something of a minor obsession for him over the past couple of months.

The writer has already diverted his attention to capping his pen and taking his coat from the back of his chair and slipping it on. The teenager has been dismissed, like the Bubblegum Woman before him. He's missed his chance to have a real conversation with the writer.

"I feel like Life After Death is sort of a gay allegory," the teenager says, the words coming out almost automatically, springing not from conscious thought but from subconscious contemplation.

This gets the writer's attention. His head snaps up and he sinks back into the chair from which he had only started to rise. His coat is only half on but he doesn't seem to notice. "Gay allegory, huh? What makes you say that?"

The teenager feels his face burn with heat and knows he must be turning bright red. Could he explain what before this moment had merely been a feeling? He supposes if he is serious about becoming a writer himself, he needed to learn to put feeling into word.

"Something about the relationship between the two male vampires, Sullivan and Delano. It felt at first like a seduction, then a relationship. By the end of the book, they were bickering like an old married couple."

"You know, there was an article in The Advocate after the third book that accused me of queer baiting."

"Oh, that's not what I would call it," the teenager says quickly. "No, more like you're coding your work so that it might slip past most people but a certain audience will still pick up on it."

The writer stares at the teenager with a laser focus that makes the teenager uncomfortable. Then the writer smiles and says, "Very astute observation for someone your age."

The smile and the compliment help the teenager to relax. "So I'm right?"

"Let's just say no comment," the writer says and winks at him again.

A pleasurable chill works its way through the teenager's body, and he thinks his suspicions about the writer are correct. He decides to test another theory. "In a different way, it's what Anne Rice did with Interview with the Vampire."

There, that grimace again. Slight and gone in a flash, but definitely there.

"I knew it," the teenager says with a laugh. "You don't like her work."

"I don't like to comment on other writers who work in my genre."

"You don't have to comment with words. Your expression gives you away."

The writer gives a slight nod of acknowledgment. "You are very astute, indeed."

"It'll be our little secret," the teenager says and tries a wink of his own. It feels awkward, but he's never attempted to openly flirt with anyone before. And he realizes that is what he is attempting to do, as ridiculous as that may be.

The writer finishes putting on his jacket then leans forward, resting his chin in his hands. His stare is piercing. "So tell me, did you find something relatable in my work?"

The teenager knows the question has a deeper meaning than what appears on the surface, and the heat in his face travels all over his body. Mustering all the courage he can, he nods his head. "I do, and I try to bring that into my own stuff."

"Oh, so you write, do you?"

The teenager mentally kicks himself. He told himself he wouldn't bring up his own writing. "A little. I'm working on a thing, a novelette or maybe a novella, about a high school kid who becomes a werewolf and has to hide it from all his friends and family, terrified he'll lose everything if they find out he's technically a monster."

"Talk about allegory."

"I do kinda worry that I might be making the metaphor too obvious, like I'm beating the reader over the head with a hammer or something."

The writer tilts his head. "It is easy to forget in today's literary climate just how effective subtlety and ambiguity can be in a work of horror."

"I'm trying, but I still have a lot to learn."

"Who are your mentors?"

"I don't know. I mean, I have writers I admire and like to read, but you're the first real writer I've ever actually met."

This is, of course, a lie. The teenager has been raised by another writer, but he certainly wouldn't call his father anything close to a "mentor." His father has taught him nothing about writing, and the only advice he has ever given amounts to "quit!"

The writer glances around, but this area of the bookstore by the cookbooks has emptied. The manager is over by Reference, seemingly caught in a conversation with a chatty customer. She keeps glancing this way, and even holds up a finger, indicating she is trying to extricate herself and come over, but for now the writer and the teenager are for all intents and purposes alone.

Still, the writer lowers his voice when he says, "Would you like me to offer you some pointers?"

The teenager isn't certain he has heard the words correctly, or is misinterpreting. Maybe what the writer is offering are dogs, English Pointers.

"I am staying at a hotel not far from here," the writer continues. "I was planning to order room service and spend the rest of the evening reading before bed. However, if you have time to spare, we could talk for a while about the writing process, character development, or anything you want."

The words linger and the teenager wonders if this is how jackpot lottery winners feel, if they have this much trouble believing their extreme turn of fate is real. "Are you sure? I don't want to take up any of your time. You must be tired after all this."

"What kind of writer would I be if I didn't lend a helping hand to the up-and-comers? Of course, if you have plans and don't want to spend a few hours with an old fogie like me, I'd understand."

"You're not an old fogie. You're the sexist man I've ever met."

The words pour out like verbal vomit before the teenager can stop them, and he clamps a hand over his mouth to staunch the flow. He feels mortified and considers turning and bolting from the store.

But then the writer smiles, and the smile is sly and almost seductive. He winks again. "Let me finish up with the manager, and I'll meet you up front in fifteen."

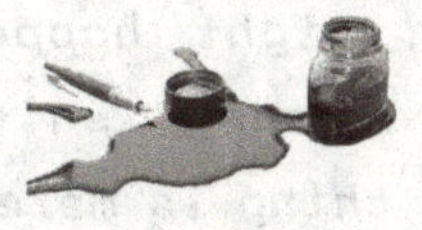

The hotel room isn't as nice as the teenager expected. It is nice, roomy and clean with a large bed, desk area separated by a half wall, and a large screen TV resting on the dresser, but for a best-selling author, the teenager expected a multi-room suite with its own kitchenette and a balcony overlooking the city. By comparison to what he'd imagined, the teenager finds the reality of the room somewhat basic and plain.

The writer goes to the mini-fridge and pulls out a bottle of beer, not one of the brands the teenager is familiar with but something with a weird label covered in foreign writing. No doubt nothing the hotel provides, something the writer must have brought with him.

"Drink?" the writer asks, holding up the bottle dripping condensation like sweat.

The teenager hesitates, but he isn't sure why. It's not as if he has never had beer before. He's been to his share of parties where the booze was flowing and he didn't hesitate to partake then. So why now?

Something about this situation, being alone in a hotel room with a sexy older man, makes him feel he should keep his wits about him in the event something untoward happens.

And yet isn't that why he is here, hoping something untoward might happen? If he really examines his motivations, isn't he wishing that the whole mentoring thing is merely a ruse and that the real reason for this tête-à-tête is something altogether less wholesome?

Another childish fantasy. The writer is a sophisticated man of the world who could likely have anyone he wants; what interest would he have in some kid with no experience in carnal matters?

He realizes the writer has raised his eyebrows expectantly, still holding out the beer.

"I'd love a drink, I'm parched," the teenager says, inwardly wincing at how dorky that sounds.

The writer uses a small bottle opener to remove the tiny tin caps then hands the teenager a beer before gesturing toward the far corner and a little blue loveseat. Loveseat, the word reverberates in the teenager's brain like a voice in a well. He takes a seat and the writer squeezes in next to him, so close their thighs press against one another. Neither adjusts and the contact remains, and the teenager isn't sure if he is imagining the electricity said contact sparks or not.

The writer takes a pull on his beer then says, "So, tell me about this werewolf story of yours? It's a metaphor for being in the closet, right?"

The teenager takes a swig of his own beer, noting the taste is richer than what he's used to. More bitter yet more flavorful. He nods, not quite able to meet the writer's gaze.

"And you're worried the metaphor is too blatant?"

The teenager nods again.

The writer leans over and bumps his shoulder against the teenager's. "Mentoring is a two-way street, you know."

The teenager laughs, realizing he is caressing the neck of the bottle—up and down—in a suggestive way. He stills his hand, trying to come up with something to say. He had thought earlier of this meeting as a tête-à-tête, but if he doesn't contribute his end then it's nothing more than a tête.

"I want to tell a story within the story," the teenager says, trying to put into words what had only been thoughts before. "Like if all the reader wants is an exciting werewolf story, then that's exactly what they'll get. But for readers with a more discerning eye, they might see the story within the story. The story of a boy who feels different with no one he can talk to, knowing the world at large would consider him a monster if they knew his secret even though he doesn't feel like a monster. Does any of this make sense?"

The writer reaches over and squeezes his shoulder, the sparks from before becoming a full-on electrical storm. "Makes perfect sense. You picked up on the gay story within the story of Life After Death, and as the series develops it is both an epic tale of vampires trying to take over the world but also it's about how gay people shouldn't feel pressured to conform to the heterosexual societal norms. Monogamy, marriage, children, none of that has to be the model on which we pattern our lives.

We can reinvent what relationships mean, seek our pleasure and happiness outside the confines of what we've been taught we should aspire to. Most readers won't get that, it'll fly right over their empty little heads, but for those with a more discerning eye, as you said, they'll pick up on it almost subliminally."

"That's the part I'm worried about, the subliminal part. I want it to be that way, but everything I do feels too on the nose."

The writer leans forward and adjusts the cushion at his back, but the teenager notices in the process he inches even closer, so that now their legs are pressed even tighter together. The teenager feels the stiffening in his pants, and he puts his signed book in his lap to try to hide the incriminating evidence of his lust.

"So tell me," the writer says, now so close the teenager can feel his breath like a mint-scented breeze, "what happens in your story? How does the character become a werewolf?"

"He sneaks out one night with a fake ID and gets into a bar. He goes to the bathroom and when he opens the stall door, there's a wolf in there that leaps out and bites him."

"Sounds a bit goofy." The writer is blunt, and the words sting mostly because the teenager knows they are true. "And yes, too on the nose. A teenager sneaking into a gay bar and hooking up in the bathroom. Maybe something less parallel to real life. Maybe he did sneak out to a bar and he's walking home drunk down a dark, narrow alley, and he hears footsteps behind him and a growling. He assumes a wild dog and starts to run, the dog chases him. Jumps on his back, takes a nip before the boy finds something to hit the dog with and gets away."

"I like that," the teenager says, wishing he had his notebook so he could jot some of this down.

"Okay, so what happens after your character realizes he is a werewolf? What's the plot?"

"Well, he tries to find ways to cure it and goes to great pains to hide it from his family and friends."

The writer is silent for a few moments, as if waiting for more. When he doesn't get any more, he says, "And…"

The teenager shrugs. "I haven't figured out the ending yet."

"You haven't figured out the ending because you have no actual story to end. You have a concept with no meat to it, so basically a skeleton. Do you plan to have your character seek out the one who made him a werewolf, meet any others of his kind?"

"I hadn't really planned on that."

"There's your problem. You are making it only about a character who realizes he is gay and tries to deal with it, but you threw a hairy rug over it hoping people wouldn't notice. You have to have more going on than just the metaphor."

"Like what?"

"That's for you to decide," the writer says with a laugh that has an almost hard edge to it. "It's your story, so you figure out what should happen, but make it exciting."

The teenager sinks back into the cushion, chewing on his bottom lip. "Maybe he doesn't go seeking the one who bit him. Maybe the one who bit him comes seeking him. Maybe he wants to teach him, introduce him to others of his kind."

"There you go. Created families, they are very big in the gay community."

"Yeah, and maybe there's someone hunting the werewolves, poisoning them with silver or something. Could be a whole AIDS metaphor."

"See, you're just full of ideas."

"I don't know why I didn't think of any of this before."

"Sometimes you merely need a sounding board to bounce ideas off of."

"I don't know how to thank you," the teenager says then leans over and plants a kiss on the writer's cheek. It is a spontaneous move, instinctual and not considered, and he instantly wonders if he has made a horrible mistake.

But the writer only smiles at him, a smile that makes the pressure under the book even more uncomfortable. "If you really want to thank me…"

When the writer leans in for his own kiss, this one on the mouth, the teenager doesn't resist. He responds with gusto, knowing this is what he wanted *all along, even more than advice on his writing. The book falls to the floor, replaced by the writer's hand, fondling at the crotch of his jeans.*

The teenager isn't exactly a virgin, but receiving one drunken blowjob and giving two hand jobs doesn't exactly make him an expert. Still, when the writer unzips his pants and places a hand on the back of his head to guide him down, the teenager knows exactly what to do.

I came out of the memory with a hard-on. The arousal brought on a fair amount of shame. Yes, the sex had been great, and I couldn't claim I'd been a naïve pup taken advantage of by an older man. I had been eager and more than willing. Hell, I'd been jacking off to Gregg's author photo for months before our encounter.

No, the shame came from what happened after. Gregg's charm had dissipated once he'd ejaculated. He'd revealed a bitterness to his personality that had been concealed before. Complaining about how his books, while still best-sellers, were selling less and less with each subsequent release. How he hated meeting his fans, but his publisher had pressured him into this tour to try to get the sales numbers trending upward again. He didn't seem to realize he was talking to one of those very fans he was bitching about.

He hadn't kicked me out exactly, but he kept talking about the early start he had the next day, about how my parents must be wondering where I was, and even at my age I could read those signs pretty easily. I had gathered up my clothes without showering and got out of there. Looking back, he'd given me fair warning in the guise of literary advice. All that talk of gay people not having to mimic heterosexual societal norms, rejecting monogamy. He'd made it clear, I simply had been too drunk on my own lust to listen.

He had asked for my number, but that had felt perfunctory and I hadn't really expected he'd ever call. And yet for almost a year after, every time the phone rang in the house I had allowed myself to hope. I had been an idiot.

Even more idiotic, when my first novel was about to be published, Greta had started talking about writers to send the manuscript to for cover blurbs, and I had actually suggested Gregg Nigel. Thinking perhaps he'd recognize my name, that he'd remember our brief time together. All we'd gotten back was a note from his representative that said, "Gregg Nigel does not blurb unknowns."

So stupidity, obliviousness, an inability to recognize a hopeless situation when I'm smack dab in the middle of one... All Rick Justice trademarks.

Near tears, I reached into my underwear and began to stroke myself. Thinking about Gregg. Thinking about Don. Hell, even thinking about Michael. I was nearing climax when the delivery person pulled up outside. The start to so many pornos, but life was not a porno. I didn't even stop stroking as the delivery person, an older black man, placed the cases of beer at the front door. If he'd glanced through the sidelights, he would have been able to see me, but part of me didn't care. If he caught a glimpse, I'd just raise my free hand and wave.

He didn't look though, simply left the beer then returned to his car. I couldn't tell if I was relieved or disappointed.

I splattered all over my bare stomach and chest. The act was unsatisfying, and I wanted to cry because it had been so long since anyone had touched me. Without cleaning myself, I stumbled to the door and opened it.

As I bent to retrieve my beer, Bubba came out of his backdoor across the street. The semen still glistening on my chest, I nodded at him and said, "How's it hanging? Want a beer?"

He glanced at me then scurried to his truck, backing out of the driveway fairly quickly without another look in my direction. Did this mean he would no longer protect me with his gun if I needed him?

Not that it mattered. Bullets didn't work on ghosts.

I went back inside and closed the door on a world that now felt alien to me.

SUNDAY, APRIL 19, 2020

I DREAMT OF MY father.

We were in his coffin, lying side by side. It was tight but not uncomfortable, like a casket built for two. At first I thought I had been buried alive with his corpse, but then he turned and looked at me, asked if I was hungry.

Next thing I knew he was at the stove, frying a couple of eggs. I knew that we were still in the coffin, only in the kitchenette area. The ceiling was low and the walls close, like being in the kitchenette of an RV. I stood to the side as my father flipped the eggs while managing not to break the yokes.

"You shouldn't have to make breakfast," I said. "You should be resting."

"In peace, you mean?"

I started to laugh before I realized he wasn't joking. "Well...yeah. I figured at least after you died you wouldn't have to cook anymore. Although I don't honestly remember you cooking much when you were alive."

He turned to look at me and we were no longer in a cramped kitchenette but the large kitchen from the house we lived in when I was a child. It wasn't exactly the same, the center island was much longer than I remembered and the fridge as massive as the doors leading into Jurassic Park, but I knew where we were. My dad put a plate of bacon on the island top then motioned for me to take a seat

242

on one of the stools on the other side. Only when I had to climb up onto it did I realize I was a kid again.

"I was resting peacefully," my father said, leaning forward to plant his elbows on the island. "But you woke me up with all that noise you were making, running around and breaking shit."

"You know about the lamp?"

"I'm not talking about the lamp you knocked over and blamed on the cleaning lady. I'm talking about my work, my legacy. It's bad enough you have shattered your own life into pieces; now you're coming for everything I worked so hard to build. What could I do but get up and punish you for the mess you're making?"

I slid off the stood, adult-sized again and took my coat from Greta who was dressed like a 1940s cigarette girl. "I don't have to take this," I said, taking the banana that Brooke Simpson handed me through a computer screen. "I'm going home."

"This is your home," my father said from next to me.

We were back in the coffin, but now it was incredibly tight. I was pinned on my side, nose-to-nose with my father. I felt panic seize hold of me, but I barely had room to even shake. I tried to scream but my voice came out thin and weak.

"Let me out of here," I said and it sounded more like a whine than a demand.

My father smiled and shook his head, as much as the space would allow. "This is where you belong. The world above doesn't need you, no one will really miss you. Not even that college kid you stupidly thought had the hots for you. Myself, however, the world definitely misses me. They want me back. The universe heard this and decided to make a trade."

"A trade? What are you talking about?"

"Don't be dense, son. Me for you. I'll get to return to the world above, tell more stories that people love and cherish, and you will remain here in the box to rot and decay."

Suddenly I was flat on my back, looking up at the coffin lid. Actually *through* the coffin lid. I could see my father standing up at the edge of the open grave, staring back down at me.

"This is for the best," he said, and I thought I detected a hint of actual tenderness in his voice.

Then he took up a shovel and began heaping dirt into the grave. The clods should have landed on the translucent lid, but instead they landed directly on my face, filling my mouth with sour-tasted earth and wriggling worms. I tried to scream but instead choked on the dirt.

I went to sit up but banged my head on the lid that wasn't there, but then I realized I was no longer asleep, no longer in the dream. So why was I still in the coffin?

The answer, of course, was that I wasn't. I was under my bed. How had I gotten there? No clue since I couldn't remember most of what happened after my last beer delivery. I could only guess the concepts of moderation and responsible alcoholism had flown right out the window.

Rolling over onto my stomach, I dug my fingers into the carpet and dragged myself out from under the bed. The TV was playing some techno music that was all pounding bass, and my first order of business was to turn that racket off. I felt certain the neighbors would have thanked me if they could.

I stumbled into the bathroom to relieve myself then checked the time. 4:50 a.m. I did a tour of the house to survey the damage, and there was quite a bit. In the living room, a lamp lay broken on the floor, the shade trampled. I also discovered a small indention in the wall next to the door; my sore and scraped knuckles suggested I had tried to punch a hole though the plaster. In the kitchen, the fridge door stood open, items scattered on the floor and the counter, as if at some point I'd decided to try to invent a new snack by using everything I had. The sink contained the pieces of a shattered plate and a cracked glass with milk residue staining the inside. In the guest bathroom, all the contents from the cabinet under the sink were dumped out as if I had been rummaging for something. I couldn't for the life of me think what that could have been. Perhaps in my drunken state, finding a pair of fingernail clippers became the most important thing in the world. Though I couldn't remember, I felt certain I had been unsuccessful if that had been the quest. Nail clippers disappeared almost as often as socks in the dryer.

As I completed the circuit back to the bedroom, I noticed my Biktarvy in a trail like fairytale breadcrumbs leading from the closet to the bed. I didn't panic this time, didn't feel much of anything truth be told, and I didn't even bother to collect the pills. Let those brats die in the woods, baked up into a witch's pie.

I crawled into bed, wrapping the covers around me. Part of me thought I should cry or rage or call someone for help, but I couldn't muster the motivation. I felt drained of all the fear and anger I had been experiencing lately, but nothing had come to replace it. Thus I was completely hollowed out, devoid of emotion and energy.

Why was I fighting so hard against my father? What was I trying to save? My life. I wasn't really using it anyway. I had done nothing of note with it for over five decades at this point; it seemed unlikely I'd get a second wind at my age. For all my father's faults, he had at least followed his passions and accomplished something of significance, leaving a mark on the world that would last long after his death.

What right did I have to mess with that or stand in his way if he wanted to preserve his legacy?

From somewhere in the house, I heard my cell ringing. I didn't even consider getting up to find the phone, nor considered answering it. There was no one I wanted to talk to, no one in my life that mattered. No real friends, no real partners, no one to turn to for support or encouragement. Before that might have depressed me, but again there was no reaction.

I had been dreaming lately of myself in a coffin, and the fact was that I felt dead already. Dead but still going through the motions of life. Not only since I had started on the *Senior & Junior* book, but ever since I had lost the deal with

New Blood and accepted that I was not a writer. Everything from that point on had been pretense.

I had expelled so much energy trying to prove to my father that he was wrong about me, but now I could see I had been attempting to prove that to myself. Knowing deep down the whole time that he was right.

Monday, April 20, 2020

I wasn't sure how Sunday slipped away from me. I ordered more beer. I had been ordering so much beer, I started to worry the grocery store might stage an intervention for me. It would have to be virtual, of course, which meant I'd be able to drink all the way through it.

This thought made me laugh, but the sound was so jagged and hysterical that I bit down on it, silencing the hyena that had apparently taken up residence in my mouth. I was naked again, and I stank of stale sweat and cheap beer. I could afford better stuff, but I didn't want to be snooty. I could still relate to the common people.

My phone told me the date was April 20th. 4/20, the national day for pot smokers. This year it was also 4/20/20 so maybe that meant extra weed for everyone. Or gummies. Wasn't the younger generation into gummies? I found myself wishing I had some to sample.

I was hungry but I didn't eat. I'd left the fridge door open since yesterday, everything was probably spoiled by now anyway. Mostly I didn't eat because feeling the hunger pains was at least feeling *something*. I had heard that some Buddhists meditated on their pain to better understand the human condition, or some such shit. Maybe I was becoming a Buddhist.

Of course, they probably didn't drink quite so much.

Sitting on the edge of my bed, I looked down at the pills that still littered the carpet. I bent over and snagged one, popping it in my mouth and dry-swallowing it. Had I taken one yesterday? I couldn't remember. Just to be safe, I took another one.

Then I laughed like my whole life was a joke.

Tuesday, April 21, 2020?

I FOUND MYSELF LYING in the grass in the backyard. Stars twinkled overhead. Late night or early morning? I wasn't sure. What had I done all day? Wasn't sure about that either.

I rolled over onto my stomach, head turned to the side. My cheek rested in a large batch of clover like a pillow. Glancing toward the house it looked as if all the lights were on inside. I got first to my hands and knees then up to a standing position. I felt unsteady, but I walked around to the front of the house and stood at the end of the drive. The lights in Bubba's house were all off, as were all the lights in all the houses I could see on the street. Everyone snuggled up in bed, enjoying blissful dreams.

But what was life if not a dream? Maybe truly waking up meant realizing everything in the world was ugly and harsh and meaningless.

I stumbled back inside the house, wrinkling my nose at the stench. Not just of my own body but of all the ruined food in the fridge. I thought about closing the door which still remained hanging open, but instead I collapsed onto the sofa and fell back into nightmares that were preferable to reality.

I woke up when the sun streaming through the windows pierced my eyelids. I rolled off the sofa, clipping my elbow on the glass-topped table. I cursed then laughed then cursed again. I saw my phone lying nearby, but the battery was dead. All the better. I no doubt had all kinds of messages from Edwin, and I didn't want to know. Either way, whether Schrödinger's cat was dead or alive, I wanted to remain in denial.

None of it mattered anyway. Keep the deal or lose the deal, ultimately both outcomes were meaningless because they would both end in failure.

Everything I touched turned to shit, after all.

Using the edge of the sofa to pull myself to my feet I saw Amazon packages sitting on the table. When did those come in? What day was it? How long had I been wandering around in a drunken fugue state?

This was no doubt the crystals, Saint Benedict medals, and herbs I had ordered. Which meant I know had everything I needed for the baptism ritual. The exorcism. Yet I felt no motivation to follow through. My life was already ruined; at this point, banishing my father's spirit seemed unlikely to fix anything.

I left the packages unopened, wandering into my father's office. I no longer thought of it as mine, and I wasn't surprised when I booted up the computer and found the file for my version of *Reborn* had been deleted again. Good riddance. No great loss to the world. In fact, I could think of no compelling reason to continue resisting. Why not give the world what it really wanted, which was the book my father would have delivered had he not died in the middle of writing it?

I had heard of automatic writing, where mediums went into a trance and channeled spirits who wrote out messages on pieces of paper. I was sure it could be done on a computer as well. I placed my fingers on the home keys, ASDF

JKL;, and closed my eyes. Inviting my father to take control. No more fighting it. He could use my body to write whatever he wanted.

At first nothing happened, and I felt an odd disappointment. As much pain as my father had brought me, at least it had kept me from being utterly alone. If even his tormenting spirit abandoned me then I truly had nothing.

Yet after a few minutes, I felt an odd tingling in my fingers and then they began to move. Seemingly of their own volition, but I knew my father moved them. He was using my body as a vessel so he could continue to create even after death.

All writers dreamed of achieving some kind of immortality through their writing, and perhaps my father had found a way to take that concept to the next level.

I emptied my mind, which was surprisingly easy, allowing myself to become a completely empty vessel. I ceased to exist as anything other than that vessel, and I allowed my father to write.

WAS IT LATER THAT night, was it the next night? I had no idea. Time had lost all sense of coherence, unraveling like an old sweater. Perhaps I had come unmoored from the flow of time altogether and become stuck in a bubble of *untime*, where time had stopped moving altogether. Trapped in a single moment that would never end. It seemed like a concept out of a Jack Finney story or possibly a *Twilight Zone* episode. In fact, life with COVID felt like *The Twilight Zone*. We were all trapped in a single moment in time that never ended.

I sat on the sofa, getting ready to take my medicine. I needed to take better care of myself. Yes, that was important, necessary, vital. If I didn't have my health, what did I have?

I held the pills in one hand, a glass of water to wash them down in the other. Everything would be better once I—

Wait, pills. I looked down at my palm, the fog lifting enough for me to realize I held over a dozen pills. And they weren't my Biktarvy. At first I didn't know what these blue oblong pills were, but then it came to me like a hammer to the back of the head.

Sleeping pills. These were from the bottle I kept in the bathroom cabinet. I had been ready to take a handful of sleeping pills.

I dropped the pills to the carpet and tossed the glass of water away from me. It struck the wall by the front door and shattered. I got to my feet and stumbled away, wondering if I should go to the bathroom and stick my finger down my throat. How could I be sure I hadn't already swallowed some pills and that was to be my second handful?

I seemed to move aimlessly through the house, finding myself back in the office. The computer was on, Word open on the screen.

I had been writing, or my father had been writing through me. That was the last thing I remembered. A morbid curiosity drove me forward so I could see what he'd composed. As I read the words on the screen, I slowly sank into the chair.

What's the point of living when there's nothing to live for? Surviving isn't living, that's what I've come to realize. Simply going through the motions, breathing and eating and shitting and sleeping and repeating, it isn't enough to justify the space I take up in this world.

And that's what I am, a waste of space. A drain on resources that could go to someone who is doing more than scraping by, someone who is actually taking life by the balls and making the most of it.

Someone who isn't me.

I'm barely a person. I am more of a ghost than my father. Long before the pandemic, I was merely coasting through life. No real friends or relationships or purpose. All that was keeping me alive was force of habit. I got out of bed in the morning because I was used to doing it, not because I had anything to look forward to.

The pandemic merely forced me to examine all this and realize how useless I am, how meaningless my life is.

So why keep something you aren't using? It's time to do a little spring cleaning, starting with myself.

A suicide note. My father had written a suicide note.

For me.

I remained frozen in the seat, staring at the screen. Deeply disturbed. Not so much by the message my father had written, but by the fact that I agreed with so much of it.

With all of it really.

My father had said in an interview once that the secret to great fiction was writing the truth at the heart of the lie. And there was much truth in this note. Truth I had tried to deny, but which always lingered in the back of my mind.

My life was worthless; I was worthless. My life was meaningless; I was meaningless.

Waste of space.

Why was I fighting so hard to preserve an existence I wasn't even using? Like hoarders who kept magazines from 1965 but would never read again. I was hoarding life that never got utilized. Perhaps it was time to clean house.

I was in the bathroom, the tub filled almost to the top. I doubted I had used the filtered pitchers to purify this water, though I couldn't remember for sure. I could spot crystals settled on the bottom and herbs floating on the surface, and I was naked except for the Saint Benedict medal around my neck on a flimsy gold chain.

I lifted one leg and tentatively put a toe in the water, unsure if I should expect it to be hot or cold. Lukewarm, right in the middle. Middle of the road. Average. Nothing special. Just like me.

When I climbed into the tub and sank back, it displaced some of the water, sloshing over the rim to waterfall onto the tile. I didn't care. Let someone else clean up my mess for once. I was tired of doing it myself.

I was tired.

I still felt numbed, hollowed out, a shell. I thought of all that had happened since my father died, since the deal with Doubleday, since inheriting this house. Looking back in retrospect, I could see a pattern, a design. Seemingly random events all leading like a trail of breadcrumbs to this very moment.

It had all been driving me here.

I slid down even further, letting my head sink beneath the water. I held my breath until my lungs began to burn, and I noticed flashes of light behind my closed eyelids. Actually alternating light and shadow, a combination that churned and melded until it formed images. Images that formed memories. All my lost memories, flooding back into my brain at once.

The writer stands in the kitchen, left foot on the pedal to keep the trash can open. He uncaps the bottle then upends it so that the little blue pills come cascading out, most pouring into the can but one striking the edge and ricocheting onto the floor. He doesn't know why he keeps taking these pills when they are only delaying the inevitable, and for what?

The writer sits on the sofa, phone in his hand. He pulls up the app on his phone and orders two more cases of beer. He knows he shouldn't, has promised himself he wouldn't, well aware of the fact that getting drunk will be counterproductive to what he needs to accomplish in this house. Yet part of him fears he is not up to the challenge of accomplishing the task, so at least with the beer he'll have something to blame his failure on.

The writer drags the two cases of beer out of the pantry, right into the middle of the kitchen floor. He tucked them away there with the ridiculous thought that he could avoid temptation, out of sight and out of mind, but now he recognizes the ridiculousness of that thought. And a part of him always recognized that, which is of course why he has kept the beer in the house. To drink, once the other part of him gave up its Pollyanna illusions and admitted it was hopeless in the face of temptation.

Tearing into the top case, the writer smiles because both parts of him have joined as one and announced that time is now.

The writer sits at the desk, reading over his work on the screen. Garbage, utter garbage. He laughs to think he ever thought he could do this. The story he previously considered so clever and innovative is, in fact, laughable. He is laughable, will be a laughing stock if this book ever gets released. He sees clearly now what a mistake it was to ever accept Doubleday's offer.

He deletes the file, from every location it had been saved, then empties the computer's Recycle Bin. He sighs with relief, knowing he has done the world a huge favor.

The writer sits at the desk again, ready to start a new project. However, this time he will try his hand at something new. Nonfiction. Autobiography, one might even say. He starts by typing the first three words. "I'm a fraud." Then again, then again, then again, eventually cutting out the spaces in between. *He realizes only distantly that he is crying, but it feels like a weight off his shoulders to finally be writing nothing but the truth.*

The writer pulls his books off the top shelf, letting them fall to the floor like bombs that don't explode. Like duds. Appropriate terminology, as these books definitely failed to explode onto the literary scene. He kicks them around for a while, considers tossing them in the toilet and pissing on them. In the end, he sits down on the floor and begins ripping the pages out, methodically shredding each page into confetti. He brings to the destruction of his books much more determination and focus than he ever brought to the creation of them.

The writer stands at the sink, holding his bottle of pills. Last time he threw them in the garbage, but then foolishly retrieved them in a moment of weakness. He has always been weak, his father was right about that, but now is the time to be strong. There is no strength in prolonging pain and uselessness, no strength in sticking something out even though you know it's over. He has never understood people who sit through an entire movie they are hating instead of simply getting up and walking out. And what is his life if not a movie he is hating? Time to walk out. He turns the bottle over and lets the pills fall into the sink and rattle down the drain.

The writer sits in the darkness, in the quiet, which is conducive to deep thought. Something he *normally avoids, but tonight it helps him see things clearly. Earlier he had been thinking how much he had liked his second novel, how it had perhaps been the best of his books. Now he recognizes the truth. Yes, it is perhaps the best of his books, but it is still utter shit so what does that say about the rest of his books? Even at his best, he is terrible.*

"Trash," he growls, reaching out and snatching the book from the table. He goes into his kitchen, moving like a blind man who knows the layout so well he doesn't need the aid of sight. By feel, he turns on all the burners of the stove then tosses the paperback onto one of them. "I always thought cremation was more tasteful," he says then returns to the living room, feeling preemptively cleansed by fire.

The writer closes his eyes and lets out a shuddering breath, standing before the open closet in his bedroom. "So I'm trending on Twitter already?" he asks, opening his eyes and punching in the code to open his safe.

"You didn't know?" says his former student on the other end of the line.

The writer takes out his bottle of pills. "I saw the clip on YouTube and the comments there, but I didn't realize I'd crossed social media platforms already. What are they saying over on the little blue bird? More of the same?"

"Pretty much. There's a hashtag going around."

"Let me guess, #Justice4Justice?"

"Yeah, how'd you know?"

"Has the kind of ring to it that would catch on," The writer says, walking into the kitchen.

"I still can't believe your own father would have said such nasty and vicious things about you."

"I wish I could claim to be surprised," the writer says as he unscrews the lid off the bottle.

"It's all such bullshit. You have mad skills, and you're going to do a fabulous job with this book. I know it."

"You're awfully sweet, Michael. If only every-one—"

The writer's words cut off as if severed with a scalpel as two of his pills clatter into the sink, one of them going straight down the drain and the other bouncing off the rim. He wants to keep rotating his wrist until they all get swallowed down the pipe, but something stays his hand. Some nagging part of him that is afraid to do what he knows in his heart must be done. His weakness is the strongest part of him.

Crying out, the writer drops the phone so that it clatters on the tiled floor, only its sturdy case keeping it from shattering. He slings the bottle away from the sink. It lands on the counter, the pills scattering across the faux-marble surface.

After starting his bath, the writer walks into the bedroom to check his phone. The message from his editor depresses him. The publisher isn't planning to cancel the contract. How is that possible? What more has to happen to sabotage this deal?

He goes into the living room and grabs the copy of what he considers his worst book. So bad that it almost infects everything it touches. A disease that can't be cured, can't be eradicated through vaccine.

Some diseases, however, can be temporarily halted by being frozen.

Enjoying the symbolism, he takes the book into the kitchen, opens the freezer, and tosses the book inside. He turns his back on it, as if to deny its existence as he waits for the disease to be frozen.

The writer wakes up in the night, covered in a stinking film of sweat. Before bed, he had written, daring to think he was doing good work. He now recognizes this as self-delusion, a desperate need to believe the glass is half-full when in reality there is nothing in the glass besides the sour caked-on residue of spoiled milk.

He needs to stop this madness before it goes any further, but he is in so deep, he can't see a way out. If only the publisher would terminate his contract, but they seem to be stubbornly holding on, refusing to cut the writer loose. Probably didn't want to admit defeat. Perhaps the writer could help them along.

Grabbing his phone he goes into the bathroom and opens the Twitter app. Time to make a little noise.

Tired of sitting out by the fire, the writer goes back inside. He feels the itch to hit the keyboard again, which surprises him. He had thought that impulse would be as dead as his father. Yet like his father, the impulse has returned as a ghost.

In the office, he sits and starts to type, slow and unsteady at first but then picking up steam. This one isn't nonfiction, but it also isn't exactly fiction. He gives the story the ending he feels his life should have. The ending that feels inevitable for him.

Once he's done, he grabs his pills and a copy of his first novel and goes back outside to the fire.

The writer tears through the house in a rage. Smashing things, punching the wall, opening the fridge and throwing everything out. His emotions are a complicated knot of rage and fear and self-loathing and sadness, creating a cyclone inside him that has to be let out, leaving nothing but destruction in its wake. He feels so hopeless, like no matter what he does he can't find a solution to end his pain. Every choice is bad, every decision wrong.

Of course, on some level he recognizes there is a solution. The final solution, and the majority of his pain is caused by his refusal to face that head on.

He takes his pills again and scatters them all over the bedroom as he makes his way to the bed and crawls beneath it.

The writer takes the sleeping pills and pours a pile into his palm then tosses the bottle. He has been taking the wrong medicine all this time. The Biktarvy didn't cure anything, in fact only prolonged the suffering. These pills, however, could cure the suffering.

Under the water, I opened my eyes, overcome by all these memories. All my blackouts brought into the light, those gaps filled in. All the times I thought my body had been taken over by my father's vengeful spirit.

And yet, in the memories I didn't feel like a passenger. It felt like I was in the driver's seat, making all the moves myself. Was that what real possession felt like, convincing you that you were in complete control so you would only have yourself to blame for the ensuing mess? They said the devil was an insidious deceiver, and what was my father if not a version of the devil?

How long are you going to go on blaming your father for all your fucking problems?

That voice in my head sounded like my own, but could that also be a trick?

Or did I just not want to face the truth, which was that the only one responsible for the mess my life had become was me? In some ways, that should be a comfort. No haunting, no ghost, no spirit out to get me. But it wasn't a comfort, because that meant I was my own worst enemy. Sabotaging myself every step of the way because I didn't think I deserved anything but misery.

That was so much more frightening than the idea of a wraith out for revenge.

I was sick. Not only the HIV, but sick in the head. Sick in the soul. There might not be a pill for that kind of illness. Only one cure that had been staring me in the face, a cure my subconscious had been pushing me toward all along.

My lungs burned and screamed for oxygen, but I remained submerged. Closing my eyes again, I opened my mouth and took a deep breath.

THURSDAY, APRIL 23, 2020

THERE WAS NOTHING. No tunnel, no light. My life didn't flash before my eyes, no departed family or friends welcomed me to the other side. I couldn't even say there was blackness. There was nothing, a total lack of something. There wasn't even me. Looking back, I had no sense of self or anything. I simply ceased to exist. Not so much me drifting away from the world, but more like the world drifting away without me.

Then the world came rushing back.

My first awareness was of another mouth on mine. I had the absurd thought that I was in a fairytale, a prince awakening me with a kiss. But the mouth on mine was hard and I could taste the breath on my tongue and it was garlicy and sour. Then I felt a rhythmic pressure on my chest, like someone pounding on me to a beat that seemed familiar. Something that made me think of bell bottoms and disco balls.

Then I felt water rushing up my esophagus to be ejected from my mouth like a geyser. I coughed furiously, until my throat was raw, and rolled over onto my side. I realized I was naked and wet and shivering.

"Jesus Christ," I heard a deep voice say and I turned my gaze toward that voice. My vision was blurred, and at first the shape seemed only a blob before finally coalescing into the form of my neighbor. Bubba, kneeling on the floor by the toilet. For a second I thought he was naked too, but then I realized he was in his boxers. Just like the night he showed up at my door after hearing me screaming in the living room.

My thoughts were as blurry as my vision, and at first I couldn't figure out what he was doing here. Had I invited him over and we had some tryst in the bathroom? After all, I had felt his mouth on mine.

Then I realized. I remembered submerging myself in the tub and swallowing the water. He had performed mouth-to-mouth, and the rhythmic beating on my chest had been chest compressions. He had done CPR and saved my life.

But how had he known? I wanted to ask, but I couldn't form words. Then I noticed someone standing behind him. My gaze shifted upward and as if through the haze of a smudged window I saw my father towering over us both. His face was slack and pale.

"Dad?" I managed to croak before the world drifted away again and I passed out.

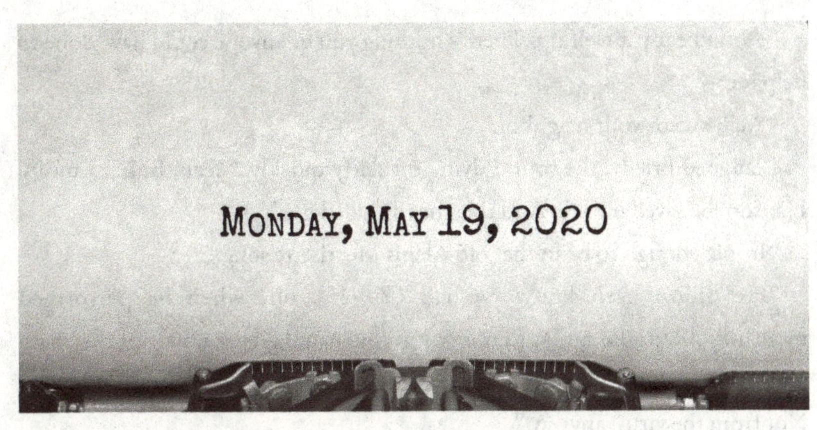

I listened to the phone ringing and almost hung up, but I clutched the cell tight against my face until the call was answered.

"Rick? Is that you?"

I sat up in my hospital bed, feeling weak. Too weak for this conversation, but I couldn't put it off any longer.

"It's me, ET," I said.

I heard Edwin sigh on the other end. "I'm so glad to hear from you. I've been worried sick. How you holding up?"

"I'm making it."

"I wanted to come visit you, but of course the hospitals aren't allowing visitors right now."

"Yeah, I know," I said, feeling more like I was in a prison than a hospital. Only here they were keeping me isolated for my own protection as opposed to protecting society from me.

"I'm really sorry about everything."

"You don't have anything to be sorry about. This is my mess; I made it."

"Yes, but I knew something was wrong. I should have been more proactive in getting you the help you needed."

"Don't beat yourself up. There's nothing you or anyone could have done to help me."

"Well, except your neighbor."

I laughed briefly, the sound dying off fairly quickly. "Yeah, Bub… I mean, Hanson, he saved my life. And then nearly killed me."

"Ironic enough to be in that old Alanis Morrisette song."

"He didn't even know he had COVID, but when he performed mouth-to-mouth he gave it to me. It was touch and go for a bit, but they have me stabilized. I still get short of breath a lot, but I'm not in any danger of dying. Not from the virus, anyway."

A pause on the line. Then, "I don't mean to be nosy, but why was your neighbor even there?"

A good question, and one I had gone over in my head a lot over the past month. I had yet to come up with any good conclusions. I knew what the official story was, but it didn't make any sense.

Bubba said he heard screaming coming from my house again. So loud it woke him up at half past midnight. At first he'd almost ignored it, remembering the last time, but he said it was one word being yelled over and over. "HELP! HELP! HELP!"

So he'd come over, pounded on the door. No one answered, but the yelling continued. He tried the door, found it unlocked, and went inside. The yelling led him to the bathroom then abruptly stopped when he walked in and saw me lying in the tub. He dragged me out and started CPR. He didn't have any training but had seen it performed enough on TV and in movies he had tried it.

But who had been screaming? It certainly wasn't me.

I thought about seeing my father standing behind Bubba after I came to, but that had been in my mind. Like the entire haunting, only a projection of my own self-hatred and self-destructive tendencies.

Right?

"Rick? You still there?"

"Yeah, ET. Sorry, I'm exhausted. I don't want to stay on here too long, but I wanted to let you know I was going to be okay."

"That's great. I, um… Well, we can talk more later."

Hi tone told me he had something important to say. "What is it, ET? Spill."

"I did want to tell you that Doubleday has decided to release you from your contract."

Release me. What a nice way of saying that I was fired, as if they were doing me a favor. Although in all honesty, they probably were.

"I understand. I may not be able to pay back the advance all at once, but maybe we can work out a payment plan."

"Don't worry about that. I convinced them to let you keep the advance. After all, you did a lot of work on the book. Under the circumstances, however, we don't think it would be in anyone's best interest for you to continue."

"I don't disagree with that," I said, thinking a prouder man would have refused the money, done anything he could to return every cent. But I wasn't a prouder man so I kept my mouth shut on the matter.

"You take care of yourself, Rick. And call me if you need anything."

"Absolutely," I said, knowing in my heart that this would be the last time I ever talked to Edwin.

We hung up and I leaned back into my pillows. The conversation had left me winded and drained. I closed my eyes, wanted a nap, but instantly the voice started up in my head. The voice that told me I was pathetic for losing the book deal, that I was pathetic for not being able to stand on my own outside my father's shadow, that I was pathetic for trying to kill myself, that I was pathetic for failing to kill myself. That I was pathetic.

The voice sounded like my father's, but I knew it was mine. The same inner voice that had crippled me with doubt my entire life, wrecked my mental health, led me to where I was today. It was me; it had always been me. Now that I could face it, maybe I could finally tell myself to shut the fuck up!

It was time I gave myself permission to be quiet, to rest.

SATURDAY, OCTOBER 16, 2021

"Here I go," I said to my reflection in the bathroom mirror.

"Here *we* go," Hank said, coming up behind me and adjusting my collar.

I met his eyes in the glass. "I'm nervous."

"I know, but it's okay. I'm here to keep you grounded."

I turned around and embraced Hank. He did keep me grounded, more than anyone else I'd ever known. "I'm so glad you're here."

"Where else would I be?"

I couldn't quite put into words the fact that most every other man I'd ever had in my life might have answered that question, "*Anywhere* else."

"Okay," Hank said, gently pushing me aside to get a good look at himself in the mirror. "I need to fix my hair."

"Why? Your hair is perfect."

"Sure, a perfect rat's nest."

Laughing to myself, I left him to it. Hank's obsession with his hair was one of his trademarks I'd come to love, like the way he could only drink room temperature water. I let him work and went into the living room. We had the laptop set up on the coffee table, two cushions on the floor so we could both appear on camera. I found myself flashing back to my appearance on *The Brooke*

269

Simpson Show a year and a half ago. So much had happened since then, so much had changed.

I had changed so much.

Settling on one of the cushions, I pulled up the email with the invite link and clicked it, signing into the Zoom meeting. I appeared in a small square in the bottom right of the screen, and I made a few adjustments to make sure there would be room to fit me and Hank in the shot.

Wendy appeared on the rest of the screen, her backdrop a collection of posters depicting a variety of comic book characters. Batman, Wonder Woman, John Constantine, Swamp Thing, Sandman, Eric Draven. She looked cool with her hair streaked black, magenta, and fuchsia, cat's eye makeup, and oversized black T-shirt hanging off one shoulder. By comparison, in my button-up shirt and tidy hair, I looked like the Mayor of Square City.

"Hey, Mav," she said, insisting on that sobriquet. "Where's the other half of the dynamic duo?"

"Fixing his hair. That's his super power, perfect hair."

"It's a power a lot of people would kill to have."

Wendy, though we'd only spoken to her online a few times, seemed as cool as she looked. She hosted what I had been told was the most popular podcast discussing comics and graphic novels, *Word Bubbles*. Hank said we should be incredibly grateful that we got booked on the show.

And I was grateful. Not only for this opportunity, but for everything. Gratitude was one of the new Rick Justice trademarks.

"You two aren't starting without me, are you?" Hank said, coming into the room and plopping down on the cushion next to me.

I didn't actually think his hair looked any different than when he started fussing with it, but I wasn't going to tell him that. He had probably made some minute adjustments, slight rearrangements of a strand or two, that no one else might notice but which would make Hank feel more confident. His hair was like a talisman; as long as he had it the way he liked, he felt he could do anything.

I was still looking for my talisman. In some ways, Hank was my lucky charm, but I realized a person's true source of strength and confidence should come from within. I hadn't found mine yet, but the fact that I kept seeking was something.

"We'd never start without you, Hankie," Wendy said with a smile. "Now you both know this isn't live, I'm pre-recording and will edit it and get it up next month. You can use whatever foul language you want. My audience doesn't give a good goddamn fuck. I'll keep it conversational, like we're all just sitting around chatting. Sound good?"

Hank and I both nodded.

"Okay, I'm just going to start right in."

I felt a tightness in my shoulders, a rumbling in my stomach, so many bad associations trying to dig their way out of fresh graves. As if sensing this, Hank reached over and squeezed my hand. A simple gesture, but it really grounded me. I took a deep breath and got ready.

"Welcome back all my fellow comic book geeks," Wendy said, her tone and intonation switching from her normal speaking voice to performance mode. "I think you all will be excited about my guests this episode. I have the creators of the new graphic novel *Imposter Syndrome*, and they are going to tell us all about the inspiration and the creative process behind the project. Why don't you two handsome fellas introduce yourselves?"

I cleared my throat and laughed, as if she'd just told a joke. "Well, my name is Maverick Justice, and I wrote the story."

"Then I came along and gave the story form," Hank said, exuding his usual unshakable confidence. "Hank Tyler here, artist extraordinaire."

"Pleasure to meet you both. Maverick, let's start with you. How did you get the idea for the story?"

"Well, it's based on real events. You see, my father was Bentley Justice."

"The famed young adult author?" Wendy asked as if she didn't already know.

"That's the one. When he died, his publisher hired me to finish the book he'd started shortly before he passed. I published a few novels in the 90s and it seemed like a good idea. But like most good ideas, it turned sour pretty fast."

"What happened?"

"Well, there was a lot of pressure. From the publishing company, from the public, from myself. I have had a drinking problem since my teens, and that became even more out of control. That all got compounded when it came out that my father and I had had a complicated relationship, and he wasn't the biggest fan of my work. Then on top of all that was the pandemic, the isolation and uncertainty. I've had some untreated mental health issues my whole life, and this took me to the breaking point. Literally, I had a mental breakdown and ended up trying to take my own life. I had developed these delusions and convinced myself my father was haunting me, trying to kill me, but it was really me. I was trying to kill myself."

A beat of silence, as Wendy let that heavy confession sink in. "That's devastating. But you survived."

"Barely, but it was the wake-up call I needed. I finally managed to stop drinking, fifteen months sober, and I went into therapy. I'm also on some medication now to stabilize my mood. I don't mean to make that sound like it was a sudden turn around. It has been hard, and it still is. Not to be all cliché, but it truly is one day at a time. However, I feel like I can do it."

"That's great. Was writing about the experience part of the healing process, therapeutic?"

"It was actually my therapist's idea," I said with a laugh. "At first I resisted, because I figured I was done with writing. He said it didn't have to be anything formal, nothing for publication if I didn't want. It could be journaling or poetry, simply a tool to get my feelings about what happened out onto page. I didn't want to fictionalize it, because the idea of writing fiction right now is not one I want to entertain. I also didn't want to do a straight memoir, but then I was flipping through TV and came across a rerun of that old MTV show *The Real*

World, the season with Pedro, the guy with HIV. I remembered after he passed away, a friend of his created a graphic novel about their friendship and the grief he felt. That gave me the initial inspiration to try to do a graphic novel. The only roadblock being that I can't draw and I didn't have any artist friends."

"Then how did Hank enter into the picture, if you'll pardon the pun?" Wendy said.

"I consulted with Greta, an editor friend of mine. She had some connections in the comics world, and she suggested Hank. He was talented, having just come off a run on a title from Hill House Comics, and he lived in my area. She put us in contact, and we hit it off instantly. The rest is history."

"Hit it off in more ways than one, am I right? You two are a couple now, correct?"

"He couldn't resist my charms," Hank said, making it a joke but it was true. Instantly I felt drawn to his charisma and self-assurance, his humor and emotional openness. "I loved the idea of turning Rick's experience into art, and I was all in. We worked well together, and there was an instant attraction on my part. Halfway through the creation of *Imposter Syndrome*, we officially became an item. Now we're joined at the hip."

I realized a huge smile had stretched across my face. Smiles used to be hard to come by in my world, but now it was like I couldn't stop. Another new trademark.

"And the graphic novel was just released through Top Shelf. So far the response has been glowing."

"The critics are raving," Hank said.

I felt a blush creep into my cheeks. I wasn't accustomed to praise; I was more comfortable with criticism. Of course, the book wasn't selling the way the superheroes did, but the critical approval moved me, I couldn't lie.

"Not to bring up a painful subject," Wendy said, "but the newest *Senior & Junior* book also released from Doubleday recently, the one Maverick was originally supposed to finish. Was that painful for you?"

I shrugged with more casualness than I felt. "I didn't expect them not to go forward with the project simply because I wasn't mentally stable enough to do the job."

"Have you read the book?"

"No," I lied. I had read it and found it pretty bad. Not that the writer they hired wasn't competent, but he had followed my father's original outline to the letter and it made for a very lackluster story. The critics had noted that as well, but the public had gone wild for it and it was one of the biggest best-sellers in recent memory.

"Can I ask an impertinent question?" Wendy said.

"Better than anyone I know," Hank answered.

We all shared a laugh then Wendy said, "Maverick, I know you recognize that so much of what happened to you was a product of your mental health issues, but I have to ask, considering the subject of so much of your father's work and everything that transpired in that house during the pandemic... Do you believe in ghosts at all?"

I found myself flashing back to the night I tried to kill myself. Bubba showing up because he had heard screaming that led him right to the bathroom, and the blurry image of my father standing behind him. I thought about all of this and told another lie.

"No, I don't."

Acknowledgments

Writing is a solitary endeavor, done mostly alone in a room, just the writer and the keyboard. However, there is so much that goes into creating a story that is not merely the writing of the tale. I want to take a moment to acknowledge some of the people who helped me.

My oldest friend Mo. She has been there from the beginning and knows where all the stories come from. Reconnecting with her over these last few years has really helped me reignite my love of storytelling in a major way.

My husband Craig. Always supportive and encouraging and interested in my work. He inspires me to be a better storyteller, and he is always looking for new and interesting things to do which will feed my imagination.

My friend Ryan. He provided invaluable insight into paranormal investigation which really helped shape the story. I rewarded him by popping him into the book for a little cameo.

I dedicated this book to my work family, because at 50 years old I finally achieved my dream job working in a library. I feel so at home there, and my coworkers truly feel like my family.

I am grateful to all the queer authors out there who are telling their stories. You are my heroes and my inspirations.

A huge thank you finally to David-Jack. Slashic is doing great work to elevate queer voices, and I'm so grateful you allow me to be part of that.

And thank you to each and every person who takes a chance on this book. I hope it provided some entertainment.

About the Author

Mark Allan Gunnells loves to tell stories. He has since he was a kid, penning one-page tales that were Twilight Zone knockoffs. He likes to think he has gotten a little better since then. He loves reader feedback, and above all he loves telling stories. He lives in Greer, SC, with his husband Craig A. Metcalf.

www.ingramcontent.com/pod-product-compliance
Lightning Source LLC
Chambersburg PA
CBHW010341170726
48283CB00009B/2900